Books by Elisa Braden

MIDNIGHT IN SCOTLAND SERIES

The Making of a Highlander (Book One)
The Taming of a Highlander (Book Two)
The Temptation of a Highlander (Book Three)—Coming soon!

RESCUED FROM RUIN SERIES

Ever Yours, Annabelle (Prequel)
The Madness of Viscount Atherbourne (Book One)
The Truth About Cads and Dukes (Book Two)
Desperately Seeking a Scoundrel (Book Three)
The Devil Is a Marquess (Book Four)
When a Girl Loves an Earl (Book Five)
Twelve Nights as His Mistress (Novella – Book Six)
Confessions of a Dangerous Lord (Book Seven)
Anything but a Gentleman (Book Eight)
A Marriage Made in Scandal (Book Nine)
A Kiss from a Rogue (Book Ten)

Want to know what's next? Connect with Elisa through Fa
and Twitter, and sign up for her free email newsletter
www.elisabraden.com, so you don't miss a single new re

Desperately Seeking a Scoundrel

ELISA BRADEN

Dedication

*This one is for my Granny, who had a cowgirl's stories,
an affinity for pink, an obsession with M&Ms,
and a tireless, generous heart.*

Nothing can steal the memories you made in us.

Chapter One

"Avoiding the discomforts and indignities of desperation requires cleverness. Sadly, no amount of pleading will increase your allowance of that coveted commodity."

—THE DOWAGER MARCHIONESS OF WALLINGHAM to her nephew upon receiving his request for an increase in funds.

August 20, 1817
Keddlescombe, East Devonshire

"HE FANCIES YOU, MISS BATTERSBY. WHEN DO YOU SUPPOSE you might marry?"

Sarah avoided her young student's gaze, focusing instead on the basket of apples at her feet. Little of the fruit in this tree had yet ripened, but there was enough for today, and that would have to do.

"We are not engaged, Miss Cresswell."

A leafy branch recoiled and shook as the long-limbed, redheaded Lydia Cresswell plucked another blushing-green apple and plunked it into Sarah's outstretched hand. The girl was thirteen and positively enraptured by anything to do with courtship and romance, which made her companionship trying. Still, while she was ten years younger than Sarah, she had already sprouted taller by an inch and possessed frightfully long arms, so she had been assigned ladder duty.

"Oh, but Mr. Foote has been saying so."

Sarah frowned. "To whom?"

"Well, everyone, I suppose. He insists you have accepted him."

Throat tightening, she glared up at the girl's narrow back. "You must not fall prey to gossip. Do you recall our recent lesson from Proverbs?"

Lydia sighed loudly and recited, *"He that keepeth his mouth keepeth his life."*

Sarah propped her hands on her hips. "Very good. God approves discretion. Let us practice that virtue, shall we?" She considered the basket. "I believe this is sufficient." Her stifling tone must have penetrated, because the loquacious Lydia glanced over her shoulder and nodded before descending the ladder.

They had managed to procure twelve apples—enough to make the pies Sarah had been promising the girls. Picking up the basket, she worried her lip between her teeth. Flour and sugar remained. For that, they must visit the market in the village square. And for those items and her mother's tea, she must spend her last few shillings.

She glanced at Lydia, who was liberating loosened leaves from her fiery hair. "Here," Sarah said, heaving the basket into the girl's arms. "Carry this back to the school and inform Mrs. Blake she may heat the oven. I shall be along shortly with the remaining ingredients."

"Oh! Are you certain you do not wish me to come al—"

"Quite certain." The last thing she needed was for the budding young gossip to observe her haggling with the miller over every ounce of flour. Poverty was humiliating enough. Sarah waved at the road toward the vicarage. "Off with you, now."

Watching Lydia descend toward the northern end of the long, green valley, Sarah pressed her lips together and fought against the despair that always crouched nearby. She let her eyes drift to her right, where the valley widened before ending at the sea, then left, where St. Catherine's Church stood in a narrow, emerald juncture. Most mornings, it was surrounded by mist, but by afternoon, one could see it from anywhere in the valley. The Norman-era church with its proud, thirteenth-century stone tower and oversized oak doors was as familiar to her as her own hands. Her father had been the vicar here since before she was born.

On the opposite slope of the valley, halfway up the hill from the church, sat the vicarage—a white, two-story cottage nestled beside a larger, older stone building that had once been part of an abbey, now home to St. Catherine's Academy for Girls of Impeccable Deportment.

Behind her lay the neighboring valley, where the white, cob-and-thatch cottages of Keddlescombe dotted the lush, green landscape.

She closed her eyes. These twin valleys by the sea cradled her home—the stalwart church that had withstood time and turmoil and Tudor suppression; the cottage where she had been born and reared; the school that gave her both purpose and income; the village where no stranger lived. All of it should bring her comfort. *Should.*

Her hand covered her mouth, a moment of weakness. No. She would not cede ground. She would fight, as she had for two long years. She would find a way.

Dropping her arms to her sides, she tightened her jaw and

patted the pockets of her worn, striped overdress. The quiet jangle of sadly few coins only raised her chin higher. With a determined stride, she took the hill road down to the village.

As she entered the central square, the blacksmith, Mr. Thompson, shouted a greeting. She forced herself to smile and gave him a friendly nod. Glancing around, she noted that the open green at the heart of the village was fair teeming with farmers, fishermen, and their wives. She had hoped to encounter fewer people on this particular day, but now was the thick of harvest time, and such busyness was to be expected. Lowering her eyes and the brim of her straw bonnet to avoid drawing attention, she headed for the miller's cart, spotting it in its usual location on the east side of the green.

"Ah, Miss Battersby," the tall, aged Mr. Miller said as she approached. "Good day to you. Come to fetch a bit of flour?"

"Indeed." She smiled politely up at the crinkle-faced man. "One pound, if you please."

Mrs. Miller, his rounder, much-younger wife, appeared from behind him to say, "So little, Miss Battersby? Cannot make more'n a single loaf with that paltry amount. Why not purchase ten? 'Tis less costly per ounce and lasts a good bit longer."

Sarah's smile tightened. "One pound is all I require for now," she said quietly.

Mrs. Miller's eyes darted past Sarah's shoulder and widened. It was all the warning she had before an unwelcome hand pressed her lower back and a loathsome voice said, "Nonsense. Make it ten pounds, Mr. Miller." The man she despised with all her being leaned close to murmur lovingly against her cheek, "I shall not have it said my betrothed has been deprived."

Using her elbow and the brim of her bonnet, Sarah discreetly shoved against his lanky form, creating much-needed distance. His hand fell away. "I am *not* your betrothed, Mr. Foote. Kindly desist in claiming so."

Dark hair, slick and shining with the lard pomatum he used, was pulled straight back from a shortened forehead. This was at odds with the relatively small eyes, long nose, and comically prominent chin. Mr. Foote was a most unhandsome man, but that did not bother her overmuch. In fact, if his soul were not far uglier than his face, she might be more amenable to his suit, particularly since he was one of precious few eligible males within miles of Keddlescombe who were neither old enough to be her grandfather nor young enough to require parental consent for marriage. He was also a landowner with four tenant farms and a sizable income—as he was fond of reminding both her and her mother.

His dark eyes narrowed on her. Small lips peeled back to reveal brown, overlapping teeth. His grin did little to enhance his attractiveness. "There, there, my dear. Mr. and Mrs. Miller surely understand the passions of youth. I see little need to disguise our affections, despite your father's ... condition."

Heat flared in her chest, rising into her face. Her skin prickled with it. "Do not speak of my father," she hissed. "You are unfit to utter his name."

As usual, Felix Foote refused to be insulted. He shot Mr. Miller a patronizing grin. "Ladies must be forgiven their upsets, for they are delicate in their constitution. I fear my dearest Miss Battersby is overwrought by the Reverend Mr. Battersby's unfortunate ill health."

"For the last time," she gritted, her rising nausea mingling with despair and frustration. "I am not *your* Miss Battersby. We are *not* engaged! Do you hear me? Not! Engaged!" By the time she had finished, her voice was loud enough to carry across the green. She knew because everyone—simply *everyone*—in the square stopped to stare at her: Mrs. Jones, who managed the bakery and secretly gave Sarah five loaves of bread per week. Mr. Walton, who had taught her to ride when she was seven. Ann Porter, with whom she had played cricket in this very green. And a dozen more she had known since childhood. They all stood silent and round-eyed as the vicar's daughter screamed her foolish temper past its boiling point.

Mr. Foote grasped her elbow and pulled her closer, his rotting-fish breath wafting across her face. "It is not unseemly to declare ourselves, Miss Battersby. Everyone in the village comprehends your *position*. You will need the care of a husband soon." His fingers dug into her flesh. "To argue otherwise is foolhardy."

Heart pounding, Sarah glared up at him. Her fury had nowhere to go. He was right. Soon, her father would be gone in body as well as in mind. The living provided by the church would cease. And she and her mother would be—she swallowed and breathed against the tightness in her chest—quite destitute.

For over a year, Felix Foote had been circling, constantly reminding her he was her only choice. She had searched and scraped for another, but it had not appeared. She had stalled and resisted, hoping his eye would wander elsewhere. But she was cornered, and she hated it, hated being so impoverished that she could only buy one pound of flour at a time. In fact, the only thing she hated more was Felix Foote.

"Impossible," she muttered to him now. "I cannot marry you. Ever."

That oily, nauseating grin reappeared. "Cannot marry me? Whyever not?" he laughed loudly. "Scarcely a line of suitors clamoring at your door, I daresay."

Quite when the decision to lie entered Sarah's mind, she could not say. It was not in her nature. She was, in truth, horribly inept at pretense, possessing a fair complexion that reddened with guilt at even the most innocuous deception. Her students had once begged her to perform in one of their dramas. They had never asked again.

She had many faults—pride first among them—but she was no deceiver. Except for today. Today, the lie escaped her lips with such ease one would have thought it a frequent visitor.

"To marry you is impossible, Mr. Foote," she announced, her voice carrying across the green. "For I am promised to another."

Shocked murmurs and speculative whispers sounded

through the village square. Mrs. Miller's eyes grew as round as the wheels of their cart while her husband's brow lowered in a puzzled scowl. At last, Mr. Foote's grin faded, slowly replaced by a snarl of displeasure. "Who? Look around, Miss Battersby. 'Another' does not exist for you. Perhaps in your grief, you have taken to inventing phantoms."

She tilted her head and gave him a tight, satisfied grin of her own. Hatred, it appeared, could lend one boldness one did not otherwise possess. How else to explain her scandalous reply?

"Believe as you like, Mr. Foote. This *phantom* shall be my husband, not you. *He* shall father my children. Furthermore, if you do not cease your despicable attentions"—she yanked her arm from his grasp—"*he* shall deliver the punishment you richly deserve."

August 25, 1817
Whitechapel

DEATH WAITED, PATIENT AND FOUL. BLOOD MARKED COLIN Lacey's wrists where they were bound above him, wetting his arms down to his shoulders, but the flow had long since slowed to a stop, replaced by numbness. The butcher's hook held the ropes fast, held him at the butcher's mercy.

None would be granted.

"Pity you did not exhibit equal reticence at the tables, my lord," the butcher murmured. "A modicum of restraint might have saved us both much aggravation." A sigh, then the snick of a knife leaving its sheath served as reviled punctuation.

Bright, cold agony sliced. Silver light flashed behind swollen eyelids as air hissed through teeth and into lungs. The flesh over his ribs gaped and wept in a warm flow.

"One word, my lord. A name. And this shall end."

His shirt had been torn from his back hours earlier. It now hung in three rags from the waist of his trousers. He fancied if he ever managed to break loose from his bindings, the cloth would prove convenient for soaking up his blood.

Rusty laughter shook inside his chest. He was never leaving this putrid place, thick with late-day heat and the odor of animals that came here to die. No, his bones would join those of cattle and swine. He was not so foolish as to believe a name would save him, either his or anyone else's.

"Come now. You are the brother of a duke. His heir at present, yes?" The butcher paused as though Colin might answer, then answered himself in his oddly soft, cultured voice. "Yes. The heir to the Duke of Blackmore has little need for credit at my humble gaming houses. After the Home Office took an untoward interest in my businesses, the coincidence was rather more than credulity could bear. To whom did you provide information?"

Long silence earned him another stripe, just below the last. This time, although pain flashed, it was but a white peak amidst a range of equally jagged mountains.

A door creaked. Boots shuffled. "Beggin' your pardon, Mr. Syder."

"Benning. I trust this interruption is of a vital nature."

"Y-yes, sir." Boots scraped and shambled again, then the low London voice came from only feet away. "Johnstone sent word the Gallows Club was raided. Roughly an hour past."

If Syder ever grew angry, Colin suspected it would sound like the dark silence that followed Benning's news. But Syder had not built an empire of thievery, brutality, and vice by being a slave to intemperance.

"Who was it?"

"Two of Kirkwood's men, along wif seven more we never seen. Took Johnstone, they did."

More silence, then a sigh from Syder. "My lord, I fear I must leave you in Mr. Benning's tender care. Might I suggest you loosen your tongue? He is less subtle than I in his ministrations."

Reflexively, Colin swallowed against his rising gorge. Footsteps, calm and evenly paced, receded until a door squeaked open and closed. Knuckles popped.

"You lasted longer than most, m'lord. Grant ye that." Benning, whom Colin remembered as a massive, pockmarked brute with hands the size of millstones, shifted near enough that his bulk deadened the noise of livestock outside the door. His breath wafted over Colin's swollen face. It smelled of ale and onions.

"Kill me," he whispered, his aching jaw scarcely able to form the words. "For I have nothing to say to you."

"You're like to die, sure enough." Colin sensed the grin in the brute's voice. "But not just yet." Heavy bootfalls thudded against the hardened dirt, heading in the direction of the table on the far side of the space. It was where Syder had assembled his tools—knives and other blades mainly, but also hammers and saws. After Benning's initial beating, Colin's eyes had swollen shut. In some ways, that had been a mercy. But now, he wished to know what Benning was retrieving, which instrument would be the source of his next dose of agony.

Metal scraped wood as Benning lifted the tool, whatever it was, from the table. Colin's heart lurched into a frantic rhythm. Why he now panicked, he could not say. It could be no worse than what he had already endured. Could it?

Benning drew close. A damp breeze of ale and onions bathed Colin's forehead. A millstone fist gripped his forearm, just below the rope.

Dear God. Was he about to lose his hand?

He heard himself wheezing, struggling, hectic and piteous. His mind flew backward from the horrifying reality, crouching at the rear of his skull.

His hand. He would never play again. Never feel a woman's flesh.

Dear. Holy. God.

His arms jerked. The blade bit. He could not feel it, could only sense the motion and pressure as Benning worked it back and forth. Suddenly, his hands released, his arms falling agonizingly down. His legs left him, and he collapsed. Stunned. Useless. A heap at Benning's feet.

"Eh," the brute grunted, nudging Colin's knee with his boot. "No time fer that, m'lord. I's paid to cut you loose. Not get nipped by Syder."

Colin's blood pounded inside his head, at war with his panting breaths, forming a deafening cacophony. "P-paid?" he managed.

The rope binding his ankles was yanked and severed. "Aye."

Attempting to move his arms, Colin groaned as needles flared across the numb flesh. The fire slowly spread until he had to grit his teeth to keep from screaming.

The scraps of his shirt were yanked from his waistband, torn into strips, and wrapped tightly around his ribs. A massive thumb stretched his eyelid. A blurry, pockmarked face peered back at him, thick lips downturned. "You'll 'ave to force 'em open. They'll come right in a day or two, but by then you'll be dead iffen you don't run fast and far. Understand?"

"Yes." He felt the wormy trembling begin beneath his skin. Sensation returned to his shoulders, making him want to vomit up the pain. He could scarcely move his arms, but at least he still had his hands. For that, he was most thankful. "Who paid you? Was it my brother?"

Benning stood from his crouch and moved to the corner where Colin's coat had been tossed. He stooped to retrieve it. "Nah. Doubtful he knows anything." The man's dialect was thick and round, sounding more like, "Dow'foh 'ee knows anyfing." Before this year, having rarely associated with men of Benning's ilk, Colin might have had trouble following his mutterings. Much had changed.

"Then, who? I took you for Syder's man exclusively."

Benning circled behind him, gripped him beneath his arms and pulled him to his feet in a rough motion. Colin could not stop his pitiful groan as excruciating pain tore through his shoulders. His legs at first refused to hold him. Shamefully, he slumped against Benning, who steadied him with a heavy forearm around his chest and began forcing his arms into the sleeves of his coat.

"Things change. The nob pays better."

Panting roughly, head swimming, Colin paused to catch his breath as Benning came around to face him and quickly fastened his buttons like a nursemaid dressing an infant. "Who is the nob, Benning?"

The blurry brute finished his task and moved to the door, cracking it to peer out. "I can get you to your 'orse. No more'n that."

"Whoever it is, he must have offered a princely sum. Syder will not pursue only me for this."

Benning returned to Colin's side, grasped his arm and hauled him forward, dragging his stumbling, bleeding, weakened body toward the door. "It's touched I am by your concern, m'lord. Fact is I don't plan to stay put. Best you do likewise." Benning stuffed a hat onto Colin's aching head, tugged it low over his swollen brow.

The darkness at the end of dusk disguised their movements as they crept through the stockyard. A few cows shifted and lowed at their passing, but no shouts of alarm sounded. Soon they entered a stable, where Benning apparently had already saddled Matilda. The pretty bay mare snuffled Colin's outstretched hand.

"Good to see you, love," Colin whispered, stroking her warm nose. His arms, still weak, quickly fell back to his sides as Benning led her to a mounting block.

"Think you can manage it?" he asked.

Forcing his eyes to open further and swallowing down his lingering nausea, Colin gave his best imitation of his old self.

"The day I cannot mount a female is the day I am cold in the grave, Benning."

The man snorted and waved to the block. "Them's prophetic words, m'lord. Prophetic words, indeed."

Chapter Two

"Indeed, one's mettle is tested and forged in battle. And, of course, whilst traversing England's disgraceful roads."

—THE DOWAGER MARCHIONESS OF WALLINGHAM to the Duke of Wellington upon his triumphant return.

"ME ARSE'LL NEVER BE THE SAME." THE GRUMBLING OF OLD Mr. Hubbard did not faze his wife, who sat beside him on the driver's bench of the wagon. Mrs. Hubbard simply sent a wry glance over her shoulder at Sarah then returned to her knitting.

Sarah, however, commiserated heartily with the old farmer. Three days to London and three days returning to Keddlescombe in this unsprung, uncomfortable wagon over the pitted, rutted, muddy roads of southern England was enough to solicit complaint from Job himself.

If it had not been absolutely necessary to replenish St. Catherine's coffers, she would not have accompanied the kindly couple at all. However, the school simply could not function without funds, and rather than wait weeks for her letters to be answered with payment for the autumn term, she had elected to visit the four fathers who resided in London and retrieve the funds herself. Absently, she stroked the thick leather of her father's coin pouch, now fat and full. Temporary discomforts were as nothing—the funds she had acquired would keep St. Catherine's Academy for Girls of Impeccable Deportment operational for another month.

The fact that this journey also removed her from the storm of village gossip, well, that was simply a happy coincidence.

"We'll soon be home, husband," Mrs. Hubbard said soothingly. "Another half-day at most." She nodded to the barrels and crates and sacks of supplies stacked around Sarah's seat. "Daresay we shan't require another journey to London until summer next. Ample time for all yer aches to recover."

Mr. Hubbard grunted in response and pulled his wide-brimmed hat lower over his eyes, clearly preferring a stew of misery to his wife's reassurances.

Her good humor, however, was not so easily dampened. "Least we're ou' the rain. Is that not somethin' for which to thank the good Lord, Miss Battersby?"

Sarah glanced up at the oiled canvas suspended on arched ribbing above them. "Indeed." Her voice shook as the wheels encountered a deep hole. She braced herself against a creaking crate and stifled a groan. "What more could one ask?"

The steady downpour had begun hours earlier and had turned the road to soup. She eyed the hem of her blue woolen gown. The wagon had already been bogged down twice in the slick, red mud, which had necessitated their exit from the dubious comforts the wagon offered and resulted in stains that would require a good deal of scrubbing on laundering day. Her hands stung at the mere thought.

Halfway through their ascent up the next hill, one of the horses stumbled, causing the wagon to jolt and shudder in a hard turn. Mr. Hubbard wrestled with the reins to regain control, but the vehicle began slipping. "Hold tight!" he shouted as the horses scrambled for their footing. Sarah gripped the flat wooden seat with one hand and the rim of the wagon's side with the other, bracing herself as best she could.

A whining, grinding protest echoed from the wooden frame, mingling with the frightened whinny of the horses as their efforts to remain on their feet caused the wagon to veer sideways and begin tipping.

"Dear God," Mrs. Hubbard moaned, while Mr. Hubbard yelled to his team in nonsensical, guttural sounds of "haw" and "yip."

Sarah squeezed her eyes closed. Heart pounding, stomach dropping, she felt the wagon jerk and drag to the right. Then, the jangling, thudding sound of horses running accompanied the sensation of being pulled at higher speed. Her eyes flew open. Downhill. They were headed in the opposite direction, back down the hill. Mr. Hubbard leaned back on his bench, pulling desperately on the reins as the heavy load pushed the horses faster than they should go.

It must have been only seconds, but felt like hours, before he finally regained control. By then, they were hundreds of feet in the wrong direction, and Sarah's fingers felt permanently imprinted with the grain of the wagon's wood.

"Heavens," Mrs. Hubbard cried, wrapping an arm around her husband's shaking shoulders. Her tear-stained cheek turned toward Sarah. "Are you 'urt, Miss Battersby?"

"N-no." She cleared her throat and forced her hands to release their grip. One by one, her fingers lifted. Little by little, her breath came back.

Mr. Hubbard was now holding his wife while she sobbed quietly. Sarah's hand came to rest over her still-drumming heart. Rising to a crouch, she reached out to stroke Mrs.

Hubbard's back. "We are safe, now," she said, her voice low and calm. "All is well."

The old woman turned creased, watery eyes to her and gave a trembling smile while she squeezed Sarah's hand. "You are such a dear girl."

Sarah returned the smile and asked Mr. Hubbard, "Do you suppose we should try the hill again?"

He shook his head. "The load's too heavy, ye see. We passed the turn for the road to Littlewood a half-mile back. 'Twill add several hours to our journey, but far more likely we arrive ... safe."

A sob from Mrs. Hubbard earned her a gentle pat and a murmured "There, there, Margaret," from her husband. After checking the horses for injury, they climbed back into the wagon and headed for Littlewood, which was more than twenty miles northwest of Keddlescombe. Mr. Hubbard was right—it was a longer, but much flatter, route.

An hour later, just as the enervation of their near-disaster receded and the chill of her damp gown brought shivers to her skin, Sarah felt the wagon slow. They were on a heavily wooded stretch of road and hadn't seen another soul since they had turned onto the seldom-traveled route to Littlewood. Consequently, she was surprised when she heard Mr. Hubbard mumbling, "Damned swells. Leavin' their mounts to wander about and hinder a workin' man's progress."

Curious, she rose up from her seat, bracing one hand against Mrs. Hubbard's shoulder and peering out at the road. There, perhaps ten yards distant, stood a bay mare, her red-brown coat darkened by rainwater, her saddle empty. She nickered and nodded her head at them.

"Where do you suppose the rider be?" Mrs. Hubbard asked, resting her knitting in her lap.

Mr. Hubbard sighed and shook his head. "Likely taking a p—er, havin' a rest. Some lackwits reckon a country lane has no need for courtesies, ye see. Blasted gentry, presumin' others will always give way. Beggin' your pardon, Miss Battersby."

Sarah blinked in surprise. "No need for pardons. It has been a generation since my family could rightly be considered gentry, Mr. Hubbard."

He grunted a neutral response.

She squinted through the soft gray rain, looking to either side of the road. "I do not see the rider. Perhaps the horse has strayed—"

"Ponder if ye like," the old man said impatiently, handing the reins to his wife. "Someah' must clear the road if Oi'm to see me bed this night." With that, he climbed down from the wagon and approached the horse. Although he spoke gently to the animal, it shied away from him, the reins dragging in the mud.

"Stay here, Mrs. Hubbard," Sarah said, stepping carefully over the driver's bench. "It looks as though he could use my help."

Mrs. Hubbard's words, "such a dear girl," followed Sarah as she climbed down. She gathered her skirt in her fist to keep her hem from further damage, but the mud was near ankle-deep. It sucked at her boots, slowing her progress and threatening her footing. The mare whinnied and tossed her head to avoid Mr. Hubbard's hands. Sarah watched her sidling toward a thicket of beech and field maple on the right side of the road.

"Have a care now," Sarah crooned as she revised her direction to intercept the skittish mare. "You wouldn't wish to mar that beautiful coat, would you?" As she came within feet of the animal, the horse suddenly turned and bolted through the shrubbery, clambering down a shallow incline before stopping beneath a stout tree.

Sarah's eyes met Mr. Hubbard's. He shrugged and started for the wagon. She turned to where the horse stood nudging at something on the ground.

Distantly, she heard Mr. Hubbard calling her name. She held up a finger, then picked her way toward the edge of the road where grass and thorny vines had begun to intrude. Shielding her eyes from the persistent rain, she craned her neck and squinted through the leaves. The horse was prodding something brown. And weighty, given the object's resistance to her motions. And it looked to be covered in ... cloth.

"Mr. Hubbard!" She waved frantically before shoving aside dense brambles and beginning her descent toward the base of the tree. "Come quickly!" Sliding down the incline, she grasped at a sapling to steady herself. Soon, she came close to the object the horse had been nudging; it was lying very still beside the broad, sprawling tree trunk, covered in a brown wool coat. She was afraid to touch it. Touch ... him. For, it was most certainly a man, either dead or sleeping very soundly.

"Sir," she said, hoping her voice alone would rouse him. Most emphatically, she did not wish to touch a dead man. The very thought made her shiver worse than five days of cold rain. "Sir, are you ... unwell?"

He did not smell dead. The only scents around her were those of musty damp, loamy soil, wet horse, and washed leaves. Behind her, she heard the racket of Mr. Hubbard blaspheming as he thrashed his way through the brush. Reluctant for the old farmer to witness her cowardice, she poked at the man's upper arm. Muscles beneath the wool were warm and quite firm, but he remained unmoving.

"'Ee breathin'?" Mr. Hubbard asked from behind her.

She shook her head. "It is difficult to say." The man was lying on his belly, his head turned away with his hat plopped awkwardly over his face. The arm she had poked was tucked protectively against his side, the exposed wrist raw and discolored and coated with dried blood. Long and lean, he was both filthy and well dressed, his coat a fine, worsted wool common to gentlemen of means. It was damp and stained with mud. Carefully, she moved closer and bent to remove his wide-brimmed, oddly shabby hat, revealing a tumble of pale-gold curls. She gasped, stumbling backward into Mr. Hubbard.

"Damn me," the old man muttered. "This one's either been trampled by a team of plow horses or 'ee presumed too far with a blacksmith's wife."

Indeed, his face was a mottled mess. Where the flesh was grotesquely swollen, it was various shades of black and yellow. In the precious few places it was not bruised or torn, the skin was ashen.

"We must turn him. If he is alive, he will need our help," she said.

Turning him was easier said than done, for he was quite tall and, while lean, heavy. But with Mr. Hubbard at his shoulders and Sarah at his feet, they managed it. For the second time in only a few minutes, she leapt back with a gasp. He wore no shirt. His coat was unfastened and fell open to reveal a lean, muscled chest and ribs wrapped tightly in linen. The cloth was stained brown with mud, but also bright red with ...

"Ye should return to the wagon, Miss Battersby."

"He is bleeding."

"Aye."

Almost against her will, she stared at the man's naked chest. It was pale, a light thatch of golden hair dusting the area between his nipples and up toward his collarbone. As she watched, the muscular surface moved. "He is breathing."

"Aye," Mr. Hubbard said again, resting his gnarled hands on his hips in a considering pose.

She returned to his side. "If we can get him to the wagon, perhaps—"

"Now, Miss Battersby," he interrupted, pointing down at the prone man. "This here is trouble. And not the sort a foine girl like you should be tanglin' with. Your load be heavy enough without a stranger adding 'is miseries."

Her mouth tightened and her chin rose. "My father did not raise me to ignore the plight of those in need."

He squinted at her, adjusted his hat, and snorted. "Very well, then." He nodded toward the mare. "Take 'er in hand. We'll need 'er help."

It took them nearly an hour, but using rope previously employed to secure the wagon's load, they wrapped it beneath the stranger's arms, leveraged it over a low-slung limb, and managed to drape his body over his horse. They then led the horse back up onto the road and positioned her at the back of the wagon. There, Mr. Hubbard yanked and slid the man lengthways across the wagon's floor, dragging him to where Sarah sat waiting with a blanket. It wasn't much, and far from comfortable, but at least they could transport the unconscious man somewhere safe.

"Like as not, we done him more injury than good," the old man panted as he climbed down to secure the horse to the rear of the wagon.

Sarah glanced up. She was seated on the floor, the man's golden head in her lap as she examined his swollen, discolored face. Delicately, she brushed cool, surprisingly silken curls away from his forehead. "He would almost certainly have died had we left him here, Mr. Hubbard."

"Likely to anyway."

"At least it will not have been due to our callousness."

The wagon shook as the old farmer clambered back up onto the driver's bench. Mrs. Hubbard handed him the reins and commented over her shoulder, "Ye have the right of it, Miss Battersby. The Bible doesn't laud the good Samaritan because 'ee kept on 'is way."

At that moment, the injured man groaned, his head writhing against Sarah's thigh. He did not awaken, but Sarah took the movement as a good sign.

"Aye," grumbled Mr. Hubbard, urging his team forward with a jerk. "Does the Bible mention a salve for a man's bruised arse? Because by the time we reach Keddlescombe, moine'll be in sore need of such a cure."

HIS BED ROCKED AND CREAKED LIKE A SHIP UPON OCEAN swells. Perhaps he had once again traveled all the way to Liverpool.

Perhaps he was en route to America at this very moment.

Distantly, he heard an equine snort and the wet, thudding clop of hooves.

Unless he was bedded down in the hold with the horses, he was not, in fact, at sea. At least, not bodily.

Fingers softly threaded through his hair. Every single inch of him hurt: his head and face, his ribs and shoulders and wrists. But that delicate touch sent unexpected thrills of pleasure rippling through his scalp and across his skin.

With great effort, he forced his eyes to open. The light above was a dull, yellowed blur, striped with brown wood. Blinking several times, the blur came into focus. A canvas. It was a canvas stretched above him. And the whooshing, pelting sound was rain.

Those sweet, gentle fingers played with his hair. His head was elevated, his neck cradled against something soft yet firm. Although it pained him, he turned his head the few inches necessary to see who touched him.

Wide, golden eyes met his. Soft, bowed lips rounded into an O. "You are awake!" she gasped.

Yes, he was awake. With his head lying in a woman's lap, apparently. When had he died? He recalled being taken by Syder, beaten, tortured, and questioned. And then ... released by Benning. He had ridden southwest, toward a property owned by a friend. A safe place, he had thought. But he had only gone two days before collapsing beneath a tree.

"A—angel," he croaked, the word a question.

Her fingertips stroked the skin at his hairline, while honey-gold eyes smiled wryly. "No. Quite human, I fear."

Without thinking, his gaze slid from her face to the swells of her bosom. Viewed from this angle, they appeared rather round and tidy, neither small nor particularly large.

She cleared her throat and halted her fingers. "Perhaps you would like some water. Can you sit?"

He sighed. He did not wish to admit to this woman that he

could not be certain he was alive, much less functional enough to raise himself from her lap. He nodded nonetheless. With her help, he rolled onto his side and pushed himself up. His arms and shoulders shrieked with pain so intense, he nearly collapsed, bright dots dancing in his vision. But she was there, *her* arms surprisingly strong, bracing him against a wooden crate.

"Here," she said, holding a flask to his lips. Cool water tipped down his throat. At the first taste, his body grew so greedy he nearly choked. She responded immediately, controlling the flow for him. Automatically, his hand came up to clasp hers where she held the flask. "Slowly, now," she murmured, her voice calm and low. It gentled him, soothed him.

After drinking his fill, his head began to swim. He was weak as a bloody newborn kitten, his arms nearly useless, his vision a black-spotted fog, his entire body steeped in pain of varying degrees. Without meaning to, he slid toward her, his head landing on her shoulder as the light grew dim and gray. He blinked, and a moment later, his nose was buried in soft wool over softer flesh. Her breasts. He groaned.

"Gracious me," she murmured, her hands cradling his neck and leading him down into her lap.

The world went dark. When the light returned, she was once again stroking his hair, this time absently, while speaking to someone.

"... bit of water, but I do not know what else to do."

A gruff, masculine voice responded, "Not much we can do. Or should, truth be known."

Then, a third voice—female, elderly—advised, "Keep 'im warm. Let 'im sleep. When we reach the village, we can better see to 'is comfort."

Panting and disoriented, he attempted to open his eyes again. She was there, a golden girl stroking his hair. "Where—" he rasped, "where are you taking me?"

Her fingers paused and settled against his scalp. "Our village.

Keddlescombe. In east Devonshire. We shall arrive within a few hours."

He did not reply, his eyes closing as the sounds of rain and horses and creaking wooden wheels faded in and out.

"... somewhere else you would prefer? What was your destination?"

Her voice, so calm and steady, made him want to look at her—her honey eyes and delicately pointed chin and up-tilted nose. She was not beautiful. He had known beautiful. Possessed beautiful. But she drew him, this woman whose soft, firm flesh weakened pain's grip, invited him to take refuge.

He could not. He must warn her.

"I am ..."

She waited while he gathered his breath. "Yes? You are?"

"I am ... danger."

"What's that 'ee says?" the old man asked.

"He is in danger," she replied.

He tried to protest, but no further words would come. He had never been so weak, his muscles leaden and aching, his head throbbing.

"Well, one would suppose," the elderly woman commented. "I wonder if 'ee was set upon by thieves. Why they would take 'is shirt and not 'is coat is bewildering, Oi must say."

"Or 'is boots. Fine-lookin' Hessians, those," the gruff man opined.

The honeyed girl said nothing.

They did not understand. He must make them understand. Swallowing against a dry throat, he whispered, "Leave."

She bent closer, turning her ear to his mouth. Golden brown curls that had escaped her pins coiled tightly close to her head, creating a halo. One of the longer escapees brushed his cheek. "Leave?" She sounded amused. "Where do you wish to go?"

He tried to shake his head, but the motion was slight. "Leave. Me."

She straightened and turned back to meet his eyes. A glint

appeared in hers, the gold turning hard and fierce. "I shall not leave you, sir. Of that you may be certain."

Frustration building, he pulled air into his lungs determinedly. "Misunderstand. You must ... leave me. I am ..." He panted, gathering strength from he knew not where. Already, the light around him was dimming. "I am a danger to you."

He allowed his eyes to close, struggling to stay awake, to explain why she should run as far from him as possible. But somehow, he failed to convey his message properly. Rather than taking heed and ordering the old man to stop and remove him from her sight, she merely grew pert, the muscles of her thighs tensing beneath his neck.

"No," she said, her voice coming to him through a gray mist. "It is you who misunderstands." The last words he heard before all sound receded did little to ease his mind, but he suspected that was not her intention. From what he had seen in her eyes earlier, her final statement was a declaration of truth without varnish: "You are now in my care, do you hear? I will not leave you. And that is that."

Chapter Three

*"Softheaded sentiment has numerous causes
but only one result: calamity."*

—THE DOWAGER MARCHIONESS OF WALLINGHAM to Lady Berne
upon hearing said lady's plans to acquire a cat.

"WHAT COULD YOU HAVE BEEN THINKING?" ELEANOR
Battersby hissed to her daughter. "We can scarcely provide for
our own needs."

It had been well after dark when they'd arrived in the
village, and past midnight before the stranger was settled into
Sarah's bedchamber. Using the blanket as a sling, Sarah, Mr.
Hubbard, and Sarah's mother had managed to haul the
unconscious man into the cottage. Together, they had

removed his coat and boots then unwrapped stiffened linen from his ribs, where they found obvious signs that he had been deliberately sliced multiple times with a sharp blade, exposing muscle and bone. After Mr. Hubbard's warning that the man's wounds and signs of binding along his wrists signaled torture, they had all agreed to keep silent about their unexpected visitor, at least for the time being.

Now, the Hubbards had departed, and Eleanor stood on one side of the narrow bed, her white nightdress glowing in the lantern light, her expression one Sarah had not seen often since childhood. "Have you an answer?"

Unable to meet her mother's eyes, Sarah busied herself with wringing out a cloth into the washbasin. "No one knows our hardships better than I, Mama. What else was I to do? Leave him to die?"

Eleanor folded her arms across her bosom. "You could have left him in Littlewood, at the inn there. The Fox and Cocks."

"It is the Fox and Fowl," Sarah corrected absently, smoothing the damp cloth across his forehead. The man had accrued a copious amount of grime on his ignoble journey. "And who would care for him? Who would pay for his lodgings?"

Reaching across the bed, Eleanor grasped Sarah's forearm. "Everything we do must be carefully considered now. We have little room for error. I thought you knew this."

Sarah straightened, sliding her arm through her mother's grip until she could clutch her hand. "I do." She squeezed her reassurance before retrieving her arm and dipping the cloth in the basin again.

"This impulsive behavior is most unlike you, daughter. And most worrisome."

Her back stiffening, Sarah cleaned the man's face with a feather-light touch, taking care with the swollen, bruised flesh along his eyes and cheeks. "It is no less than Papa would have done. I do not call an act of Christian mercy 'impulsive.'"

"Then explain how you justify inventing a false betrothal,

declaring it before the entire village, if not an act of rash haste. Hmm?"

The heat of shame bloomed beneath her skin. She had no answer—aside from her abiding hatred for Mr. Foote, of course.

"I thought as much."

"It has held him at bay thus far, has it not?"

Eleanor came around the foot of the bed to stand beside her. "It was a lie. A very public, obvious lie. Few believe it, though most understand your reasons. More than anyone, your father and I wish you did not have to marry for reasons other than love. But you do, Sarah. You know this. When he is gone—"

"Please do not speak of it, Mama," she begged, her voice hoarse.

Her mother's hand settled on her shoulder. "When your father dies, we will lose his living. We will lose our home. The school, as well."

Sarah knew she was correct. The curate they had hired to perform her father's church duties had no interest in maintaining a school for girls. For now, since they paid the young, ambitious Mr. Dunhill out of her father's meager income, they controlled his decisions regarding church property. But he had appealed to the bishop to be appointed as the new vicar after her father died. Once Mr. Dunhill was vicar, he would decide what was done with the old abbey, and he had made it clear that he considered St. Catherine's Academy for Girls of Impeccable Deportment a distraction that did not produce enough additional income to be worthy of his time. Indeed, he intended the abbey to become his new residence and the cottage to become a home for his wife's parents.

Neither Sarah nor Eleanor begrudged Mr. Dunhill the right to his decisions. However, those decisions would leave her and her mother with neither home nor income. Sarah had known for months that she must either secure a position or marry. And Mr. Foote had made himself her only choice of husband.

"I cannot marry him, Mama. I cannot."

Her mother's hand stroked her hair, the calluses on her fingers catching on the unruly curls. "Neither can you marry a man who does not exist, Sarah. Your lie will not protect you for long."

She turned to meet Eleanor's eyes. For all the similarities she and her mother shared—the rebelliously curling, light-brown hair, the pointed chin and upturned nose—their eyes were different. Her mother's were green, resigned and dimmed with the burdens she must bear.

"What if it were not a lie?" Sarah whispered. "Or, at least, appeared to be true long enough for me to secure a new position?"

Eleanor sighed and shook her head. "A new position. After two years of failed inquiries." She chuckled dryly. "Your father is the believer in miracles, Sarah. Not I."

"A month. Perhaps two. That is all I need. Ann Porter said she knows of a school in Sussex—"

"We do not have a month or two."

Sarah's heart squeezed painfully, her throat tightening. "Please do not say that."

"Do you know what your father ate yesterday? A crust of bread. Nothing more. He will leave us soon."

"Please ..."

Eleanor's arm wrapped around her daughter's shoulders, simultaneously shaking and squeezing her. "Lie to others if you must—to me, even. But do not deceive yourself."

"I cannot marry him. You know what sort of man he is."

"Yes. I know. I also know if you do not accept him, he has promised to increase rents on those who can ill afford it—Mr. Hubbard, young Mr. Lovejoy. He has you in a fair bind, daughter."

For long minutes, they swayed together, their bone-deep weariness rocking them as a mother rocks a babe. Sarah let her head fall forward, let the cloth slide down the curve of the porcelain bowl into water now stained with dirt and blood. "Please, Mama. Just ..." She swallowed hard. "Please let me try."

Her mother gave her one last squeeze before releasing her. "Very well." Eleanor plucked the lengths of fresh linen she had torn from an old bed sheet, rounded to the unconscious man's opposite side, and dabbed an experimental finger at his wounds. The cuts were red at the edges and slowly oozing blood. They were not healing well on their own.

"We'll need a name for your mysterious suitor. Sending you to London with the Hubbards put you beyond the reach of gossip and speculation for a time, but the villagers already suspect your lie, and that will become a problem soon." She poked and pressed, then without glancing up, held out her hand, her fingers waggling. "Cloth."

Automatically, Sarah complied, wringing the wet cloth and setting it in her mother's palm.

"Mr. Foote is a shrewd man—detestable, I grant you, but passably clever. If you are to deceive him, we must name someone real. Believable," Eleanor continued, wiping the blood away. The man did not move. Thankfully, he appeared quite oblivious to her mother's ministrations. "Someone for whom you would have had occasion to develop a fondness."

Nodding, Sarah retrieved the thread and needle her mother had fetched earlier and placed it in her outstretched hand. "I agree."

Eleanor went to work stitching the man's flesh, her needle poking and piercing. "And he must be either too distant to hear of your deception, or—"

"Or a willing participant." Sarah picked up the candleholder and held it above the man's wounds.

Her mother's hand paused after tightening one of the loops. She glanced at Sarah's face, then at the unconscious man's bruised, distorted features, then back at Sarah. Her eyebrows rose with dawning realization. "Oh, daughter. This plan of yours is mightily flawed."

"I am aware."

"Even if he recovers—"

"He will."

"—you have no idea who he is. He could already be married."

"It is possible," Sarah sighed. "But I do not need him to marry me. Only pretend to be promised to me. For a while."

"What makes you think he would agree to such a thing? He is a man of means." Eleanor waved her free hand toward the coat that had been draped over a wooden chair in the corner. "Hardly in need of anything we have to offer."

"At the moment," Sarah retorted, "He needs us quite desperately."

Resuming her stitches, Eleanor gave a slight shake of her head. "Gratitude is a precarious limb to hang your hopes upon, Sarah. You know nothing of this man or his character. These wounds are not scrapes caused by being thrown from his horse. What if he is dangerous—a criminal or a ... a scoundrel?"

Sarah eyed the man's bare chest, taking the steady rise and fall of his breathing as a positive sign. "I will be asking him to lie for me." She sat on the side of the bed, her hip gently bumping his arm, her free hand brushing his hair back from his forehead. "A scoundrel?" She smiled through her exhaustion. "I do hope so."

CLACK, TAP. CLACK, TAP. CLACK, TAP. THE SOUND OF HIS bootfalls approaching the library door sent fine tremors over Hannah's scalp. Clack, tap. Clack, tap. Patient and measured, the sounds nevertheless grew louder, closer, punctuated with the sharpness of his walking stick.

She sat very still, the book heavy against her thighs. Clack, tap. Clack, tap.

The knob twisted. She heard the small squeak. Felt the whoosh of air upon its opening. Clack, tap. Clack, tap.

Her eyes remained fixed on the page she could no longer see.

"Good morning, Hannah." His voice was soft, warm. She had heard him speak to others and knew that, with her, he was different. A hand gently stroked her hair. Once. Twice. "What is it you are reading?"

He always wished to know. "The sonnets of Shakespeare," she answered.

Another stroke of her hair, then an amused, "I should think you would have them all memorized by now."

"I do. I like to see the words."

With a quiet "hmm," he came to settle in the chair beside her, twisting his walking stick between his fingers. "You mustn't neglect your mathematics, Hannah. Poetry is edifying of human nature, but a thorough knowledge of sums will be required to manage the accounts. In some ways, numbers can also tell you a great deal about human nature."

She did not reply, instead fingering the page and struggling to keep her breathing even and slow.

"For example," he said, his tone that of an instructor. "I recently discovered an imbalance at one of the clubs. A minor thing, really. It made me curious. So I gave the thread a tug, and do you know what I found?"

She shook her head.

"A man I believed loyal had been lining his pockets. Imagine." He chuckled lightly. "Naturally, I dispensed with him. By stealing from me, he steals from you. I cannot allow that."

Controlling her reactions had become automatic over the years, as the consequences of provoking him proved too dear. But every time he spoke like this, as if the things he did were as normal as taking a cup of tea, her stomach clenched and sickened. Fortunately, his visits had been less frequent of late.

"These are the lessons you must learn. I do nothing for myself; it is all for you, Hannah. One day you will understand. Threats must be identified swiftly, else they fester and grow intransigent." The walking stick tapped once quietly, causing a flinch that she immediately stifled. Then, it resumed its slow, back-and-forth spin. "Over the past months, I have had occasion to rediscover this critical understanding. A new foe has taken an interest. Not to worry. The weapon he chose is feeble and frivolous. However, like imbalanced numbers, that weapon is a thread that may be followed."

A hand stroked her hair. She kept her eyes on the words, kept her hands and body motionless.

"You are my treasure, dearest Hannah. My resolve to protect you is steadfast." The hand drifted away with a sigh. "Mathematics. Apply your remarkable mind to those subjects which will serve you faithfully." He rose from the chair with a tap of his walking stick and light brushing of his coat. "For now, your fond Papa will work to follow the threads that may damage the tapestry." His steps retreated. Clack, tap. Clack, tap. Clack, tap. The squeak of the knob. The rush of air. "And, once found, I shall cut them away with swift and uncompromising force."

SARAH AWAKENED WITH A GASP, HEART SKITTERING INSIDE her chest. The dream had come again. She pressed her lips together to imprison the whimpers inside. Every time, it was worse, requiring greater effort to recover her composure.

Rolling over onto her side, she pressed the back of her hand over her mouth and stared up toward the window. It was difficult to see anything other than the sky from her position on the floor. Pre-dawn light painted the world dusky blue while stars clung like dust to a curtain. Sunrise was perhaps an hour away. She could go back to sleep. The good Lord knew her body needed the rest.

She squeezed her eyes closed. No. Someday, perhaps, she could afford the luxury of a full night's sleep. Not this day.

A gasp, a creak, and the rustle of bed linens drew her attention to the man in her bed. Strange to think of it. She had never been kissed. Not seriously, anyway. Surely Bertie Lovejoy's attempts did not count, for they both had been twelve years old and subject to a dare from Ann Porter. Still, by her reckoning, she had never been kissed by a man, and now one lay in her bed. Most peculiar.

His breathing changed, quickened. Bracing her hands against the bed frame, she sat up to look at him. His eyes, less swollen than they had been yesterday, opened to meet hers. They were blue, surrounded by red instead of white. "You—you are still here."

She pushed herself up to stand beside him, smoothing the skirt of her white dressing gown. "Yes. How do you feel?"

He grimaced and promptly ignored her question. "Matilda."

She blinked then shook her head. "Sarah," she corrected. "Sarah Battersby. Yesterday, we brought you to our village. You are in my home. Do you remember? Is—is Matilda your wife?"

Closing his eyes for several seconds, he appeared to be gathering his wits. Perhaps he could not see very well. That would certainly explain mistaking her for another woman. Or his head might have been damaged severely, his mind addled.

His lips twitched and tightened. "Matilda. My horse. Is she ... safe?"

"Horse? Oh! Yes. She is in the care of Mr. Hubbard. His stable is quite sound."

"I am relieved to hear it."

Why did she get the impression he was amused? She smoothed her unruly hair, which was frizzed and ill-confined by the plait over her shoulder, then forced herself to lace her fingers together over her belly. "Are you in need of anything? Water? Broth, perhaps? It is early yet, but—"

"A chamber pot, Miss Battersby. That would be most welcome."

It took a full minute for the flush of embarrassment to rise and bloom. She swallowed, then nodded and looked away. Cleared her throat. Turned. Stumbled as her pallet of blankets tangled her feet. "I—ah, I do have one." She indicated the wooden privacy screen in one corner of the small bedroom. "There. I can retrieve it for you if you like."

He rolled and twisted up onto one elbow, gasping as the motion stretched his injured flesh and her mother's careful stitches.

Rushing to his side, she admonished, "You must take greater care, sir. Your wounds are deep."

As he slung the blankets aside and slid one leg to the floor, he grumbled, "I do not need you to tell me about my injuries, Miss Battersby."

She straightened, hands planted on her hips. "No? It seems to me the reason you are here is that you have underestimated their severity. Much to your detriment."

He grunted through his teeth as he pushed himself into a sitting position on the edge of the bed. Her skirts now brushing his knees, she prepared to assist him, reaching for his bare forearm. Instantly, he jerked away, his curling golden head bowed as he gathered his resolve to stand. "Another thing I do not need? Help with taking a piss."

Well, she thought, her chin rising. *It appears Mama was correct. Gratitude is a fragile limb, indeed.*

Understanding pride better than most, however, she simply nodded and stepped back, giving him room to rise. She also knew the limits of his strength, so she remained close, just a few feet away, arms folded beneath her bosom, back resting against the plaster wall.

"Bloody hell," he muttered, the muscles in his arms visibly shaking as he braced his hands on the edge of the mattress and attempted to support some of his weight. He relaxed, slumping fully back onto the bed, panting as though he had just lifted a horse.

She waited, one finger tapping on her opposite arm.

He tried again, his muscles straining, elbows shaking as he leaned forward, forcing himself onto his feet with an agonized groan. His standing position—more of a crouch, really—did not last long, as weakness sent him teetering. Swaying. Falling.

Toward her.

"Ooph!"

His arms caught most of his weight as they crumpled against the wall, but the sudden pressure of a man's body flattening her as she attempted to catch him drove the air from her lungs. Warm, naked skin covered in crisp hair pressed against her cheek, then slid downward until her nose was buried against his throat. He was trembling. Everywhere. She tried pushing against his chest, but to no avail. For a lean man, he was dreadfully heavy.

"Dyah enk iss pozbul to mff a bih?"

His chest was heaving, sweat beading along his throat with the strain of remaining upright. "Wh-what did you say?" he panted, his own forehead pressed against the plaster above her shoulder.

"Can't brth."

"Oh. Right." One of his arms buckled, allowing him to slide sideways into the wall. "Better?"

"Yes." Drawing precious air, she slid her arms around his waist, taking care not to disturb the cuts along his ribs, and flattened her hands on the muscles of his back.

He stiffened. "Were this any other time," he said, his voice strained and thready. "I would answer your ... eagerness with abounding vigor. At present, however, I confess seduction is not foremost in my capabilities."

"Seduction?" she squeaked.

"Not to worry. I heal quickly." He traced a trembling finger down her cheek, the light touch causing disturbing sensations to dance along her spine. "Within a day or so, I should be fit to thank you properly."

"Th-thank me?"

"Mmm. You are quite fetching in your way." He considered her with eyes still swollen and bruised, yet sparking with a bright blue flame. "Tightly wound, but then, the tighter the coil, the more powerful the release."

She barely understood a thing he was saying. And yet, it

washed everything from her feet to her scalp with prickling heat, made the air in the room insufficient to satisfy her lungs. "Sir," she said firmly, as she would to an impudent student. "I was attempting to assist you."

A corner of his lips lifted. "Of course you were."

"To the chamber pot." Her voice was clear and crisp, each word enunciated with cutting precision.

Both his lips and his eyes lost their smile. "Ah. Yes." The same corner of his mouth lifted again, but this time, the grin was wry, as though he now laughed at himself. "Forgive my impertinence. An old habit, you might say."

"Come," she said briskly, sliding one arm around his waist and lifting his arm over her shoulders. She seemed the right height to act as his crutch. "I shall help you to the corner."

He slumped against her as he staggered away from the wall. Her knees buckled and she nearly gasped at the sudden weight, but it lasted only seconds before he grunted and took most of the burden back onto his own weakened legs. They stood swaying for a moment, he using her for balance more than strength.

"It is all right, you know," she said. "Lean on me. I am accustomed to heavy loads."

His head fell forward as they dragged and shuffled toward the screened corner. "Are you implying I am fat?"

"No!"

"Because some women prefer a portly gentleman. Or so I have been told."

"Oh, for the love of—"

"Presumably they mistake strong appetites of one sort for those of another. Or perhaps it is simply a fondness for padding."

"I believe your mind may be addled."

They paused together as they moved into the small area behind the screen. "Undoubtedly," he said. "But that was true long before my injuries."

She unwrapped his arm from around her shoulders and ducked beneath it to place his hand against the wall. "Can you—" She swallowed and cleared her throat, waving in the direction of the wooden chair her father had fashioned for use with the chamber pot beneath. "Can you manage on your own, or ...?" Although she refused to meet his eyes, she watched as his free hand hooked above the fall of his riding breeches. The waist sank lower, exposing the lean, defined muscles of his lower belly. *Not fat,* she reflected. *Not fat at all.*

"If I cannot, then I daresay we have greater problems than an addled mind."

His voice, a rich baritone roughened by sleep, pulled her gaze to his mouth—which grinned teasingly. He had rather lovely lips, surprisingly untouched by whatever had damaged his eyes and cheeks. They were firm instead of full, defined at the edges and curled slightly upward at the corners. Clearly, his was a mouth that smiled readily and often.

"Miss Battersby."

She liked the way he said her name. The aristocratic diction was crisp, whereas the tone was warm and smooth, like melted butter soaking a hard crust.

"Ordinarily, I would not oppose indulging a lady's more peculiar desires."

The way he formed the words, his lips mobile and shapely, rounding and pursing along the vowels, was fascinating. Of course, it was likely the only part of his face that did not pain him to move, so perhaps that explained—

"However, in this instance, I must protest."

Blinking, she repeated, "Protest?"

"Your watchful presence whilst I relieve myself. A tad undignified, I'm afraid."

She stumbled backward, her shoulder knocking into the screen. Grabbing it blindly to keep the thing from toppling over, she gasped. "Oh! Gracious me!"

He merely grinned like the devil while her entire being fired

red. Unwilling to further relinquish composure, she steadied the screen and nodded firmly, spinning toward the bedchamber door.

"I—I will fetch you some broth. A-and bread." She twisted the knob, exited the room, and closed the door behind her with more force than necessary. Wincing at the loud slam, she leaned back against the wood and covered her cheeks with her palms.

How will I ever look at him again? The empty corridor did not answer.

She sighed and patted her chest, then fanned her hot cheeks and made for the small kitchen at the rear of the cottage.

What must he think of me? she asked cold ashes as she stooped to light the fire beneath the pot. For, never had she looked upon a man in such a way. Of course, most of the men she had ever known were either married, old enough to be her father, or so familiar to her, they might as well have been brothers. In Keddlescombe, her options for male companionship were few.

Mr. Foote did not signify.

Which brought her to her third and most pressing question: *After such a humiliating interaction, how in heaven's name do I tell this stranger he shall act as my betrothed?*

Like the empty corridor and cold ashes, the dancing orange flame beneath the iron pot offered no answer, and instead seemed only to be laughing.

Chapter Four

"'Scoundrel' appears to be the new definition of 'dashing' this season. Perhaps I shall perish soon and be spared the redefining of 'regal' to include beggars and vagabonds."

—THE DOWAGER MARCHIONESS OF WALLINGHAM to Lady Atherbourne in a letter explaining the pitfalls of romantic nonsense.

WHEN NEXT COLIN AWAKENED, THE LIGHT FROM THE WINDOW was afternoon-bright, and the inimitable Miss Battersby was gone. Their last interaction had been a mite terse, with she setting a bowl of broth and a slice of bread on the side table and he barely conscious, head swimming after collapsing back onto the narrow bed.

"You should eat something before you sleep," was all she said before departing, face red and eyes downcast.

Perhaps he should not have teased her so. Something about her prim manner and authoritative speech provoked him. She reminded him of every governess he'd ever had. Except he had never longed to kiss the starch out of his governesses.

Tossing aside the blankets, he managed to sit up and plant his feet on the creaky wooden floor. The flesh over his ribs stung and protested, but he could not let a little pain prevent him from leaving. He was a danger to her, to anyone who aided him. He must find his coat and boots, find Matilda, and then complete the journey to his original destination.

"Ah, I see you are awake."

His head swung toward the door. There, an older twin of Miss Battersby stood, a stack of folded cloth between her hands, a stern look on her pixie face.

"You must be her mother. Mrs. Battersby, is it?"

"Mmm," she affirmed. "And you? What is your name? Or shall I call you 'stranger'?"

He hesitated before answering, "Perhaps that is best."

She stepped forward to place the folded stack on the foot of the bed. "Some clothing for you. My husband's. There is water and a bit of soap on the washstand."

"Thank you."

"You appear much improved." Her eyes landed on his hand where it rested over his ribs. "Any signs of fever?"

The first two days after he had fled London, he had been feverish, but by the time Miss Battersby had loaded him into her wagon, that had broken, replaced by debilitating weakness. He shook his head in answer to the mother's question. "I am on the mend, it seems. As soon as I can locate my horse, I shall trouble you no more."

The woman's mouth tightened. "When you leave is your choice, naturally. However, my daughter did not save your life, nor I mend your wounds, only to have you perish for recklessness."

He blinked, unaccustomed to being chastised by a female. Occasionally, his sister would do so, but Victoria had not spoken to him in months. His mother had been dead for years, and before that, could scarcely be bothered to offer a greeting, much less a scolding. He gestured to his ribs. "This was your handiwork?"

She nodded, her pointed chin elevating. "Have a care how you exert yourself. Your wounds are deep and will not heal well on their own. You must keep the stitches intact for at least a fortnight."

"My thanks to you, madam, for your kindness. Please convey the same to your daughter."

"Perhaps you should thank her yourself."

He stood, steadying himself against the same wall where he had collapsed against Miss Battersby that morning. "I should think you would prefer distance between a strange man and your unmarried daughter. Are you not concerned she slept here last night?"

The woman's hard stare softened, and she crossed her arms in an oddly familiar pose. "Sarah insisted. She refused to leave you."

He huffed out a chuckle. "Now, that I believe." Moving to the foot of the bed, he picked up the stack of clothing: linen shirt, dark trousers. Simple, well-made garments that had been mended numerous times.

"Where is your husband? I should like to thank him as well for your kind hospitality."

Her shoulders stiffened. "He is asleep."

He frowned. "A bit early in the day for—"

"I have much to do," she said tartly. "I shall leave you to dress and ..." Her nose wrinkled. "Well, as I said, the soap is on the washstand, and more water can be found at the well in the garden. There is a stew in the kitchen when you are hungry."

"Mrs. Battersby." His voice halted her as she opened the door. "I must leave—and soon. Where will I find my horse?"

Without turning, she answered, "Ask my daughter." Then, she closed the door behind her as though being chased.

"Blast," he muttered, tossing the clothing back onto the bed before limping to the washstand. Infernal stubbornness must surely run in families, for the ladies Battersby both possessed that quality in abundance.

Glancing at the sizeable bucket of water at his feet, the full basin on the washstand, and the sliver of homemade soap placed neatly beside a washcloth, he sighed. Stubborn they might be, but they were also kind. Miss Battersby—Sarah, he preferred to think of her by that name—had stubbornly refused to leave him to die. She had stubbornly cared for him, even sleeping beside his bed ... which was not his at all, but one she had provided, and at some risk to her own safety and reputation.

Glancing around the small chamber, he noticed a few details he had earlier missed. The pillow on the wooden chair near the window was embroidered with small flowers and framed with a ruffle. The coverlet was a patchwork of fabrics—ginghams, sprigged muslins, and floral cottons—all in shades of lavender, white, and sunny yellow. He ran a hand over it. Such fine stitching. The fabrics themselves were wash-worn, clearly reutilized for a new purpose, but great care had been taken in the design and crafting of the quilt. The dark, wooden bedstead was plain, but solid and in good repair, the feather mattress plump and comfortable.

"This is your room, is it not, sweet Sarah?" He grinned slowly, seeing the place in a new light. Why it should delight him that he had slept in *her* bed, he could not say. But it did.

"Bloody hell," he muttered in an ongoing conversation with himself. Shaking his head, he stripped off his filthy breeches, took up the cloth, and sloshed it in the basin.

He needed to leave.

Briskly scrubbing his skin, he cringed at the flash of cold water and the sting of soap. It was hardly the baths he was accustomed to, but it would have to do.

He needed to leave because if he did not, his stubborn, honey-eyed Miss Battersby would be in danger, not just from the man who hunted him, but from Colin himself.

"YOU LET HIM LEAVE?" SARAH HURRIED FROM THE COTTAGE parlor, past the staircase and the front door, and into the corridor to her bedchamber. Seeing the room was empty, she swung around to confront her mother, who had followed behind. "Why did you not stop him?"

"Calm yourself, daughter," Eleanor chided.

"We need him, Mama. _I_ need him."

"This foolish plan of yours was never going to—"

Rubbing at her eyes, Sarah tried to ease the dry ache behind them. Unfortunately, her fingers had little effect; the only cure was sleep. "Did you at least discover where he means to go?"

Her mother sniffed. "The village, then the Hubbard farm. He mentioned a horse. Marigold, or some such."

"Matilda."

Eleanor waved a hand dismissively. "Regardless, it is several miles, and given his condition, that is approximately as manageable as leaping across the Channel to take tea with an odious Frenchman. I would guess he has either collapsed near the old orchard or recognized his folly and is even now making his return here."

Sarah's chest tightened at the thought of him lying unconscious—again—on the side of the road. Brushing past her mother, she headed for the front door. "You knew he was weak, and still you allowed him to leave."

"What would you have me do? Bind him hand and foot? Lock him inside your bedchamber? That man is not our prisoner. He is wealthy, likely gentry. He may even be titled."

That stopped Sarah where she stood, hand resting on the knob of the cottage's front door. "Do you ..." She took a deep breath and turned to face her mother. "Do you think it is possible?"

Eleanor stepped forward to grasp Sarah's free hand. "If he agrees to help you—and that is, at best, uncertain—it will be because he seeks to settle a debt. Agreeing to your absurd charade is not the only possible method of repayment. Perhaps he will settle funds upon us, once he returns to his family. A far better reward, I daresay, than this silly pretense, which shall gain you only a temporary reprieve."

Her jaw clenched, the tight squeezing of her heart and throat clamoring to be eased. "If he should die, or leave without an understanding ... He is the only hope, Mama."

"That is his choice, not yours. For pity's sake, Sarah, you cannot bend everything and everyone to your will. It is long past time you learned—"

Sarah yanked her hand away, jerked the door open, and slammed it behind her. Blindly, she strode past her father's rose garden, through the small gate, and out onto the narrow road. The late-day sun lavished the church's valley in rich, amber gold. But she took little note.

Her mother was wrong. Eleanor had surrendered to the ill fortune looming like floodwaters overtopping a dike. But *she* was not the one who must marry Mr. Foote. No, that wretched duty belonged to Sarah.

It was Sarah who must agree before God to obey him.

Sarah who must allow him to touch her.

Sarah who must bear his children.

Her head spun as it swiveled back and forth in denial. Eleanor did not understand. Sarah would sooner starve to death. If her mother's fate and that of Foote's tenants did not also rest on her shoulders, she would have left Keddlescombe rather than entertaining his suit for even a moment. Eleanor might consider the battle already lost, but Sarah had no such luxury. The price of failure would be paid by her, not her mother. And it would be painfully dear.

Her footfalls along the hard-packed soil of the village road blended with the steady, soughing breeze coming off the sea. The air was cool today and smelled of brine, the waves of the Channel a distant drumbeat. Ordinarily, such fine conditions would be just the balm she needed. But nothing could ease the knot in her chest—nothing except finding him and persuading him to lie. For her.

She let her eyes travel the road ahead, where it wound gradually down to the floor of the valley, then back up the opposite slope past the old orchard. Beyond the peak of the hill, it descended again into the village.

He was weak, with much healing yet to do. He could not have traveled far.

Passing the school—a looming stone structure with Gothic-arched windows and one ivy-covered wall—she slowed her stride. It was quiet there. Too quiet. She stopped and swiveled to peer across the open valley, shielding her eyes from the setting sun. When she turned back to the old abbey, her fears were confirmed. No movement. No screeches of outrage or delight. No giggling or shouting. The girls had gone somewhere, perhaps to explore the beach, as they were fond of doing. She had warned them not to go anywhere without her. Keddlescombe was a tiny village populated with good people, but it only took one moment with one despicable man for a young girl's future to be shattered. A man like Felix Foote.

The thought quickened her pace. By the time she reached the hilltop orchard, the tension riding the muscles along her spine had gripped her stomach and flushed into the surface of her skin. Why could everyone not simply do as she instructed? If they had, the stranger would still be at her cottage, and the girls would be safely ensconced at the abbey, and she would not feel this crawling urgency to shake them all until they understood the precariousness of—

"Miss Battersby! Er—we did not expect to see you ... that is, we were thinking ... it is such a lovely day, is it not?"

Sarah blinked as Caroline Thurgood, the oldest of her students and the one in charge when Sarah was not present at the school, emerged from behind one of the thicker apple trees, her apron hem lifted to hold what looked to be a dozen or so of the rosy-flushed fruits. The girl was sixteen, dark-haired, and passably pretty with a fair complexion and thick-lashed blue eyes. Like nearly all the girls at St. Catherine's Academy, she was the daughter of wealthy, ambitious parents who sought to purchase the one thing they lacked: a title. In a few months, Caroline would return to London, where she would be offered on the marriage mart to a certain breed of gentleman—those with pockets to let, but a bloodline to compensate. It was Sarah's task to teach them the skills required to be first debutantes, then wives. But, above all, she must to deliver them back to their parents in perfect health and virtue, which was impossible to ensure if she could not control them.

Quickly examining the grove where chatter and laughter had turned to guilt-stricken stares upon her arrival, she counted nine of the twelve girls, all similarly attired in aprons currently used as cloth baskets. "Where are the others?" she snapped. "Miss Pritchard and Miss Parnham and Miss Colton. Did you leave them alone at the school?"

Caroline swallowed visibly, her cheeks reddening to match her apples. "No, Miss Battersby. A few of the village lads were playing cricket on the green, and I thought there would be no harm—"

"Miss Thurgood," Sarah bit out. "It is my job to determine what is potentially harmful and what is not. That is why I set out rules. Your job is to follow those rules and to ensure the others do likewise in my absence. I thought you were capable of bearing such responsibility. It appears I was mistaken."

Moving away from the ladder where she had been plucking apples, the crimson-haired Lydia came forward to defend her best friend. "Caro only wanted us to enjoy the light for an hour or two, Miss Battersby." Lydia glanced at Caroline before turning back to Sarah with her chin a fraction of an inch higher. "It has been nothing but rain for a week. And these apples are going to waste. And Mary Elizabeth is better on the pitch than any boy—"

"Indeed," Caroline nodded eagerly, her voice breathless. "She is a true all-rounder; even the boys say so."

"And Susannah wished only to watch the match whilst Penelope purchases a bit of butter and cream for Mrs. Blake, for we have run out. And—"

Sarah's patience with the chattering girl expired abruptly. "Miss Cresswell!"

The girl's red eyebrows rose nearly an inch, her eyes rounding. "Yes?"

"That is quite enough."

She bit her lower lip and nodded, clutching her apples close.

"Miss Thurgood, take the girls and return to the school. I shall continue into the village and retrieve the others."

Caroline swallowed and curtsied awkwardly, dislodging one of the fruits from her makeshift apron basket. It plopped onto the grassy ground and rolled to a stop at the toe of Sarah's boot. Wide eyes met Sarah's.

"Take your apples with you."

Nine girls rushed into obedience. If only they had been so compliant to begin with, Sarah thought, careful to maintain her stern countenance. As she watched them haul their fruited loads back toward the vicarage, she slowly stooped to retrieve the escaped apple. A helpless smile tugging at her lips, she shook her head, tucked it into the pocket of her unfashionable, striped overdress, and resumed her brisk walk to the village.

Keddlescombe was nothing like London. Fewer than twenty buildings crowded together along the floor of the valley. Most of the structures were white with thick thatched roofs, and they surrounded a modest square with a tidy, open field of grass at the center. This time of year, farmers and merchants converged on the square daily to offer the bounty of the harvest. But if one wished, the entire village could be traversed on foot in five minutes. That did not include the time required to respond to all the greetings and polite demands for conversation, of course. She reckoned it at a full thirty minutes for either her or her mother. The village might be small—around sixty residents at last count—but everyone knew everything about everyone. And what they did not know, they speculated upon.

This was Sarah's first foray into the square since her impulsive, public declaration to Mr. Foote. She took a deep breath, keeping her pace deliberately steady, her gaze determinedly forward. If she appeared ashamed, then they would pity her. So, she must not allow the enormity of her lie to intrude upon her thoughts.

First, she must retrieve her students, then locate the injured man before he did something to further hurt himself ... or her.

"Sarah! Good day to ye," called Ann Porter from the east side of the green, where she watched the impromptu cricket match.

Sarah approached her oldest friend. "Ann." Pressing Ann's outstretched hand, she smiled and nodded toward the children. "Who is winning?"

"Who d'ye suppose? Miss Colton there is a right terror as a bowler and even stronger at the bat. 'Tis a wonder the lads allow her to play."

Glancing sideways at Ann's freckled countenance and wistful expression, Sarah observed quietly, "You could join them, you know."

Ann chuckled. "Bertie'd like that, would 'ee not? His intended wife playing a boy's game instead of returnin' to tend the crops."

"Everyone deserves a respite now and then."

Ann grew quiet then slid an arm around Sarah's waist. "Everyone except you?"

Stiffening, Sarah kept her eyes fixed on the game. Mary Elizabeth had just scored again, causing four boys on the opposing team to drop their faces into their palms.

"You 'pear half dead, Sarah."

She closed her eyes and sighed. "Not this again."

Ann's arm squeezed tighter. "Yes. Until you confess Oi'm right. In three months, this is our longest conversation. Ye're always workin', and obviously get no more'n a few winks at night. Continue as you are, and ye're like to take up residence in the grave before—"

"My students rely upon me, as does my mother. I should let everything come apart because I am *tired?*" She laughed dryly. "How far your opinion of me has fallen."

With one last pat on Sarah's waist, Ann pulled away. "Mr. Foote was askin' after you this morning. He expressed ... concern."

Acid filled Sarah's stomach, rising into her throat. "Mr. Foote has long been overly familiar for the tenuous nature of our acquaintance."

"Mmm. Per'aps this mysterious gent—of which you have told me nothin'—will persuade Mr. Foote of 'is folly. When were you plannin' to share the glad tidings with yer dearest friend? Oi ask merely out of curiosity, mind."

The heat in her cheeks caused Sarah's feet to shift in discomfort. "I ... I intended to tell you ... that is, I would have done so."

"Had it been true."

Denial lodged in Sarah's throat, but she could not bring herself to lie. Not to Ann.

"Oh, stop frettin'. Oi've been keepin' yer secrets since you found me muddyin' me gown behind the church, Sarah. Oi see little reason to change course now."

"You were four."

Ann smiled. "And you were horrified. The vicar's girl, whose gowns were ever lovely and spotless."

Sarah glanced down at her hem, worn and frayed and discolored with the dirt she could never entirely wash away. "That was a long time ago." A shriek from the green was a welcome distraction. Mary Elizabeth's team had scored again. "I should gather up my stray lambs and take them home. Those boys have been crushed soundly enough for one day."

Ann snorted.

Sarah cast her a sideways glance. "First, though, I must tend to some ... tasks here in the village. You will watch them for me? I shan't be long."

Her friend's eyebrows arched, her freckles gleaming in the fading sunlight. "Certainly."

Sarah paused as she brushed past her friend. Over her shoulder, she said quietly, "Thank you, Ann."

Ann gave her the crooked smile she remembered from their youth. "Certainly."

Relieved that she could resume the mission for which she had left the cottage in the first place, Sarah hurried along Limekiln Lane, glancing side to side down each narrow cross street. Admittedly, there were only four. Keddlescombe was a tiny village. A cursory search of the main streets between shops and houses at the center took minutes.

As she headed back toward the green, she turned east and spotted the cheerful green door of the bakery. Perhaps Mrs. Jones had heard something. Her ear for gossip was well known.

The bell chimed as Sarah entered and smiled at the large, frost-haired woman entering the small room from the bakehouse, her arms piled with loaves. "Mrs. Jones. A rather substantial order you have there. I expect I shall soon see you in Mr. Canfield's shop, admiring his new glazed crockery."

The woman chuckled, her voice like coarse pebbles. "Nothin' so fortunate as that. This 'ere's for the Reverend Dunhill's Sunday picnic. Christian duty is more costly for some, I gather." She dropped the loaves on the wooden counter and began wrapping them in brown paper. "Still," she continued thoughtfully, "that cranky old butcher must contribute a pig for the occasion, so I suppose me lot's better than some."

"Picnic?" Sarah blinked.

"Aye. In the churchyard. Entire congregation is invited. Mr. Dunhill announced it at the end of his sermon, Sunday last. Missed that, did you? Not surprisin'. Never seen a man talk so much and say so little. Full of blather, that one. Unlike your dear Papa. Lord, I do miss those days."

Sarah smiled noncommittally. The young curate was brimming with ambition and fervor, but his oratory skills sorely needed refinement. "Mrs. Jones, I was wondering if you had heard any news of a visitor to Keddlescombe."

"Visitor?" Her thick hands deftly knotted a piece of twine, set the wrapped bread neatly in the growing stack, then grasped a bare loaf and continued wrapping without breaking eye contact with Sarah. "What manner of visitor?" Sharp brown eyes topped by prematurely white brows sparked with curiosity. "Don't see many of those 'round here."

Sarah felt her shoulders slump as she sighed. "So, you haven't heard anything?"

"Never said that."

Sarah tilted her head and narrowed her eyes. "What do you know?"

The woman snorted. "Would take decades to chronicle, dearie. If 'tis recent arrivals you wish to learn about, I only can repeat what Mr. Canfield's wife reported, and you know how she favors exaggeration."

Sarah waited impatiently while Mrs. Jones tied off the next package and disappeared through the door to the bakehouse, returning moments later with another armful of bread.

"Now then, where was I? Oh, yes. Mrs. Canfield. She said a man came into the shop earlier today and tried to sell 'is boots. Fine ones they were, too. Hessians, made in London. Rather odd, she said, as 'ee had no others to wear."

Her breath caught as her heart kicked her breastbone.

"When was this?"

"No more'n a quarter-hour, I'd say."

Sarah turned and flung open the green door, throwing a "Thank you, Mrs. Jones!" over her shoulder. Two doors away, Mr. Canfield's shop—filled with a mishmash of items from fabric to fishing nets to Mrs. Canfield's dreadful feathered hats—was thankfully still open. Upon entering, her eyes landed on the handsome boots prominently featured in the front window. Clearly, the stranger had been here, and had already departed, for the portly proprietor was the only other soul present.

"Miss Battersby!" The expression of shock on the man's round face would be comical if she did not understand the reason for it—she had avoided his shop for months. Why court temptation, after all, when fabric for new gowns or fine leather gloves or even the lovely beeswax candles near the counter were beyond her reach?

"Good day to you, Mr. Canfield," she said with a calm she did not feel. "I understand there was a gentleman here earlier who sold you his boots."

The shopkeeper's pleasant smile turned puzzled. "Yes. How—how did you hear—?"

"Can you tell me where he went?"

"Well, I ..." Mr. Canfield rested a hand on his round belly and scratched his head with the other. "As to that, I cannot be certain. 'Ee asked for directions to Mr. Hubbard's farm, but 'ee was lookin' rather peaked. Poor man appears to have suffered great misfortune and was not in the best of health. When 'ee learned the farm was several miles' walk, 'ee seemed a mite discouraged."

Sarah's jaw tightened on a sigh. "He did not tell you anything more, perhaps how his plans have changed?"

Mr. Canfield shook his head and shrugged. "Traded 'is boots for another pair, plus a bit of coin, and then left. Do you know 'im, Miss Battersby?"

In answer, she only smiled tightly. "Thank you for your help, Mr. Canfield."

"Surely. Ye've always been the dearest girl. We've been hopin' you would come visit the shop every week, as you did before. Our five boys are dear to us, but we were never blessed with a daughter of our own. Mrs. Canfield so enjoys your comp'ny."

Sarah glanced down at her hem, feeling the weight of something cold settle into her chest. Something like guilt. "My apologies, Mr. Canfield. I fear my work at St. Catherine's Academy has occupied much of my time of late. I shall try to visit more often. Perhaps I will bring some of the older girls with me."

The man's beaming smile was her reward for the concession. "Mrs. Canfield will be most pleased."

With a nod and a farewell, Sarah exited the shop and glanced down the length of Limekiln Lane, first one direction, then the other. When she saw a crowd of boys along with her three girls and Ann Porter huddled around something near the green, she squinted and started for the square.

As she approached, she heard one of the boys exclaim, "'Ee walked straight into the path of the ball! 'Tweren't my doin'."

"Robbie," Ann replied, "No one is accusin' you of hitting him on purpose."

A masculine groan was followed by Penelope and Mary Elizabeth's simultaneous gasps and Susannah's cry of "He is awake!"

The words spurred her feet to a full run. In seconds, she was shoving aside Mr. Canfield's youngest and Mr. Hubbard's grandson. And there, sitting up on the grass with the assistance of Ann's hand beneath his arm, was the man she had been seeking. The man who wanted so badly to leave that he had sold his boots for a bit of coin.

He was pale, panting weakly. Sarah knelt beside him, running a hand over his muscled shoulder. "What happened?" she demanded.

"Robbie hit him with the cricket ball," said Susannah.

"Told you 'tweren't me fault! And 'is face were like that before—"

"Quiet, both of you," Sarah commanded. She glanced up at Ann. "Where did it strike him?"

"'Ee was crossin' this side of the green when Robbie made a bruisin' shot. Would'a been a sixer if the ball hadn't struck the man's head—"

A masculine throat cleared, and the man in question squinted at Sarah, his blue eyes flaring with a trace of temper. "My facility for language remains intact, Miss Battersby. I can answer for myself." He waved a lean, elegant hand toward his face. "The swelling makes it dashed difficult to see anything not directly in front of me."

"This the gentleman you were askin' about, Miss Battersby?" The voice of Mr. Canfield brought Sarah's head up, along with her sense of alarm. The shopkeeper stood at the edge of a growing crowd, which now included Mrs. Jones and four other proprietors.

Blast. This time of day, they were all closing up their shops and heading home. They must have noticed the commotion and come to investigate.

"I—yes, he is."

"Then you must be acquainted," Mrs. Jones interjected. "'Ee seems to know your name, at least."

Her mind scrambled for a response, something that would make sense but would not force her to lie. Were they acquainted? Yes, she supposed they were. She nodded in answer to Mrs. Jones.

But the baker was far from satisfied. "How do you know one another, then?" she demanded, folding her thick arms across her chest and turning a steely gaze toward the stranger. "Never seen you before. Where do you hail from?"

"Aye," added Mr. Canfield, a gleam of suspicion entering his eye. "Sellin' your boots. Seems a mite peculiar."

The stranger closed one eye and lifted one blond brow.

"That is not what you said when you paid me half what they were worth."

"Now, listen 'ere, young man," Mr. Canfield protested. "Our Miss Battersby's a good girl. We'll not abide her associatin' with scurvy knaves."

"Indeed," came a loathsome voice from mere feet behind her, causing lead to fill her legs and close off her air. When had Felix Foote arrived? The snake hovered incessantly whenever she entered the village, as though he watched for her, ready to slither to her side at a moment's notice. "I believe we would all like to know who solicits such concern from our dear Miss Battersby."

She wanted to vomit every time he said such things, laying claim to her like a mare he'd won at auction. Well, she did not intend to be granted as property to the highest bidder. She would do whatever she must to thwart him. Whatever it took.

Rising slowly to her feet, she kept her hand on the man's shoulder and her back to Mr. Foote. She did not look directly at Mr. Canfield or Mrs. Jones or Mary Elizabeth or Susannah or Penelope. She especially did not wish to meet the stranger's blue, blue eyes. Instead, she caught Ann's warm gaze. It was the only tether available to steady herself before she strode off the precipice.

"We are acquainted, yes," she confirmed.

"Oi knew it!" Mr. Canfield cried as though he had discovered a new continent.

Still, Sarah's eyes did not leave those of her dearest friend. Ann's perplexed expression was subtle to others, but Sarah saw her confusion clearly. "In fact, we are more than mere acquaintances. I have been caring for him in my home."

Gasps from several villagers sounded in her ears. *They should reserve their outrage*, she thought. *They will need it for what is to come.*

"Your charity is admirable." Mr. Foote's tone was far from admiring. "However, it is also reckless when it causes you to bring strange men into your home."

"He is not a stranger," Sarah said, feeling the air at the edge of the cliff beneath her feet. One more step, and she would be flying. Would he catch her? Despite the time they had spent together, she did not know him well enough to say for certain. She did not even know his name.

"Sarah," Ann whispered, her eyes wide and alarmed and glued to Sarah's own.

Swallowing, Sarah took that final, dangerous step and left the earth for the vagaries of the fall. "We are more than acquaintances," she said. "We are betrothed."

Amid the gasps and cries of "Oh!" and "Oh, my!" and "Oh, my God!" from the crowd of villagers, Sarah watched Ann's eyes first flare with shock, then dart past her shoulder, then dawn with realization, and finally, soften and darken with sympathy.

"Preposterous," Mr. Foote growled. "You are lying."

Sarah did not answer. She was flailing for solid ground. It *was* a lie. A very, very big one. Falsehoods on this scale were foreign to her. She had no experience as a scoundrel, no instruction in deception.

Fortunately, Ann Porter was a friend whose loyalty remained steadfast, even amidst Sarah's leap into moral failure. "No," her dearest, oldest friend said. "She speaks true. They are to be married."

A strong hand came up to grip her wrist tightly where it rested on his shoulder. "What do you think you are doing?" the stranger hissed, his words clipped but quiet, overshadowed by the murmurs of those around them.

"What I must," she answered just as quietly before placing her free hand over his hard grip. Then, with a deep breath, she deliberately plunged deeper into the abyss, far away from the cliff's edge. Too far to turn back. "With my father's health so precarious, we have been reluctant to share our happy news," she announced to the crowd. "Celebrating seemed ... unseemly. But now, there is little reason to keep our secret."

Finally, she dropped her gaze to meet his. Fire so hot it

burned blue shone there, a warning as blatant as if he had bellowed it. Still, she did not dare retreat. Not with Felix Foote hovering, a snake coiled to strike at the first sign of weakness.

She patted the fingers currently attempting to strangle her wrist. "This man is my intended husband. And I am his intended wife. Now, if you will excuse us, I must take my beloved home, for he has had a most trying day."

Chapter Five

"Madness is a most unfortunate affliction."

—THE DOWAGER MARCHIONESS OF WALLINGHAM to Lady Berne
upon hearing a lengthy description of said lady's new
feline companion.

THE WOMAN WAS OUT OF HER BLOODY MIND.

"You are out of your bloody mind," he growled into her ear as they slogged and staggered together along the road to the vicarage. Three young girls led the way, occasionally skipping ahead, then turning back to glance at Colin and the utterly mad Miss Sarah Battersby.

The slender arm around his waist tightened. "That is a fine way to speak to your betrothed."

"Then it is well we are *not* engaged. For the love of God, what would compel you to make such a claim? You do not even know who I am."

The woman currently acting as his crutch slowed her pace, forcing him to slow as well. "True," she conceded quietly. "Who are you, then?"

"Bloody hell," he muttered through gritted teeth. "Do you not think you should have inquired before declaring that we are to be *married?*"

That pointed chin elevated. "For most of our acquaintance, you have been asleep. A ready opportunity for introductions did not present itself. Because you have been injured. And I have *taken care* of you."

"I suppose you think that entitles you to payment—in the form of a ring and a new last name, no less. Bloody-minded females. Even when you pull a man half-dead from the roadside, you cannot resist laying a parson's mousetrap for him."

He felt her body stiffen along his side, her shoulders going rigid. "Don't be daft. I neither expect nor desire your hand in marriage. Gracious me, even now, you could be wed to another."

"Then what was that rubbish about—"

"I simply need them to *believe* we are engaged."

"You want me to lie. To your entire village."

"Do you object to lying?" She sniffed. "I had hoped you would prove a capable scoundrel."

Jaw flexing, he glanced down at the delicate slope of her nose with its impudent tilt, then watched the waning sunlight glint off the honeyed, rebellious curls that refused to remain coiled at the back of her head. Neither pins nor her iron will could contain them. Try as she might to appear composed, Miss Sarah Battersby was in need of taming.

Deliberately, he kept his voice low and smooth. "These presumptions of yours are dangerous. If I am capable of such deception, as you apparently desire, surely you cannot trust me to behave honorably. And if that is true, every moment you spend in my presence puts you at risk."

"A risk I must take."

The woman was either blindingly stupid, entirely mad, or infernally stubborn. He would wager on the latter. "When, precisely, did you decide to implement your little deception?"

Her silence was punctuated only with the scrape and thud of their footsteps and the distant giggles of the three girls.

He halted as they reached the edge of the apple orchard, drawing her toward one of the trees. Removing his arm from across her shoulders, he winced at the pain in his ribs and muscles. Although it was dull in comparison with the throbbing inside his skull, it served as a sharp reminder of why he must persuade her to recant her claim, why she must help him leave with all due haste. Carefully fingering the small lump forming between his neck and skull, he leaned against the rough bark and attempted to catch his breath. "Answer me, Sarah," he said, his voice hoarse. "When did you devise this plan? And why?"

She refused to look at him. A couple of yards away, she stood gazing down the length of the village road, her hands planted on her hips. The setting sun made her hair glow like a royal crown, lit her eyes a bright, uncanny gold. "I—I needed time. Only a month or two longer, and I shall be able to secure a position. I am certain of it."

He frowned, his impatience growing. "Speak clearly, woman. My head hurts too damn badly for riddles."

Startled honey eyes turned to him. "What is your name?"

"*Now* you want a proper introduction?"

"Yes."

He lowered his chin and gave her an intimidating glare. At least, he hoped it was intimidating. Who the hell knew what he looked like with the way his face had been battered? "Answer my questions, and perhaps I will answer yours."

She blinked, glanced toward the vicarage, then back to him. "Very well." She waved to the grass beneath the tree. "Shall we sit? It appears you could use a rest before we resume our journey."

He wanted to argue that he was fine—strong and robust and perfectly capable of navigating a bloody country lane without her assistance or a *rest*, thank you very much—but in truth, he could scarcely stand, even with the help of an old apple tree. So, instead of rebutting her assumption, he slid down onto his arse and nodded to the patch of ground beside him.

Most women of his acquaintance might grimace at such rustic seating arrangements and uncouth manners, but not Miss Battersby. She did not hesitate, instead neatly and gracefully sinking down beside him on her grass cushion, folding her arms atop her upraised knees, and releasing what sounded like a relieved sigh. "My father used to bring me here to pick apples." She peered up into the branches, weighted here and there with green and red fruit. "Every year. Except this one."

Hearing the strain in her voice, he let silence fall between them for a moment before prompting, "He has been ill, I gather."

"Yes." Her gaze dropped to meet his, then fell to a spot of ground between them, where two old apples lay, brown with rot, among a drift of yellowed leaves. "He is dying."

Perhaps it was the way she whispered the words, so quiet he could scarcely discern them from the distant echo of the sea and the light rustle of leaves. Perhaps it was the way she held herself, still and mournful. But her words caused his heart to twist painfully. She might be a liar and a fortune huntress, but he did not wish such grief on anyone.

With a deep, sudden inhalation, she gathered herself and continued, "When he goes, his living will go with him. My mother and I will lose ... everything. His income, the cottage. Even the school."

A frown tugged at his brow. "You have no other family who will take you in?"

She shook her head. "My mother's brother died three years ago, and his widow recently remarried. My father has two sisters, but neither of them is in a position to support us."

"What about the villagers? They seem rather fond of you."

Her eyes met his directly, firing a sharp gold. "We are not inclined to accept charity from those who can ill afford it. I will find another way. It is simply taking longer than I had supposed to secure a position."

He looked the length of her, from her pixie face surrounded by a frizz of honeyed curls to her worn rag of a dress, down to the scuffed toes of her brown boots. "You are attractive enough," he observed. "Not beautiful, perhaps, but—"

"I beg your pardon!"

"—put a proper gown on you, and you would be acceptable fare for most gents. Why do you not trap one of the locals in your leg shackles?"

Her eyes narrowed. "For all that your diction is perfection itself, your manners are dreadfully boorish."

"Answer the question," he said softly.

From her expression—mutinous and acidic—he would guess she strongly considered telling him to go to the devil. But she must be quite desperate to try trapping him—a virtual stranger encountered under dubious circumstances—into a false engagement.

After several minutes, she sighed and muttered, "I suppose you deserve to know." Her chin came up and her eyes met his. "There is a man. He has offered for me … many times."

His stomach gave a queer lurch. Perhaps he should not have eaten so much stew earlier. "Why have you not accepted?"

"He is not a good man. I do not wish to marry him."

In that moment, with her eyes hooded and her voice flat, Colin saw everything Sarah would not—or could not—say aloud. This man, whoever he was, had tried to force her hand, and she would resist until her last breath. Sarah Battersby might be barking mad, but she was a fighter. He saw it in the set of her shoulders, straight and proud, the curl and clench of her fists.

"Who is he? What is his name?" The questions came from Colin's mouth, but he could not recall deciding to ask them.

Her lashes rose to reveal those startling eyes, like falling into a honeypot lit from below. "Felix Foote. He was there when you"—she waved her hand around the top of her head—"succumbed to Robbie's sixer."

"Was he, now?"

"Mmm. He is always there, it seems. Every time I go into the village. Every time there is some opportunity to remind me that he is my only option. By his design, of course. Keddlescombe is home to few men of my age, and Mr. Foote has ... encouraged them to look elsewhere for a wife."

"Why would they heed his advice?"

"He owns several farms in this parish, none of which he works himself. Mr. Foote has become rather well set charging substantial rents to his tenants, rents which he can increase at any time. He fancies himself a proper gentleman."

Colin shifted as cramping built along his spine and curled around his neck. With his injuries, sitting in one position for long was painful. Besides which, his limbs currently pulsed with the desire to rise and charge back to the village. He could not say why. The disgust in Sarah's voice, perhaps. He did not like it.

"No one enjoys being cornered," he said, keeping his tone casual. "But I suspect your resistance to his suit runs deeper than mere dislike."

"My reasons are my own."

"Do you desire my cooperation?"

She bit her lip and nodded.

"What is it Mr. Foote has done to deserve your contempt?"

Her jaw clenched. Her bowed lips tightened. A tiny furrow appeared between her brows. "If I tell you, it must be in the strictest confidence. This is very important. Do you understand?"

"Of course."

She took a deep breath, released it slowly, plucked at the dusty fabric of her skirt where it puckered along her knee, laced her fingers together and squeezed. "Felix Foote is ..." She cleared her throat delicately. "Mr. Foote has done things. Things no gentleman would do. Revolting things."

As he watched the color rising into her cheeks, Colin began to wonder if the prim Miss Battersby had misconstrued a man's clumsy advances. Perhaps Foote had attempted to kiss her and had bungled it badly. Innocents such as Sarah were prone to hysterics when they did not understand what a lusty man was about.

He felt his hands curl into fists. Why was his stomach turning with such vigor? Was it the stew after all? "What things? Describe them," he barked.

Lashes lowering again, she turned her gaze away, toward the road. "Those who attend St. Catherine's Academy for Girls of Impeccable Deportment are in my care. Their welfare has been entrusted to my mother and father and to me."

"First, I am surprised you could not think of a longer name for the school. Second, you are avoiding answering by changing the subject—"

When her eyes returned to him, they cut through his pain and impatience. "I am giving you your answer."

After a moment, he nodded for her to continue.

"Last year, I came upon Mr. Foote and one of my students in the wood behind the church. He was ... forcing his attentions upon her." Sarah's voice cracked on the last word.

The churning in his stomach grew worse. But she was not yet finished.

"At first, I did not realize what I was seeing," she continued, her voice now ragged. "She stood very still. He knelt in front of her, his h-hand beneath her skirts. I thought perhaps she had been injured and he was helping her ..." She chuckled darkly then swallowed hard, like someone who was trying not to retch. "As I drew closer, I saw that she was weeping. She did not make a sound. Just stood there. Letting him touch her. As though it had happened a dozen times, and she must simply wait for it to be over."

Colin wanted to ask questions. Who was the girl? What did Sarah do after she discovered them? He wanted to know what Foote looked like so he could return to the village and pummel the rotting slime. He remained silent.

"She—she was a precious thing. Intelligent beyond her years." Sarah laughed softly as a tear tracked down her face. The drop made it two inches before she swiped it away. "She'd only just turned twelve, and yet already she had learned how vile men can be."

Twelve. The girl was twelve. Colin closed his eyes, unable to watch Sarah's face any longer. Twelve. He remembered his sister, Victoria, at that age, seated on a bench outside Blackmore Hall, sketching away in her little book, gazing out at the fish pond with a quiet smile and a wistful sigh.

"I stopped him. A stone to the head. He may suspect it was me who struck him, but he never said a word about it, even after we transferred her to another school in Exeter. Took away his plaything. Perhaps that is why he is so determined to ..."

Colin blinked and refocused on Sarah. "You believe he is pressuring you to marry him as a *replacement?*"

"Perhaps. I have not bothered to ask him. I cannot bear to be in his presence."

"Why do you not simply tell everyone what you witnessed? Surely, that would blacken his name sufficiently—"

She shook her head. "Although my father wished it otherwise, the girls who attend St. Catherine's Academy are here for one reason, and it is not to learn mathematics or study poetry. They are to be prepared for the marriage mart."

He sighed as understanding dawned. "She would be ruined."

Sarah's mouth twisted into a mockery of a smile. "Yes. Impure, they would say. Some might have sympathy for her, if they knew, but her chances of making a good marriage would be scant."

Sick to his stomach, Colin felt his veins pulse beneath his skin. It was not his fight, to be sure. He did not know the girl, had never been introduced to the vile Mr. Foote. Still, he longed to deliver an excruciating death. When had these violent impulses begun? Perhaps he should begin drinking again. He'd been quite an agreeable fellow when he'd been sotted most of the time.

"Colin," he said softly.

She blinked. "Beg pardon?"

"My name is Colin."

Her mouth formed a little O. "And your last name?"

He paused before answering. "Clyde." It was not a complete lie. Clyde was one of his names.

Nodding, she sniffed, propped her arms on her knees, and gave him a wry grin. "How lovely to meet you, Mr. Clyde. Would you consider becoming my intended husband? Temporarily, of course."

He stared at her, unable to return her smile. "I cannot stay, Sarah. What I told you in the wagon is true. I am a danger to you. The longer I remain, the greater the risk to your safety."

"If you were truly dangerous, the last thing you would do is warn me away—"

"The man who did this"—he placed a hand over his ribs—"will stop at nothing to find me, including harming those who may harbor me. You. Your mother."

She looked bewildered, her eyebrows drawing together, her lips pursing. "What does he want with you?"

Sighing, Colin braced one hand on the ground and one on the trunk behind him. Pressing his palm into the rough bark, he heaved himself up onto his feet.

Sarah scrambled to help him, tucking her shoulder beneath his arm and wrapping herself along his side. She was warm and soft, for all her slender strength. A small, honeyed woman constructed of pure determination. As weak as he was, his body reacted with startling appreciation.

Bloody hell. He must leave as soon as possible.

"I took something from him," he answered, panting the words as a wave of dizziness nearly sent him back to the ground.

He leaned on her, closed his eyes, and waited for it to pass.

"What was it?"

When he opened his eyes, she was gazing up at him, her face upturned and close. So very close. Slowly, he grinned. "Peace of mind."

"I don't understand."

Chuckling, he slid his arm from her shoulders down to her waist and gave her a pat. A trim waist it was, thin even. She needed to eat more. "I know. But he does. And that is what matters."

With that, he withdrew from her and walked slowly, gingerly toward the road. She should not be touching him. She should be outraged by his familiar manner and order him to leave her sight.

"Mr. Clyde!" She trotted to his side. Determined little woman.

"Colin will do. We are engaged, after all."

Her footsteps halted then resumed. "We—we are?"

"For the moment."

Silence fell between them as their plodding shadows grew longer on the hard-packed dirt. The sounds of distant, girlish chatter carried across the valley on a crisp breeze.

"You intend to leave," Sarah said softly. It was not a question.

Keeping his eyes forward, he nodded. "Tomorrow. I will need your help to retrieve my horse. What you tell the villagers afterward is entirely at your discretion. I shan't contradict you."

For long minutes, Colin focused on simply placing one foot in front of the other. His stitches pulled, his ribs burned, his head throbbed like a thumb stomped by a boot. Or struck with a cricket ball. Bloody hell, he longed for her bed, her hands stroking his forehead and playing with his hair, her quiet, reassuring voice telling him to rest. Apart from his sister, no woman had ever offered him such care.

"Why did you do it?" he asked quietly.

"Do what?"

"Rescue me. Was it this ruse of yours?"

When he squinted at her, she shrugged, the sunlight streaming through her frizz of hair, surrounding her face in amber. "We took you with us because ... well, because you needed us. You would have died there. I could not let that happen." Her chin tilted up a fraction. "It was only later that I wondered if you were the answer."

"To your problem."

"To my prayers."

Even to his own ears, his laugh was cynical. "Believe me, sweet, I am the last thing God would deliver to anyone worthy of His benevolence."

"Still, I needed someone to stand between me and Mr. Foote for a time, and you appeared," she replied. "Absent evidence to the contrary, I am choosing to see you as a blessing."

Again, he laughed. "First time I have been referred to in such a way, I assure you."

They reached the valley floor before she spoke again. "Must you leave tomorrow, truly?"

He sighed, his resilience sapped by his wounds and the endless, mud-plagued ride from London. Oh, and months of being hunted by a soulless butcher. That one did take the vigor out of a man. "I have told you I cannot stay."

"No, I ... I am not asking you to stay forever. The day after tomorrow is Sunday. The curate, Mr. Dunhill, has organized a gathering in the churchyard. A picnic. Would you consider ... that is, could you possibly ...?"

Squinting at her, he shook his head. "Apologies, sweet. You may tell your fellow parishioners whatever you like, but come morning, I shall be gone."

Her throat worked on a hard swallow, and she nodded.

The eastern sky turned a pale violet as the sun dipped below the hill behind them. Soon, darkness would come. Then morning, and with it, his departure. What made it such a hollow thought, he did not know.

Halfway up the slope toward her cottage, Colin's lungs and legs were burning. He paused, bending forward with his palms braced on his thighs. Bloody hell, he was weak.

A warm, gentle hand settled between his shoulder blades just as a frayed skirt swayed into his view near his newly purchased boots. "Easy now, Mr. Clyde," she said quietly. "You are still healing." Fingers threaded through his hair, there and gone so quickly, they felt like a fairy's touch. "The wayward cricket ball did not help matters."

"Colin," he panted, his heart thudding with a bit more enthusiasm than his climb demanded. He turned his head toward her. She was close, her tidy bosom inches from his face. "At least, when we are alone together."

"Very well. Colin."

He liked the way she said his name. He liked the feel of her hands. He liked her nicely proportioned bosom and pixie face. He liked ... her. This could easily turn disastrous. Thank heaven he was leaving.

"... well enough to reach the cottage?"

Dragging his gaze away from her bodice, he shook his head to clear his thoughts and straightened upright. His answer to her query was to resume his slow pace, ignoring the way the road blurred and tilted before him.

"Colin?" she said, easily keeping pace by his side. Why did she have to say it like that, the two syllables like drops of honey on her tongue?

He grunted.

"Thank you."

"For what?"

"Earlier, in the village. You could have exposed the truth. Things would have gone quite abominably if you had. For me, that is." As they neared the cottage, which gleamed white in the disappearing light, she trotted ahead to open the gate.

He replied, "If you knew me better, you would not have doubted for a moment."

She glanced back over her shoulder. "The soul of discretion, are you?"

"More like the soul of deception."

The grin she gave him—slow and wise and a bit mischievous—stole what little breath he had. Good God, when had she become such a temptation?

"Oh, I had my suspicions about you," she said.

As he walked through the open gate, she spun around to face him, close now. Close enough that he felt the differences in their height, the strange pulse of their proximity. He frowned. "Did you?"

"Mmm." She nodded, still grinning, her hands on her hips. "I knew that a man who could escape what you obviously endured must have some cleverness in him. And who could be so clever and still land himself in such a spot?"

"Not the kind of man you should bring into your home, that much is certain."

She stepped closer, her head craned back on her dainty neck. "Now, that is where you are mistaken. You were precisely the man I needed, at precisely the moment I needed you." With that, she turned on her heel and headed for the cottage's front door. "As I said before," she threw over her shoulder as she twisted the knob. "When you pray for a solution, and God sends you a scoundrel, it is best to say thank you."

Chapter Six

*"I like a good ramble as much as anyone, Humphrey.
However, there is a limit to my appreciation for precipitation.
A limit I fear we have reached."*

—THE DOWAGER MARCHIONESS OF WALLINGHAM to her
companion, Humphrey, upon witnessing said companion's
peculiar fascination with puddles.

FRANTIC KNOCKING BROUGHT COLIN OUT OF A DEAD SLEEP.
Heart thudding, he tried to make sense of where he was. It was
dark. He lay in a bed beneath a quilt. Her quilt.

"Sarah?" a feminine voice said as the door creaked open,
revealing the dim orange glow of a candle. "He has gone
wandering again."

He heard tears and worry in that voice. Mrs. Battersby. Beside the bed—which Sarah had insisted he use and he had been too exhausted to refuse—the rustle of blankets being displaced on the floor preceded Sarah's whisper. "How long?"

"He was gone when I awakened. He could be anywhere by now." The distress in the mother's voice was stark.

But Sarah, having scrambled to her feet and cinched her dressing gown, murmured calmly, "All will be well, Mama. We shall find him. Give me two minutes to put on my boots, and we will search together."

A sniff, then a nod of the mother's shadowed head, then the door closed and darkness cloaked the room once again. He watched in the faint, silvery glow from the window as Sarah hurried to the small wardrobe opposite the corner with the chamber pot, and bent to retrieve something inside.

"Does he do this often?"

She yelped, jerked, yelped again as she struck her head on a shelf inside the wardrobe, then shot upright, rubbing her head and presumably shooting daggers at him. "You should be asleep," she grumbled, her voice husky and hushed.

Pushing himself up and, throwing aside her quilt, sat on the edge of the bed as dizziness flowed over him. "It is your father, yes?"

She busied herself with donning her boots, leaning her hips against the wardrobe and bending forward to pull them on and tie the laces. Notably, she did not answer him.

"Sarah."

Her head came up, and an exasperated sigh punctuated jerking motions as she knotted the laces. "Yes, it is my father. And yes, he does this sometimes. He is ... not himself."

He retrieved his own boots from beneath the bed, quickly pulling them on.

"No," she said firmly. "No, no, no. You must rest, Colin. You will need your strength—"

Rising from the bed, he steadied himself against the wall. "I shall rest after we locate your father."

She moved to his side before he could say another word, wrapping her arms around his waist and trying to tug him back to bed. He felt her softness like a brand against his side. She wore no corset, merely layers of linen draped over her slender form.

"Sarah," he said hoarsely, easily resisting her attempts to move him. "It is the middle of the night, and you are standing in your bedchamber with your arms wrapped around a man you rightly dubbed a scoundrel. Might I suggest you instead maintain a sensible distance?"

She snorted, her arms vainly attempting to pull his body the two feet between them and the bed without pressuring his wounds. One of her hands accidentally brushed the fall of his breeches. He had to clench his jaw to stifle his groan.

"Don't be silly," she scoffed. "Even you have said I am not particularly attractive. I shall take that as assurance of my immunity from your prurient impulses."

The woman was bloody reckless. Someone should have taught her better caution before now. "You do not know me well enough to gauge my 'prurient impulses.' Furthermore, despite your impressive vocabulary, Miss Battersby, you are dangerously naïve when it comes to men."

She huffed as she continued to tug at his waist and hips, finally resorting to wrapping both arms around his elbow and pulling, putting pressure on his sore shoulder. He tugged back automatically to prevent the pain of stressing the joint, which pulled her off balance, brought her stumbling toward him, tumbling against his chest.

This time, the groan escaped. It could not be helped. Her firm little breasts pressed against him, her hips forming a perfect cradle for his—

"Rubbish. You can scarcely stand without swaying like a reed in a strong wind. I shall take my chances."

Her dismissive tone flayed his nerves, incited his desire to impress upon her the foolishness of her actions, of her assumptions about him. She needed to be taught a lesson. Before he could think better of it, his hand snaked up to the side of her slender neck and, using his thumb along her jaw to tilt her head back, he brought her mouth to his.

The first touch of her lips sent an unexpected streak of fire across his skin. He jerked away and sucked in a breath. The second pass—purely for purposes of confirmation—was worse. That bow of a mouth was soft. Responsive. It surrendered and sighed against his. Curved and caressed and tempted him to take. Which he did.

Third pass. Sweetness shifted and burned hotter. Hands tightened on her neck and elbow, pulling her hard against him. Erect little nipples brushed against his chest. Lips nibbled and parted to welcome him inside. Her mouth was hot and sweet, home to a curious tongue that curled around his as his arm went around her waist and gathered her closer, crushed her against his ribs. The resulting pain barely registered, as it was drowned by the sheer pleasure of her. Soon, however, it sharpened enough to tear into his consciousness, reminding him of where he was. Who he was. And why he should never have touched her.

"What the bloody hell is this?" he murmured against her mouth, his forehead resting against hers as he panted and struggled to ignore the aching wound of his arousal.

Her response was breathless and a little slurred. "Should that not be my question?"

A quiet knock pulled them apart.

Sarah shook her head, her hands sliding away from him to brush at her unruly hair, ill contained by a plait. "I—I must find my father." She turned away, moving to the door. When she yanked it open, her mother handed her a lantern.

The older woman glanced directly at him over her daughter's shoulder before returning to Sarah. "I shall take the church and the wood."

Sarah nodded. "And I the road and the beach. We will find him, Mama."

In the orange light, Colin saw the gleam of a tear on Mrs. Battersby's cheek, her brow crumbling, her eyes squeezing closed.

Sarah pulled her into a tight embrace, whispering something in her ear. The mother nodded, dabbed her nose with a handkerchief, and withdrew to disappear from the doorway.

"I am coming with you," he said once her mother was gone.

Without turning, she replied, "As you like."

Running a hand through his hair, he drew a deep breath and trailed her into the corridor, waited while she donned a dark woolen pelisse, then followed out the front door.

The moon was a gentle light in the valley, the air crisp and salty and blessedly cooling as they took to the road. After their kiss—if one could even call such a conflagration by that name— he needed something to douse the fire in his blood. Perhaps he should go for a swim. A frigid, distracting swim somewhere far from this peculiar woman.

His eyes tracked her strides, purposeful and swift. Her shoulders were rigid, the hem of her white linen dressing gown glowing in the moonlit dark. He rubbed a palm down his face, trying to break whatever spell she had cast.

When they reached the valley floor, Sarah left the road for a gap in the waist-high grass. It was a worn trail that led south, toward the shoreline. He might get his swim, after all.

Within minutes, his boots left hard-packed trail for soft, pebble-strewn sand. Ahead, Sarah's lantern bobbed and swayed with her strides. "Papa!" she called, her head swiveling to scan the shoreline in both directions. The motion paused as she glimpsed what he had seen a fraction of a second earlier.

"Sarah," he murmured as he caught up to her.

"I see him." Her voice was raspy and stark. She shoved the lantern into his hands and ran toward the waterline where rolling waves lapped at the knees of a lone, white-haired figure.

Loping after her, he arrived just as she looped the frail man's arm around her shoulders. She had done the same with Colin many times. This explained why she so readily touched him and took care of him. Clearly, she had been nursing her father for a long while.

"... return to the cottage now, Papa," she was whispering as he approached. The old man's shivering was visible even in the dim moonlight. His nightshirt was soaked to his thighs, revealing a frame so thin, Colin wondered if he might not shake apart like a rickety ship in a North Sea gale.

"Eleanor?" Even the man's voice was frail and cracked.

"No, Papa. I am Sarah. We must get you home. You are positively frozen."

"S-Sarah. Yes. I do recall now. But I thought you married that naval captain and moved away to ... where was it?"

She shook her head. "It does not matter now. Come. Come with me, Papa."

Colin could see her tugging at the old man, but she could not move him. He stood gazing out at the rolling waves gleaming silvery white in the distance. Suddenly, he shoved at her, causing her to stumble, her arms flailing wildly to regain her balance.

Colin wasted no time, dropping the lantern and wading in to steady her with a solid grip on her waist. She glanced back over her shoulder, eyes startled and shimmering with tears, which she quickly attempted to hide. His heart twisted painfully inside his chest, his jaw tightening as he released her.

"He—he is not well. It is not his fault."

Colin frowned. "What was that about a naval captain?"

She pressed her lips together, her eyes riveted on her father. "He does not remember."

His eyes following hers to the old man, he watched as a breeze lifted a tuft of white hair until it waved like a flag.

"He does not remember," she repeated.

"Remember what?"

She chuckled, the sound humorless and sad. "Everything. Me. He thinks I am his sister. Or my mother. Some days, I am a perfect stranger."

He had heard of this—one of his great aunts had suffered similarly before her death, even losing the ability to speak. But he had only learned of it through his cousin, who had shuddered and changed the subject before taking another drink of the brandy they'd been sharing.

"We cannot let him stay here much longer," Sarah said.

She was right. Already, the frigid water was numbing Colin's legs, soaking the cheap boots he had paid too much for. Was it only minutes ago that he had longed for a dunk in cold water? Foolish notion.

Colin's eyes narrowed. "He thinks you are his sister? And married to a captain in the navy?"

She nodded. "That was thirty years ago. Aunt Sarah has been widowed twice since then."

He waded close to the old man, coming alongside him, letting him feel his presence before he spoke. "Mr. Battersby," he said quietly. "The sea is lovely, is it not?"

Hunched, bony shoulders straightened and a white head swiveled toward him. Dim, vacant eyes shone in the moonlight, sunken in a sagging, wrinkled face. A frown drew down white brows. "Have we met, sir?"

Colin chuckled. "You usually call me 'Captain,' but I suppose we are both different men these days."

Eyes blinked wide. "Captain ...? George? When did you arrive?"

Settling his hand on the man's shoulder, Colin had to control a start as the truth of the man's frailty could be felt through the linen nightshirt. Skin over bone. "Sarah needed me here. She said you had gone wandering."

A small smile tugged at the man's lips. "I like the water."

"As do I. But it is a tad chilly. What would you say to a warm fire and some pleasant conversation?"

He did not respond for a long while, then turned to Colin with confusion in his eyes. "Where is Eleanor?"

Sarah, having moved to her father's opposite side, drew his

attention by gently cradling his elbow. "She is at the cottage. Let us return there now, and she will make you a nice, warm cup of tea."

"I like the water."

"I know, Papa. But Mama is waiting for you. Do you not wish to see her?"

"Eleanor?"

"Yes, let us go find Eleanor. She is at the cottage."

He looked at Colin. "Who are you?"

Colin's eyes met Sarah's. Hers were grieving. "I am her husband."

"George?"

Not knowing what else to do, Colin nodded. "Time to return to Eleanor now, my good man. I hear she has tea prepared."

"Well, let us go, then. Eleanor dislikes cold tea." Then, as if it had been his idea all along, Mr. Battersby turned around and waded slowly, tremulously toward the shore, Sarah holding one arm and Colin the other.

"You are good for her, George," the old man opined, his voice shaking, his steps ginger as they left the rhythmic water for the rounded pebbles and cold sand of the beach. "Mustn't leave her alone any longer. She needs you."

Feeling ice seep and root down in the center of his bones, Colin swallowed hard against the cause of it. Not the water. Not the wind. The truth. Her father would die soon. Her strength and will to fight could not last forever. She did need someone, probably a husband, very badly. But it could not be him. And for a man who had sworn never to marry, that should have filled him with relief.

Instead, the hard stone in this throat tasted bitter, like resentment.

Like regret.

Like a loss he would only fathom after it was too late.

SARAH HAD LOST A GOOD DEAL OF FEELING IN HER FINGERS and feet by the time they arrived at the cottage. Fortunately, her mother had already returned and quickly swathed Papa in three blankets, sat him next to the parlor fire, and served them all hot tea.

Colin stood at the edge of the room, staring broodingly in Sarah's direction. When she noticed him, she approached with a cup of the steaming, albeit weak, brew. "Drink," she said, gritting her teeth to prevent them chattering. "I shall fetch you another pair of Papa's trousers. You cannot afford to catch your death."

"How long has he been this way?"

She glanced back to where Eleanor knelt beside Papa's chair, her hands stroking through his sparse hair as she gazed at him with naked fear and grief and love. Sarah swallowed down the lump of her own sorrow then took Colin's arm to lead him out of the parlor. He obligingly followed her upstairs to her parents' bedchamber, where she opened a trunk and dug through a stack of her father's old trousers.

"Here," she said, handing him a clean pair. "They may be too short, but at least they are dry."

He set his tea on the table next to a lit candle and took the folded garment, staring at her out of bruised, exhausted eyes. "How long, Sarah?"

She sighed then sat on the edge of her parents' bed. Rubbing her face with both hands, she replied, "We began to notice the changes two years ago, but looking back, his illness must have begun long before then. Years, perhaps." Her hands dropped into her lap like a marionette whose strings had been cut. "At first, the signs were small. He would forget words, misplace his reading spectacles. He sometimes became difficult and argumentative with my mother. It was unlike him, but we thought it normal for a man of his years. Then, one Sunday, he failed to appear in the pulpit. Simply forgot he was to deliver a sermon. The entire church waited, and we found him here, tending his roses, oblivious that anything was amiss. My father adored his work. He never would have ..."

The mattress depressed as Colin sat next to her, draping a blanket he had retrieved from her mother's reading chair across her shoulders. "Do you know the cause?"

She shook her head, her thumbs twirling around each other, tingling now as warmth gradually returned. "The physician could tell us little, only that he would worsen, that eventually, his mind—his memories—all of who he was would be gone." She sighed again, the drawing and releasing of air deep and slow. Sometimes it helped.

"I am sorry, Sarah. Truly. I cannot imagine the difficulty of watching your father deteriorate in this way."

She glanced at him, gathering the edges of the woolen blanket closer around her. "If that were the only thing, I think Mama and I would be ... well, we would feel sorrow, of course, but we would cope with his illness as any family does. Unfortunately, by the time we realized what was happening, he had quietly spent every farthing we had, and then some."

"On?"

She huffed out a dry chuckle. "Oh, silly things, mostly. Parlor furniture we did not need. Books for the library at St. Catherine's. He bought a traveling coach too fine for a lord, to say nothing of a country vicar. Between settling Papa's debts and hiring a curate to take charge of his duties at the church, I'm afraid our well has been quite depleted."

Colin was quiet for several minutes. She could not see much of his expression, as the room was lit only with the single candle her mother had left burning on the bedside table. Then, he cleared his throat to speak. "I wish ... I wish I could do more. If I had funds, I would—"

Sucking in an alarmed breath, she stopped him immediately. "No."

"I meant only to say—"

"Whether you are wealthy or not—"

"I am not." He said it as though admitting something shameful.

She clenched her teeth and nodded. "Regardless, I would not accept. Soliciting charity is not why I told you about my father's illness or our ... difficulties."

"What was your reason, then?"

The flickering, orange light cast strange shadows from behind him, obscuring his features. Except, she imagined she could see something in his eyes. An intensity that caused a flash of sensation to shimmer along her skin. Not a chill, precisely. More of an awareness. "I don't know," she whispered. "Perhaps I simply needed to say it aloud. And you are here."

She saw a muscle jump and flex in his jaw before he turned his head away from her. "You need someone." His tone was puzzling, almost angry.

As warmth returned, her mind slowed, the exhaustion of the last few days rising like a mist, filling her head and weighting her muscles until she began to list backward. She caught herself before she collapsed, but his words were a jumble.

"I shall stay until Sunday."

"You—you will?"

"Sunday. Then, I must go."

She nodded, wondering if she was dreaming.

"Come. You need to sleep. I will take the floor," he said, rising from the bed and moving to the doorway.

Again, it took her a moment to translate his words, as everything seemed sluggish, even sounds. "No, you are—you are still recovering."

Instantly his face was inches from hers, his hands braced on the mattress to either side of her hips as he bent over her. The movement seemed sudden, but that was probably her sleep-hungry mind playing tricks. Still, his proximity was disconcerting, as were his words. "You will take the bed. Do you understand?"

She blinked slowly, seeing the flash of anger, hearing the grind of his words. "I ..."

"Say that you understand, Sarah."

Why was her heart pounding, of a sudden? And why did the memory of their earlier kiss keep dancing through her mind? "Your injuries—"

"Say it."

"Fine. I will take the bed."

His warm breath drifted over her face as he sighed. "Good." He pushed himself away from her, rising to his full height then holding out a hand.

She frowned, still mightily confused, but slid her hand into his and allowed him to bring her to her feet. He was shockingly close and warm. "Thank you," she murmured.

His arm came around her and settled at the small of her back. But, instead of the embrace she half-hoped for, he ushered her through the door, growling, "For the love of God, Miss Battersby. Do not thank a man for giving you what was yours at the start."

Chapter Seven

"For some, fine manners and skill in waltzing compensate
for many shortcomings. For others, I recommend
more frequent bathing."

—The Dowager Marchioness of Wallingham to Sir Barnabus
Malby in a Mayfair ballroom.

A SHRIEK ECHOED DOWN THE CORRIDOR OF THE OLD ABBEY,
causing Colin to cringe before he followed the sound. He knew
this was a school for girls, and ordinarily he found most females
charming company, but he hadn't slept well last night. The floor
made a bloody uncomfortable bed—cold, hard, and unforgiving.

She should never have been forced to sleep there.

His still-clammy boots thudded on the wood floor as he

approached the half-open door to what must be the music room, given the awkward notes emanating from within. Pushing inside, he was greeted by the sight of a dozen girls, ranging in age from approximately twelve to sixteen, taking a dancing lesson. In a glance, he pegged them for wealth. Their gowns were pastels, all expertly sewn, their hair glossy, their skin clean and pale. If that were not evidence enough, they appeared to be practicing a quadrille.

A gangly redhead stumbled as she spun into a curtsy. The girl across from her—a gold-haired giggler with a tendency to snort—laughed uproariously. The redhead's face turned the color of her hair.

"Miss Parnham, I will thank you to maintain your composure and exhibit the good manners you *all* have learned here at St. Catherine's Academy." The crisp reprimand instantly drew Colin's attention to its source, Miss Battersby, who stood beside the dreadfully talentless girl playing the pianoforte. "Remember, we should strive to treat others more graciously than we would like to be treated, for one never knows when we will find *ourselves* in need of kindness, only that it is certain to occur."

She looked ... fetching, a slight crease between her brows, her lips pursed, her wild hair scraped back from her face into strictly enforced order. Later, he knew, the curls would launch a daring escape, but it was early yet. Right now, her voice commanded respect, compelled the listener to straighten his posture and bow with precision and observe all proprieties.

He wanted to kiss her again. He wanted to liberate that hair and make her honey-hued eyes glaze with desire.

The object of his fancy continued, now speaking patiently to the red-haired, red-faced girl. "Miss Cresswell, as you make your turn, start with your weight on your back foot whilst allowing your front foot to lift and glide lightly above the floor. Anticipate each step, just as you would when walking across the room. Try it again."

He folded his arms across his chest, leaned against the door jam, and watched her. The instructor. The governess. She managed these girls like a ship's captain, with natural authority, and they responded with obedience.

He wondered idly what it would be like to take instruction from her. To let her make stern demands which he could satisfy one by one until she melted for him. Begged for him.

Sucking in a deep breath, he gave his head a subtle shake. No sense indulging such fantasies. She was not and never could be his.

"Mr. Clyde?"

He blinked, yanking his eyes up from her modest, brown-and-white-checked bodice to her face. "Yes?"

Her smile was both polite and puzzled. "Are you in need of assistance?"

"That depends, Miss Battersby," he replied before he thought better of it. "What are you offering to do for me?"

From her sudden frown, he deduced she understood he was teasing her, but did not comprehend his meaning. So, he merely smiled blandly and pushed away from the wall to cross the room. He gave her a polite nod as he drew alongside the compact, square pianoforte, stopping with the young music student between them. The girl's dark head swiveled to and fro, her hands blessedly still as she sought to sate her curiosity.

"Your mother mentioned you were here giving lessons," he continued. "My apologies for the interruption."

Sarah glanced down at her pupil, then back up at him. She sighed. "Mr. Clyde, may I present Miss Thurgood. Miss Thurgood, this is Mr. Clyde."

Miss Thurgood blinked slowly at him, her ridiculously long lashes like brooms sweeping the air for cobwebs. "A pleasure to make your acquaintance," she said breathlessly.

"Likewise." Immediately, his attention drew back to Sarah, who was still frowning at him. "Miss Battersby, I hoped you might assist me in retrieving my horse."

Her face tightened. "I have already sent a note 'round to Mr. Hubbard. He will deliver Matilda to the cottage tomorrow, as he and Mrs. Hubbard will be attending Sunday services."

Nodding, he watched her lips turn down at the corners as if she'd bitten into something bitter.

"Pardon me, Mr. Clyde, but are you Miss Battersby's intended husband?"

He had almost forgotten the girl between them. Miss Thurgood. Probably sixteen or seventeen, if he didn't miss his guess. Pretty enough, he supposed, but utterly uninteresting next to Miss Battersby.

He met Sarah's eyes. "So I am told."

The chatter in the room had quieted. Glancing around, he noted the stillness amongst the girls, who all stared at him with either fear or fascination—he could not be sure.

The redheaded girl—Miss Cresswell, he recalled—spoke first. "What happened to your face?"

"Did Robbie's shot do all that?" asked another.

"Are you from London?" inquired the golden-haired Miss Parnham. Vaguely, he recognized her as one of the girls present when he'd been bashed by the wayward cricket ball. Absently, he rubbed the bruise at the juncture of his skull and his nape. It still smarted a bit, but he was grateful it hadn't been worse.

"You sound as if you have a title. Do you?" asked a dainty brunette with light-blue eyes and a shy demeanor.

Another girl, emboldened by her schoolmates, added, "Please tell us about the season. Have you ever been to a ball?"

A light clap from Miss Battersby halted the interrogation. "Girls, that is quite enough. You know better than to exhibit such impertinence. Mr. Clyde was just leaving."

Sweeping over their wide-eyed faces, eager and fairly trembling with curiosity, he gave them a grin. "No harm done, Miss Battersby. Ladies, I am not a peer, only a humble gentleman, I fear. Yes, I have lived in London. And yes, I have attended a ball or two in my time."

Gasps from his feminine audience would have been better suited had he announced he had once been a giraffe roaming the African plains. However, their reaction became clear upon Miss Thurgood's stuttered question. "Could—could you describe it to us?"

"Yes, please, Mr. Clyde."

"What is it like?"

"Are there many, many gentlemen there?"

"With titles?"

"What sort of dances have you done?"

"The *waltz*?"

"Oh, the waltz! Quadrilles are so very tedious. I long to learn the waltz."

Colin tried to keep up with the questions, he really did. But they bombarded him like a volley of arrows over castle ramparts. The best he could manage was to cover his head and wait for a pause while they reloaded. Figuratively speaking, of course.

Finally, Miss Thurgood lobbed the flaming arrow they all apparently had been waiting for: "Could you teach us, Mr. Clyde? The waltz, that is."

Another volley of "please" and "oh, please" followed from the crowd. His armor could not withstand the assault. "Very well," he conceded, playfully imitating his brother's ducal hauteur. "But first, Miss Thurgood, you must learn to play one. And with greater skill than you demonstrated on the quadrille."

Ignoring Sarah's disapproving glare and ineffectual protest, he gestured for Miss Thurgood to vacate her seat at the pianoforte. Taking her place, he let his fingers settle into position. It was like coming home. "Now then," he said, stroking the ivory keys lightly, lovingly. "Miss Battersby, have you the sheet music for a waltz?"

She did not reply. Instead, Miss Thurgood rifled through a stack, ripped away the hated quadrille, then placed a waltz before him, a simple, untitled piece in three-four time.

"Lovely," he breathed. "Let's begin. First, a waltz has regularity, but that does not preclude emotion. It is a dance for two—tender rather than jolly. Observe." He played a bit, letting the notes drift and strengthen, then float and twirl, then repeat with delicate joy.

"You see, Miss Thurgood? Emphasize the first note of each bar to serve as a guide for the dancers. Your fingers should glide precisely across the keys, not plod like an overburdened mule. Come, sit beside me." He scooted to his right. The long-lashed girl eagerly sat. And, together, they played. Twice she struck an awkward note, but he murmured his corrections, and by the time they had made their third pass through the song, he could declare, "I do believe you have it. Now, try it once on your own." He stood up from the bench, watching her hands. "Breathe, Miss Thurgood, there's a good girl."

She played the repeating tune twice more, gaining confidence until her rendition could at least be termed passable, much improved over her previous efforts. He could not prevent the rush of prickling warmth at her success. It was more than he had expected, enough to explain Miss Battersby's fondness for teaching. He was—how to explain it—*proud,* he supposed. For Colin, it was a most unusual sensation.

Without a thought, he grinned his happiness at Sarah. She seemed stunned, then glowered back. He sent her a questioning look. She answered with raised brows and a tilt of her head toward their rapt audience. The girls were staring at him and Miss Battersby, their dazzled eyes betraying their romantic fancies.

As Miss Thurgood's last note faded, the titter and chatter began, as did another volley of questions. Did Mr. Clyde teach Miss Battersby to play? Was that how they met? Was he a music tutor? Did they meet at a ball? What was it like? Did they fall in love immediately? How long after they met did he propose? And on and on, giving Colin a headache to rival his drinking days.

"Girls!" Sarah said sharply. "Enough, for goodness' sake. Calm yourselves. A lady must curb her curiosity so as not to appear rude or overeager. At most, she may make a single polite inquiry, but she should never—*never*—harangue a gentleman with invasive questions."

A younger girl, likely twelve or so, bravely challenged, "Even when everyone else is doing it?"

"*Especially* when everyone else is doing it, Miss Turner. A lady follows her conscience; she does not join a mob."

Clearing his throat, he attempted to retake the lead. "I shall grant your request to learn the waltz on one condition." Twelve sets of eyes landed on him, waiting breathlessly. "Mind my instructions carefully, and afterward, if you have questions, you may raise your hand and I shall answer. But only one at a time. Understood?"

They all nodded. Then, the redhead raised her long arm. He sighed. "Yes, Miss Cresswell?"

She swallowed hard. "Will you partner Miss Battersby? She is your betrothed, after all."

Again, twelve heads eagerly nodded their agreement. Notably, Miss Battersby was not one of the twelve. Instead, she looked rather peaked.

He sighed. "Very well."

Sarah's protest came immediately. "Oh, but—"

"Miss Battersby," he interrupted, enjoying her look of startled dismay as he sidestepped Miss Thurgood to stand before her. "Will you honor me with a waltz?" He extended his hand. Gloveless, but then, he could barely afford the half-sodden boots he was wearing.

She blinked three times before dipping a perfect curtsy and sliding her hand into his. Her palm and fingertips had the most intriguing rough patches. Briefly, he considered how they would feel on his skin ... No. He must focus on the task at hand.

"Play on, Miss Thurgood," he said, now eager for this lesson to be over quickly so that he did not have to be so near Sarah

Battersby—near enough to smell her clean, womanly scent, to imagine things he should not want. He placed her hand on his arm and led her to the open space near the windows where he had seen the girls dancing earlier. With a flourish, he held his other palm up and gestured to the dance floor. "Let us demonstrate how a waltz is done."

HE WAS A SUPERB INSTRUCTOR, SARAH THOUGHT AS HE counted out the steps of both the German and French waltzes for her and her students. Engaging, humorous, forthright yet gentle, he explained what he wanted so perfectly. She remained stunned that he had managed to transform Caroline Thurgood's playing from awkward to graceful in minutes. Sarah had been unable to accomplish the same task in months.

Currently, he was demonstrating the Sauteuse waltz, exaggerating his movements and slowing and quickening his voice to comical effect. "At once, we are most grand and dignified in our posture, with our chins in the air and our noses poised to rise above unwelcome odors," he intoned in an appropriately lofty manner, pursing his lips and demonstrating the position of the head. "Whilst below," he continued in a more sprightly tone, "our feet are enjoying a flight of fancy." He performed a sudden turn, gracefully bringing his heels to the floor and winking at her.

A bubble of laughter threatened behind her tightened lips. The girls failed to demonstrate similar fortitude, bursting into helpless giggles at his antics.

He pretended confusion. "Never laugh, my dears, for the waltz is a serious business." His statement might have been more believable if he had not gone into a falsetto then dropped three octaves upon the last two words.

The bubble of laughter escaped, bursting from her in a gush. He stopped beside her, his hands cradling hers, his blue eyes dancing with light as he stared. At her.

Her skin heated. Her vision went bright. Her stomach fizzed and bubbled until she had nothing but froth inside her. She shook her head, still grinning like an idiot, but now breathless. "You are most diverting, Mr. Clyde."

He licked his lips and stared at her a bit longer than was comfortable. "As are you, Miss Battersby. Diverting, indeed."

"Eww. D'you suppose he intends to kiss her?" The question was whispered, but loudly enough to reach Sarah's ears and cause the froth to rise from her belly into her cheeks, burning her skin.

Another girl sighed, replying, "Oh, I do hope so."

That was Lydia, of course. The girl's romantic nonsense would not be stifled, to the vast amusement of all the others, including one Colin Clyde, who chuckled and pulled away to bow in their direction somewhat stiffly. His wince reminded her that he was not yet healed.

"Colin," she murmured automatically, reaching for his arm.

But he retreated, his smile fading as he back-stepped. "Ladies, you should find your partner for the waltz." He turned toward Miss Thurgood. "Begin again, if you please."

An hour later, Sarah marveled at his stamina, even as her teeth worried at her lower lip. She had taken over playing the pianoforte so Miss Thurgood could practice the dance with Colin, which gave her a chance to watch him tutor each girl in turn, correcting posture here, aiding in the search for proper rhythm there. He was surprisingly patient with them all, though she could see lines of strain around his mouth. And was he paler than before? It was difficult to judge since his face was still swollen in places and heavily discolored around the eyes, nose, and cheekbones. By all rights, she should not feel the slightest attraction to him, for his appearance was rather grotesque at present. But something made her suspect he was ordinarily quite handsome. Perhaps it was the way he carried himself, unquestioning of his own appeal, unconcerned that anyone might find him less than charming—particularly anyone of the female persuasion.

Her eyes strayed again from the sheet music to where he danced with Miss Thurgood, his hand resting lightly at the girl's waist. A sour note struck. Her fingers halted, along with the tinkling tones of the pianoforte. Girlish groans sounded across the room. "I believe that is enough dancing for today," she announced, rising from the bench stiffly. "Mrs. Blake will have luncheon prepared soon. Go and refresh yourselves for the afternoon lesson in watercolors."

They complied, but only after each one had personally bid farewell to Mr. Clyde, demonstrating their facility for curtsying and rapid eyelash movement. At last, she and Colin were left alone in the room, she leaning lightly against the pianoforte and he against the window wall.

"I can see why you enjoy it," he said, pushing away from the wall and coming toward her with an indolent stride.

"Dancing?"

"Teaching. It offers a certain gratification."

She felt a small smile curve her mouth. "Hmm," she agreed. "When one is successful, very much so. You seem to have a gift for it, Mr. Clyde. The girls learned quickly and well under your tutelage."

He grew silent as she tidied up the sheets of music, but she could feel him move closer, hear the quiet tap of his footfalls on the wooden floor. Finally, he asked a hushed question. "Where did you learn all this, Sarah?"

Startled, Sarah paused to consider the man standing mere feet away. She hadn't expected him to ask such a thing. Living her whole life in Keddlescombe, she was accustomed to everyone, from Ann Porter to old Mr. Hubbard, already knowing her story.

"I sometimes forget that you are a stranger," she murmured

absently then shook her head and sighed, sliding the pile of sheet music into her mother's carved wooden box. "My great-grandfather was titled. Baron Chalsea. My grandfather was a third son, so merely an 'honorable mister.' That was enough, however, for my mother to have a London season and a few friends among the nobility. Until she married a lowly vicar and began rusticating in Devonshire, of course." Sarah chuckled wryly. "That placed her firmly in the middle class. However, she eventually put her fine manners and tenuous noble connections to work when Papa suggested opening a school. I was educated here."

"Ah. Did you expect to have a season, as well, someday?"

She laughed. "Heavens, no. The school began in an effort to provide scholarly instruction to daughters of the aristocracy. Papa was an Oxford man, but quite modern in his convictions. He believed girls should be educated in the same subjects as boys."

A surprised half-smile quirked Colin's lips. "Your father is a radical?"

"Not a radical so much as a true believer. He sees God's reflection in all of us." Her throat tightened as sadness knotted her tongue. "He believes one should honor that by helping develop every child's full potential, whether boy or girl, pauper or prince. He hoped to eventually offer schooling to poor girls, as well."

"An unusual proposition."

She cleared her throat, shaking off her melancholy. "Yes. Unfortunately so. When he failed to attract more than two or three students, my mother suggested changing the emphasis to preparing young ladies for their debuts. After a time, the school became rather successful, but largely with the landed gentry and those who had become wealthy through trade."

"Mushrooms, in other words."

"If you like."

"Why not keep it going? Seems an ideal solution. You and your mother—"

Sighing impatiently, Sarah turned toward the door. Like most people, he simply did not understand her position. "Where? The only reason St. Catherine's Academy remains solvent is that the abbey is maintained by the church. What do you propose we use as a dormitory once Mr. Dunhill takes possession? A sheep pasture?"

He was quiet as he followed her into the corridor and toward the main entrance. "I am sorry, Sarah."

Five feet from the doors, his simple, sincere words stopped her in her tracks. She drew a deep breath, hoping to crowd out the infernal tightening inside her chest. She mustn't give in to despair. Not now. Not ever. It would serve no good purpose at all.

Warm hands settled on her shoulders. His tall, hard frame brushed her back. "I would do more if I could. I swear it."

Her eyes drifted closed. For a moment—just a moment—she allowed herself to lean into him, to let herself imagine the luxury of sharing her burdens, of relying on someone else's strength for a while. Nothing had ever been a greater temptation.

She was losing so much, and she could not stop it, only watch it happen. Slowly. Inexorably. Like a wagon sliding downhill through slick mud, breaking apart as it plummeted.

A sob gathered in her chest. She crumpled forward. Strong arms caught her, bracing across her collarbone, circling around her waist. Gathering her up tight.

"You will get through this," he whispered in her ear.

Her answer was choked. "What on earth makes you think so?"

"You are strong. Stronger than I, certainly, though that is a poor measure."

"I don't know why you say such things."

"Because they are true."

Her hand brushed over his forearm where it pressed her waist. "You do not feel weak to me."

Stiffening behind her, he laid a kiss against her temple and whispered, "Sweet Sarah." Slowly, he withdrew his embrace, his arms sliding away, leaving a cold shadow in their wake. He walked past her to the great oaken doors and pulled them open. The midday light was gray and watery where it fell on his golden hair, turning him pale as a ghost. Before the doors closed behind him, he gave her a heartbreaking smile. "If you only knew."

Chapter Eight

"The rustic nature of the country soothes me.
The rustic nature of villagers has rather the opposite effect."

—THE DOWAGER MARCHIONESS OF WALLINGHAM to her local vicar
upon his request for her presence at a village fair.

"ON THE ROAD?" ASKED MRS. JONES DUBIOUSLY.

"You two met one another on the road?" Mrs. Canfield
seconded. "To where, pray tell?"

Sarah readily acknowledged she was a poor liar, and Mr.
Dunhill's churchyard picnic was her trial. Perhaps even her
punishment. "I—I was traveling to ... er, Bath. Last year. And ...
Mr. Clyde's horse had gone lame."

Speaking of lame, her tale was taking on that character in a dreadful hurry. Where was Colin, she wondered. He was much better at this.

"I don't recall your takin' a journey to Bath," Mrs. Jones said, her brow furrowing. Her expression was reminiscent of the time Sarah and Ann Porter had pilfered an apricot tart from the counter in Mrs. Jones's shop. Ann had shoved the thing into Sarah's hands moments before Mrs. Jones returned from the bakehouse, and Sarah had hidden the sticky, delicious treat behind her back. Mrs. Jones had never been easily fooled.

"I—That is, it was a brief trip to—to meet with the headmistress of a school there. Hardly worth mentioning."

"Hmmph," opined Mrs. Jones.

"Well, luck was surely with 'im that day to be rescued by you, dear," said Mrs. Canfield, her eyes sparkling with keen interest. "And to have you tend 'is wounds after bein' thrown from the very same horse while on 'is way to see ye here in Keddlescombe! Oi might be for sellin' the horse, but 'ee should marry you proper and quick. Ye're 'is good luck charm." She glanced over Sarah's shoulder and raised her brows. "Mr. Clyde! I was just sayin' how fortunate you must feel."

"Indeed I do," came his smooth voice from behind and then beside Sarah. He was wearing another of her father's shirts today, along with a tall hat of Papa's. Colin had paired the borrowed garments with his own riding coat and buff breeches, which she had cleaned and her mother had mended. He appeared rather well put together for a man she'd found nearly dead only days ago.

"Miss Battersby is heaven sent." He gathered up her gloved hand and laid a kiss upon her knuckles. Her heart kicked and stuttered inside her chest. "My angel of mercy," he murmured, his eyes capturing hers.

For a moment, she forgot to breathe. He was that good.

They had agreed upon their tale before leaving for church that morning. *Hew closely to the truth,* he had advised, *and change only the details that must be altered.* Clearly, he was well experienced in the art of deception. But the story stuck in her throat, heated her cheeks, made her cringe to tell it. Even now, with him gazing at her with naked affection, she felt ashamed of lying to two women who had shown her nothing but kindness. And a twinge of regret that Colin did not, in fact, belong to her. That he would leave without her discovering where these new feelings led.

Presently, his blue eyes appeared as guileless as a newborn lamb. "I daresay I would have been lost without her. Quite literally." He returned his gaze to the two middle-aged women—one skeptical but softening, the other captivated—and chuckled. "And now, I must steal her away for a moment. I do hope you will forgive me, ladies."

As he led her through the throng of chatting villagers, she muttered, "This is harder than I supposed."

Still smiling, Colin tipped his hat to the Millers and slid his hand over hers where it held his arm. He gave her a squeeze. "Only a little while longer, dearest."

She raised a brow. "Dearest?"

"Sweetheart, then?"

Her nose wrinkled. "Too ... sweet, I think."

His smile warmed her belly, made her heart flit and bob like a cavorting butterfly. "Oddly enough," he said, "I often think of you in terms of honey. Honey eyes. Honey hair." Blue eyes lingered on her mouth. "Honey lips."

Gracious me, where is the air? Her head had taken to spinning, the villagers' chatter fading around her. All she could see was this man. The one who looked at her and saw not the familiar Miss Battersby, but Sarah. The woman who longed to be kissed.

Perhaps attending the picnic had been a mistake. While Colin Clyde was all too convincing, she remained a dreadful liar, awkward and self-conscious. But, then, nothing could convince Mr. Foote of her unavailability more firmly than being squired about by another man.

"Sarah!" Ann Porter waved them over to the corner of the

open green field, just near the edge of the wood. As they approached, Sarah saw her mother standing with Ann, a worried look on her face.

Sarah released Colin's arm and hurried to Eleanor. "Mama, what is the matter?"

Ann answered, "Mr. Foote cornered her earlier, asking all sorts of questions."

"If the Hubbards had not come along, I–I don't know what I might have said. He was rather forceful–"

Grasping her mother's hand, Sarah gave it a little shake. "Did he hurt you, Mama? Threaten you?"

"No. He simply asked about you and Mr. Clyde. The more he asked, the weaker my answers became. I put him off, but ..."

Sarah finished her thought. "You're worried he will become suspicious."

"He is already that," Eleanor scoffed. "I am worried he may learn the truth, which will only increase his leverage over you."

Colin stiffened. "Where is he?"

Eleanor waved toward one of the longer tables, near the east wall of the church. Sarah twisted around to see Mr. and Mrs. Hubbard conversing somewhat heatedly with Felix Foote. Before she could say a word, Colin was stalking toward the trio, aggressive intent in every line of his body.

"Oh, dear," Mama sighed. "I hadn't realized ..."

"What? Realized what?" Ann queried.

Sarah watched Colin's shoulders straighten on his approach, saw Mr. Hubbard's eyes flare wide with alarm. She could not see Colin's expression, for his back was to her, but Mrs. Hubbard appeared to be stammering a preemptive protest, and Mr. Hubbard had placed his stooped, wiry frame between Colin and Mr. Foote.

Immediately, Sarah knew she must intervene. She pushed forward through the thinning crowd, pausing just long enough to let the youngest Miller girl chase her sister in front of Sarah and run toward the wood. It was then she heard her mother answer Ann's question, a dim thread of chatter amid the bells of urgency pealing in her mind.

"I had assumed his motivation to be gratitude or even chivalry," Mama said to Ann. "Now, I see it is much worse than that."

Sarah did not waste a moment, seeing Colin inch forward against Mr. Hubbard's staying hand, his posture daring the viperous, narrow-eyed Felix Foote to take a swing. As she drew closer, hurrying across the shorn grass, she heard Foote say, "I've a far sight better claim than you, a stranger come from where, precisely?"

Colin's voice was surprisingly low and smooth, considering he looked like he wished Foote's head to fly from his shoulders. "Yet, she has chosen me. She belongs to me."

He reached past Mr. Hubbard's shoulder, bumping the brim of his hat along the way, and took a fistful of Foote's woolen lapel, drawing the other man forward until poor Mr. Hubbard was sandwiched between them, sputtering and struggling to straighten his hat.

"If I find you have forgotten that pertinent fact at any point in the future," Colin continued softly. "If I discover you have trespassed where you are unwelcome, by word or deed, you will have no more need of claims, for a dead man owns nothing but his grave." He released Foote with a shove, sending him careening into a long table.

Sarah halted, swaying in place like the bottles on that table. No one had ever defended her in such a way. No one had ever threatened violence in order to protect her. Perhaps he was pretending, playing the role to its fullest. He must be. He was an excellent liar, as she had seen for herself.

All day, as they strolled together through milling villagers, stopped and chatted about their "secret engagement," he had lied as easily as he would report the weather: *Fine day today, sunny and mild, perfect for taking luncheon outside. We fell in love on the road to Bath and have been corresponding ever since.* So nonchalant was he when speaking these falsehoods that, occasionally, reality would pause, and she found herself believing. In him. In them. In love.

So, his sudden ferocity where Felix Foote was concerned could have no other explanation. Colin was playacting, and Sarah's fantasies were nothing but a lot of silliness. She was not Lydia Cresswell, a foolish romantic with an overabundant imagination. She was Sarah Battersby, vicar's daughter, virtuous neighbor, and responsible instructor of young girls. She was a pragmatist. She could not afford to be anything else.

"Miss Battersby!" Mrs. Hubbard cried, spying her hovering like a ninny.

Sarah gave herself a mental shake and came to stand beside the older woman. Now she was near enough to see that Colin's fury was quite real and had not dissipated, his jaw flexing, his fists clenched. Additionally, Mr. Foote, who jerked at the hem of his coat and shot both her and Colin a baleful glare, appeared ready to do battle.

"Boys," Mr. Hubbard said with disgust. "We are on church grounds. Fightin' has no place here."

Mrs. Hubbard seconded her husband's admonition. "Indeed. Ye should behave as gentlemen if ye wish to please a lady. Is that not so, Miss Battersby?"

The trouble was Sarah liked what Colin had done. She liked that he had stood up for her, threatened the despicable Mr. Foote. Which was why she kept her answer to a noncommittal, "Hmm." Then, looking directly into Mr. Foote's narrow face, she calmly curled her hand around Colin's elbow and moved in close, nearly hugging his side. "While I do not condone violence, Mr. Foote, you would do well to heed Mr. Clyde's advice."

Foote's eyes became malevolent slits, his mouth a tight line. The serpent was angry. "This sudden match is so much flimflam. I cannot prove it, but I know it to be true."

Colin's voice grew softer rather than louder. "She is mine, you disgusting worm. Get it through your head."

Foote opened his mouth to retort, but Sarah had had enough. She interjected sharply, "Even if I were not, Mr. Foote,

I should never be *yours*. That is all you need to know."

The serpent's chin thrust up and forward. "If, as I suspect, your engagement is a lie, then it won't be long before your need of a real husband brings you begging at my door." He shoved away from the table, at last departing their company, but stopped as he brushed past Sarah. "I shall look forward to that day, Miss Battersby," he murmured through gritted teeth before stalking away.

She did not turn to watch him leave. His words caused chills to crawl along her skin like thousands of spiders. "I do not understand why he is so insistent," she muttered to herself. "So ... fixated upon *me*, of all women."

"Don't you?" said Mr. Hubbard.

Sarah shook her head.

Mrs. Hubbard clucked and gave Sarah a peculiar look. "Of course you do, dear girl."

"I honestly do not."

The older woman glanced at her husband, seemingly exasperated, then back at Sarah. "'Tis the same reason we agreed to go along with this"—she waved toward Colin—"flimflam, as 'ee put it. You are quite a favorite in Keddlescombe, Miss Battersby, admired by a great many of us. Mr. Foote may own land, but 'ee is not well liked."

Mr. Hubbard snorted. "No, indeed. His buttons could use a bit of polishing 'round here, that's for certain."

"Miss Battersby will not be polishing any man's buttons," Colin snapped. "Least of all that piece of—"

A loud clearing of Mr. Hubbard's throat halted further description of Felix Foote's dubious character.

Sarah blinked up at Colin, tilting her head to see past the brim of her bonnet. He was furious, his eyes flashing with outrage. He appeared to be struggling to contain himself.

Why it should matter so much to him, she did not know. This was supposed to be a pretense—it *was* a pretense—but he was obviously angry, and not merely for show.

Without thinking, she found herself stroking his arm soothingly. She gave him several pats before she felt Mrs. Hubbard's gaze on her. Sharp questions went unspoken in the old woman's eyes. Slowly, Sarah withdrew her hand from where it curved around his elbow.

Mr. Hubbard cleared his throat again. "That horse of yers is a calm and easy girl when she's not distressed about her owner. What did ye say ye call 'er?"

"Matilda."

"She's a fair beauty, that one."

After Sarah's withdrawal, Colin had cooled noticeably. One might even say he'd taken on a bit of frost. "Yes."

Mr. Hubbard nodded, sniffed, and braced his hands on his hips. "Still plannin' to depart today, then?"

A long pause. "Yes."

Such a simple word, it was. *Yes,* he was leaving. Yes, this was likely the last she would ever see of him. He was a stranger. She'd only known him a few days. Why did it feel like someone was slowly breathing poison into her lungs?

Again, Mr. Hubbard nodded, letting his eyes drop to his boots. "Well, now, that's fer the best. Horse like that don't belong on a farm. Lovely and loyal, but hardly suited to the plow." He chuckled then gave Colin a hard stare. "Not that she wouldn't try, mind ye. For the right cause, she'd run 'erself dead. 'Tis how she's made, ye see. Takes a good man—a *wise* man—to resist askin' such a thing."

Sarah's eyes darted between the two men. A muscle in Colin's jaw flexed as his chin elevated. "I may be neither good nor wise, Mr. Hubbard, but I know well what I am capable of offering." He looked away, then at her, then back to the old farmer. "And what I cannot."

Appearing satisfied, Mr. Hubbard sniffed, gave a single nod, then held his arm out for his wife. "Come, missus. If we must speak with the Reverend Dunhill before leavin', I'd as soon be over an' done with it."

After bidding farewell, the kindly couple moved away through the dwindling crowd. Sarah, still trying to unravel their coded conversation, asked Colin, "What did you mean by what you can offer?"

"Nothing of import." His smile was quick and vacant. He held out his arm for her, mimicking Mr. Hubbard. "Come, missus," he grumbled playfully in a perfectly executed Devonshire burr. "Let us set yer mother's mind at ease before Oi must take me leave."

She wanted to laugh. She could not.

She wanted this to be real. It was not.

Swallowing hard against the ache in her throat, she faced him, then glanced around to ensure they had privacy before saying quietly, "While I have the chance, I—I must thank you, Mr. Clyde." She met his eyes. The red around the blue irises was almost gone, leaving them remarkably similar to a clear sky. "I conscripted you into this battle, and you have risen to the challenge with no promise of a reward." She dropped her gaze to her worn gloves, the leather thin and cracking with age. "If I could repay your kindness, I would."

"You saved my life, Miss Battersby." A gentle finger lifted her chin. A pair of warm lips brushed her cheek with the barest touch.

Her eyes closed tightly for a moment. She did not want to say goodbye to this man. She wanted to beg him to stay. Her heart drummed out its demand that she do precisely that. *I cannot,* she answered that foolish thing. *He is leaving and I must let him.*

His lips and his hand left her. "Most would judge that a worthless cause, and they would be right."

When she opened her eyes, he was half-turned away, staring down the valley to the sea. "Perhaps it is time I raised its value to a measure worthy of your efforts," he murmured. His eyes, distant and pensive, were surrounded by discolored flesh. Strangely, over the past few days, the ugly blue, black, and yellow of his injuries had slipped from her notice.

"Every life is precious," she said, her voice constricted to a thread. "No matter who you are or what you've done."

He was quiet for a while, simply staring out to sea. At last, he faced her and once again offered his arm. She took it, and they started back across the grass toward her mother. Halfway there, he leaned in close to whisper, "I will miss you, Sarah Battersby. Truly, I will."

And I will miss you, Colin, her heart whispered back. *Fathoms deeper than I should.*

Chapter Nine

*"I am not convinced absence makes the heart grow fonder.
Perhaps we should test the veracity of this axiom more
thoroughly, you and I."*

—The Dowager Marchioness of Wallingham to her nephew
upon his fourth request for an increase in funds.

Three weeks later
Blackmore Hall, Yorkshire

"Jane," groaned Harrison Lacey, the eighth Duke of
Blackmore, to the lush woman straddling his thighs. He
attempted to sound stern. "I shall not bend in this."

Her rose-silk gown rustled as she shifted, wedging her knees against the arms of his chair and nibbling his jaw. "I will accompany you, my love," she replied throatily, the rim of her spectacles brushing his cheek. "And that is that."

"The roads are perilous this time of year." His hands came around her waist, drawing her soft, generous bosom tighter against his chest, needing to absorb her into himself. "The journey will be—"

"Unpleasant. I know." Her lips found his, and for a moment, he forgot everything. The letter from Colin. The endless downpour painting the window of the old library. Everything except her.

She sighed and panted against his mouth, her dark-brown eyes opening and seizing him by the heart.

"The risk is unacceptable, Jane."

"Would you prefer I follow after you?"

He frowned, clutching her soft, rounded hips reflexively. "You will do nothing of the sort."

She simply smiled, her dimples flashing.

Damn and blast, the woman had him dancing to her tune as easily as a puppet on a string. "You must abandon this penchant for extortion. It is ill suited to the Duchess of Blackmore."

Her pale, perfect hand stroked his cheek, the backs of her fingers tracing the edge of his jaw. "Presently, I am not a duchess."

"No?"

"I am the woman who loves you too much to be separated from you, Harrison. Particularly when your brother is in peril."

He grunted. She did know precisely how to twist him inside out, his wife.

"Besides," she continued, "he is my friend, and I wish to help."

Feeling a glower descend upon his brow, he battled an old bitterness. "The last two times you attempted to help Colin, you were put in untenable danger."

"This is different."

"How, precisely?"

Her index finger slid playfully down the slope of his nose to tap his chin. "You will be with me."

He sighed deeply and with great regret—then lifted her from his lap and rose from his chair, letting her skirts fall into place and her feet dangle a moment before setting her down.

Rounded cheeks flushed. Dark eyes behind thick spectacles flashed as her tempting lips parted in a small O. "Harrison," she breathed. "How I love it when you lift me just so." She raised her face for his kiss.

But he could not give in, no matter her infernal seduction. He must convince her to remain here at Blackmore, where she would be safe. Grasping her upper arms, he set her away from him gently. "It is more than the roads. He is being hunted, Jane. I cannot—I *will* not—have you anywhere near such danger. Never again."

He still had not entirely recovered from the last time Colin had sought shelter with them. Only a few months past, Harrison's brother had turned up at Blackmore, having been pursued by a shadowy London criminal from one end of England to the other. With nowhere else to go, Colin had come home, and when Jane had gone to visit the cottage where he was staying, the Londoner's hired man had abducted her. Harrison had spent a day tracking them—long, horrifying hours in which he had imagined every sort of barbarity being perpetrated upon his new wife. His Jane.

When he had found where the man had taken her, he'd come within a hair's breadth of blowing the weasel's head to pieces. A part of him still wished he had done. Fortunately for that pile of dung, Jane had suffered little more than a fright. Harrison would have thought the experience sufficient to dissuade her from her present course. But this was not some faint-hearted miss; this was Jane.

"Am I to wait, then? Sit here in the old library like a wobble-chinned ninny, wringing my handkerchief and begging Beardsley for any sign of your letters? Oh, I think not."

He clasped his hands behind his back and gave her his best icy glare. "You will do as I have commanded," he said softly. "Because I am your husband, and my duty is to keep you from all harm."

Sniffing dismissively, she nudged her spectacles higher on her short, round, adorable nose. "How many books do you suppose I should pack? At least four, I should think—two for the journey, and two for our stay."

"Jane. You have libraries filled with books."

"Excellent point. Why scrimp? Six it is."

"*Here.* Read as much as you like, but you shall remain here." Why did it seem every time they argued, he lost the battle before it commenced? Frustration gnawed at his gut.

She stepped into him, slipped her arms around his waist, and laid her cheek against his cravat. "You will take me with you."

"Jane—"

"I will be safe because we are together. And that will keep Colin safe, as well. We are his family. He needs us all, my love."

Sighing and unclasping his hands to slide them around her, he felt the knot of fear in his chest beginning to ease. He often found her calm affection a tonic. She knew it, of course, and used it to great effect. "What are you suggesting?"

"A man alone is vulnerable to attack, but a man surrounded by allies ... Perhaps this Mr. Syder will think twice before he rekindles his pursuit. If he chooses aggression over caution, then he may well be drawn out into the open where the threat he poses can be more readily confronted. As matters stand, Colin is running from a shadow, and we are chasing one."

Thunder clapped in the distance. Rain splattered beyond the window. Harrison held her tighter as she stroked his back through layers of coat and waistcoat. "How did you become such a strategist?"

She pulled back and gave him a brilliant smile. "Reading is a most illuminating pastime."

He stroked her cheek with the backs of his fingers. Her skin and eyes glowed with love for him. Some thought her plain. They were blind. "Perhaps Colin is your friend, but even you must acknowledge his recklessness has twice put you in danger. I cannot risk losing you. I simply cannot." His voice was raw, the words grinding and true.

As her eyes softened with compassion, she placed her hand over his, pressing into her cheek and laying a tiny kiss on the inside of his wrist. "The risk is no greater than my falling ill with consumption or slipping on the wet stones of the south terrace and cracking my head."

Cold nausea gripped him at the visions she presented. Of her suffering. Dying.

He must have paled, because her eyes softened further, and she instantly reassured him, "I only meant that while nothing is certain, I will always be safer when we are together than when we are apart. Woe be to any man who dares trifle with the Duke of Blackmore, for he is a formidable foe."

"As is my duchess," he acknowledged wryly. Letting her nearness soothe him, he laid his forehead against hers and breathed her apple blossom scent. "If I allow this, you must do as I ask, Jane. No arguments. No delays. You must let me protect you as I see fit."

"When have I ever defied your husbandly wisdom?"

Feeling a smile tug at his lips, he replied, "Only always."

She laughed, the sound husky and hitched. "Well, you have me there."

A knock sounded at the door. It was Beardsley, their butler.

"An urgent message has arrived for you, your grace." The short, balding man handed Harrison a letter stained by rainwater, then bowed and withdrew, closing the door quietly. Harrison glanced at the seal.

"Who is it from?" asked Jane.

Frowning, he quickly moved to the desk beside the window to retrieve an opener. He sliced beneath the seal, unfolded the note, and quickly read the contents. The letter was both a warning and a call to arms.

"Summon Mrs. Draper," he said grimly. "Instruct her to begin packing immediately. Then write Digby and ask him to prepare for our arrival."

Jane blinked, taking the letter from his hand as he sat at the desk to write one of his own. "I—I thought we were going to Devonshire. That is where Colin is staying. Why must we open the London house?"

"Read it."

She did, her muttered, "Oh, no," the only commentary.

"Do you still wish to come?" he asked, hoping she would concede, knowing she would not.

Her arms slid around his neck from behind, the paper crinkling in her hand. She kissed his earlobe then whispered, "Try to stop me."

One week later
Thornbridge Park, Derbyshire

VICTORIA LACEY WYATT, VISCOUNTESS ATHERBOURNE, laid her sleeping son in his cradle. "There, now, sweet Gregory," she cooed. "Mustn't let your papa's dark mood disturb your slumber."

The man in question leaned against the nursery window, arms folded, storm-cloud eyes flashing with temper. Lucien might be glowering his displeasure after their earlier argument, but he remained as beautiful as ever, like a fallen angel. Why that should arouse her so, she could not say. But it had always been thus, since the night they met, when he had kissed her past all sense of self-preservation. Scandal had followed, then marriage. Then the kind of love she had never dreamed possible.

Sighing, she folded her hands at her waist and met his eyes. He glared at her, the dimming light of the sodden afternoon painting his face in shades of gray and white.

"You know very well why I cannot agree to this, Victoria." His voice was hushed in deference to his sleeping son, but the rumble of his deep baritone sent shivers across her skin. Over a year of marriage, and still he made her belly flutter like a trapped bird.

"I would not ask—"

"It surprises me greatly that you did."

"—if the situation were not terribly dire."

His mouth tightened and he shoved away from the window, striding to the door. He held it open then gestured for her to precede him. She led the way to their bedchamber, where they could converse without fear of waking little Gregory. As they entered the opulent room warmed by a crackling fire, he sighed and ran a hand through his ink-black hair before closing and leaning back against the door. "Convince me."

His expression was shadowed—almost sinister—so she wondered for a wild moment if he was asking to be seduced past his resistance.

"Not like that," he murmured, reading her thoughts in her face. His tempting lips curled up on one side. "Well, perhaps later."

"Are you certain?" she inquired throatily, swaying toward him and letting her hand settle against the buttons of his waistcoat. "I am not opposed to such methods of persuasion."

Groaning, he answered with a swift kiss and a whisper against her mouth. "Neither am I, but I fear we must talk about this, angel."

She nodded and stroked his cheek before pulling away to walk to the blue-silk canopied bed centered on the wall near the fireplace. Sitting on the edge, she folded her hands in her lap and rubbed the knuckle of one thumb with the pad of the other. "Colin is in grave danger. Harrison has a plan, but it requires us to travel to London. He needs his family."

"You realize this is the man responsible for my sister's death."

"Yes."

"Not to mention Jane's near ruination."

"Yes."

He heaved an intemperate sigh and began to pace. "He is fortunate *I* am not the one trying to kill him, by God."

She smiled gently, remembering how much hate he had given up in order to love her. "I know, Lucien."

"And yet, you wish me to take my wife and infant son from the comfort and safety of our home and haul them halfway across England to provide shelter for Colin Lacey to escape his troubles? Troubles which, bear in mind, are almost certainly of his own making."

She patted the bed beside her. "Come sit with me."

His broad shoulders stiffened, his tall form freezing in place as he shot her a considering glance. Eyes settling on her bosom, he clenched his teeth and started toward her, his long strides eating the distance within seconds. "You may soon doubt the wisdom of your invitation, angel."

"I shall never regret wanting you near me."

He sank down next to her and took her in his arms, burying his face in her neck. His next words were muffled against her skin, but she understood. "I do not know if I can do as you wish. I would give anything for your happiness. But this ..."

She threaded her hands through his hair, thick and cool to her touch. "Shh. Just listen," she whispered. "I am younger than Colin by four years; did you know that?"

His lips left a trail of silvery tingles from her ear to her collarbone before he answered, "Mm-hmm."

"And yet, I have always felt older. Colin has a kind of sweetness about him, an ebullient, generous spirit that is inborn. Harrison did his best to protect it, but he could not be there all of the time."

Lucien's lips paused, his breath warming her skin. Slowly, he drew back to meet her eyes. "This is about your father."

Her hands fell away, landing in her lap. "Yes."

Face hardening, he sat silently, waiting for her to continue.

She swallowed and drew a deep breath. The memories made her chest hurt. "My brothers were not permitted softness. Laughter, play, affection. Love. To my father, these were cracks of weakness in the fortress he was building. And weakness was intolerable. It had to be crushed to bits and reshaped into stone."

Lucien's hand clasped hers where they were folded in her lap.

She continued, her voice growing hoarse. "Colin is gifted in music. He—he feels it singing in his blood, the way I do with painting. Like a—a force outside of your body vibrating in your bones. It is hard to explain. To hear him play the pianoforte when he thinks no one is listening ... is wondrous."

After a long silence, he squeezed her hands and stroked her back. "Go on."

The pain inside her chest had spread outward and now filled her until her joints and throat and eyes and heart ached. It sought escape in the form of tears. But she would not allow that. Lucien must understand, not grant her wish simply to stop her weeping. "Colin was thirteen when Father came upon him in the music room at Blackmore Hall. I remember ... I remember his face. He was playing a song he had composed, and his joy painted the very air around us with light."

She smiled, loving the memory of that boy, her brother, sharing his soul with her. "Father entered the room. I saw, but Colin did not. He—Father said his name. That was all. The music stopped. From that moment until my father's death four years ago, he forbade Colin to play another note." A tear escaped against her will. Lucien stroked it away with a finger and kissed her temple. "He ordered the servants to bar him from the music room, dismissed Colin's tutors, and sent him to Eton with instructions to the headmaster to enforce his command."

"Victoria, love. I am not unsympathetic, but that does not excuse Colin's behavior—"

"I know. No one is angrier than I at his wanton selfishness and immaturity over the past few years."

Lucien raised a single brow.

"Very well, perhaps someone else is angrier." Her small smile quickly faded. "But I hope you understand that this was not the first time Father had behaved so. He'd been crushing the life out of Colin for years before that, and Harrison before him. Nothing was good enough to please the Duke of Blackmore. Anything that made them truly happy was soon forbidden, as though Father could not countenance his sons having what he did not."

"So, Colin rebelled," Lucien said flatly. "The spare became a drunkard. Seduced my sister and then abandoned her."

She knew he was correct. Colin's actions toward Marissa Wyatt had shocked her, repulsed her. She still had trouble reconciling the man she had known as her charming brother with the scapegrace he had become after he'd begun drinking heavily. It was why she had not spoken directly to Colin in over a year.

"After our parents died, he changed," she continued. "Grew reckless, uncaring of how he hurt those around him. Your sister. Me. Harrison. You know how difficult it has been for me to forgive—"

"Please do not expect that I will do so. Ever."

"No, I do not. I only say these things so that you might understand why I will always love him. To you, Colin is a villain. To me, he is that boy who hugged me without thinking twice and played his music for me and made me laugh until my sides ached." The tears were spilling over now, her nose growing stuffy. She sniffed and gave her husband a watery smile. "That is the man I want to save, Lucien. Will you help me?"

She knew what she was asking, and she wished with all her heart she did not have to lay this burden upon her husband's shoulders. If this were about anything but saving Colin's life, she would not have asked at all.

Lucien was quiet for a long while, his head bent forward as he stared down at their entwined hands. When he finally raised his eyes to meet hers, she could read his decision before he said a word.

"Yes, angel," he said, raising her fingers to his lips and kissing them reverently. "For you, I will do whatever must be done."

THE CRACKLING OF THE FIRE IN THE HEARTH COMFORTED Hannah as she watched his approach through the window of the morning room. His walking stick tapped lightly on the terrace stones. Thankfully, she could only hear the fire.

"Would you care for biscuits, miss?" The voice of the housekeeper could not distract her.

"No," she murmured absently. "That will be all, Mrs. Finney."

She must watch and wait and gauge his mood. He appeared ... almost jubilant, his steps showing a faster pace, a hint of spring.

He entered the house, disappearing from her view. She continued gazing out the window for long minutes, waiting. Then, she heard it, distinct above the sound of logs being eaten by flames. Clack, tap. Clack, tap. Clack, tap.

"Hannah," he said, his voice carrying a note of triumph. Most people would not be able to discern it. But she had known him for ten years. Discovering each subtle variation in his seemingly monotonous demeanor had been necessary for survival. "Lamenting the rain, my dear? Do not despair. It shall soon pass."

She did not turn around. Instead, she watched a drop snake down one of the panes before it was replaced with another. "I like the rain," she said.

Clack, tap. Clack, tap. Clack, tap. A hand played with one of the curls on her shoulder. "Lovely," he breathed. "So like your mother's. You miss her, do you not?"

How could she? Every time she closed her eyes, the woman was there. Glassy, sightless gaze. Head at an unnatural angle. Arm outstretched for her daughter. Cold to the touch.

"As do I, my dear. And yet, I see her in you." He sighed and ran a hand over the back of her head as though petting a favored hound. "It is a good day, Hannah. I have found the thread. All that remains is to follow where it leads and then sever it." A gentle kiss fell on the crown of her head. "Patience. Acuity. Persistence. These are qualities you must cultivate, as I have done." Finally, he retreated, moving toward the fire.

She allowed herself a moderately deeper breath. There was no need for a response. This was him crowing. In his abnormally constrained way, of course.

"Rest easy, Hannah. Your Papa will dispose of this matter soon. And then, we may carry on as we did before."

Hannah did not argue. She did not speak. She watched drops slither down glass, following each other's trail until the trail itself appeared solid. And, inside, where he could never hear, her heart screamed until its voice was bloody and raw.

You are not my Papa. You are not my Papa. You are not my Papa.

Chapter Ten

*"Obtaining a position is your task. Mine is ensuring
I do not invite thieves to polish the silver."*

—THE DOWAGER MARCHIONESS OF WALLINGHAM to an applicant
for the position of lady's maid during an unusually
abbreviated interview.

SARAH CAREFULLY FOLDED HER FATHER'S WAISTCOAT AND
placed it inside one of the crates slated for the poor. Mr. Dunhill
had promised to distribute Papa's things to deserving families.
Which was strange, considering she and her mother could now
be counted among that number.

"Do you suppose we should take the teapot with us when we
leave?" Eleanor inquired as she entered the parlor with another

stack of clothing. She set it beside the pile Sarah was sorting. "It is rather fragile."

Plucking another garment from the stack, Sarah said absently, "Given we do not yet know where we will be living, I suggest we pack only what is necessary."

"Well, Mrs. Hubbard has offered—"

"I know, Mama. But how long can we stay with them, really?"

Eleanor sighed, arching her back as though it pained her. The black band of fabric around her upper arm slid down to her elbow. She tugged it back up and ran a hand over her forehead, nodding her agreement. Her hand dropped to her hip. "Have you heard anything from the school in Exeter?"

"Nothing yet."

"I still maintain we should travel to Bath. There are several fine schools there, as well as moneyed families who may be in need of a governess, and Cousin Elizabeth will have a much harder task ignoring us when we arrive at her door."

Lately, Sarah had found little to laugh about, but the vision of Mama's haughty cousin—who refused to answer Mama's letters—being importuned upon her own doorstep was rather amusing. She gave a half-hearted grin and pulled one of Papa's tailcoats from the pile. Giving it a shake, she examined the seams. A bit worn, but someone would surely get years of use out if it.

Unbidden came the thought of the last man who had borrowed Papa's clothes. For possibly the millionth time, she wondered about him. Colin. Wondered how he was, *where* he was. Whether he had found safety. Whether he ever thought about her, the madwoman who had claimed him as her betrothed.

"Be sure to search the pockets," her mother murmured, glancing around the parlor for her teapot. "Your father was always tucking things away."

Sarah laid the coat down atop the crate and fished inside the interior pocket. A corner pricked her fingers. Folded paper. She withdrew the sealed letter, noted her father's spidery scrawl on the outside. It was her name.

Tears gathered in her throat, choking her.

Across the room, china clinked. "If it cracks, then so be it," Eleanor muttered. "This pot was a gift from my mother on my wedding day. Where I go, it goes."

Sarah gritted her teeth and shoved the letter into her apron pocket. She sniffed and folded her father's coat, placing it gently inside the crate.

A knock sounded at the door. Sarah turned in that direction, but Eleanor was ahead of her. "I shall answer," her mother said, wiping her hands on her apron and weaving her way past the various crates cluttering the parlor floor. "Likely it is Mr. Dunhill's mother-in-law again, come to measure the windows for draperies or some such."

Sarah half-smiled. The woman had visited thrice in the past week, always insisting they should "take as much time as needed in this period of mourning." Yet invariably she managed to leave with a set of measurements or new furniture plan, all in preparation for taking possession of their cottage.

The voice now drifting from the open door was not a woman's, however. It was a man's—cultured, soft, unfamiliar. Sarah frowned, curious. She walked slowly across the parlor and came to stand behind her mother.

He was richly dressed, his greatcoat of fine, gray wool, his black top hat gleaming in the early sunlight. Apart from his blatantly expensive clothing, he possessed bland features and middling height that made him rather unremarkable.

"Ah, Sarah," said Eleanor over her shoulder. "This gentleman has come to inquire about placing his ward in St. Catherine's Academy for Girls of Impeccable Deportment. I was just informing him, regrettably, that we have closed the school. Our last pupil departed yesterday."

"Regrettable, indeed," the man said, his eyes shadowed by the brim of his hat, his gloved hands clasped neatly atop a silver-capped walking stick. "St. Catherine's Academy came with the highest recommendation."

"Oh?" said Eleanor. "By whom, if you don't mind me asking?"

"A friend of a friend is acquainted with a local man. Mr. Foote, I believe."

Slightly nauseated by the reminder of Felix Foote, Sarah recalled hearing he had gone to London last month. For what purpose, she did not care to know. She'd simply been relieved he had disappeared from Keddlescombe. After her father's death, the respite from his loathsome attentions had been a blessing.

Presently, she smiled with a politeness she did not feel. "I do hope you have not traveled far, Mr. ...?"

"Forgive me, Miss Battersby," he said, smoothly removing his hat. His hair was ruddy blond and thin, the wisps combed neatly across his scalp. "Syder. Horatio Syder. I traveled from London, but I have matters of business to attend nearby, so it was not out of my way." His eyes, previously difficult to see, were a flat, pale gray. He smiled gently, his expression mild and even charming. But his eyes gave her a chill.

Dismissing it as a trick of the light, she nodded and responded with the manners her mother had taught her. "Well, I am very sorry to have disappointed you, Mr. Syder. If you like, I can provide a list of recommended schools for your ward. What age did you say she is?"

"Fourteen," he said, his eyes brightening for the first time. *Yes, indeed,* she decided. *A trick of the light, surely.* "And so curious, it is all I can do to persuade her to leave the library."

Sarah smiled back at him. "Many of my students are the same." She shook her head and immediately corrected, "Former students, I should say. Their expression of wonder at making a new discovery was always my best reward."

A breath-stalling gust of wind whistled up from the sea, pushing past Mr. Syder and raising gooseflesh on Sarah's skin.

"How rude of us," Eleanor exclaimed. "Would you care to come inside? I fear we are in the midst of packing up the cottage, so it is dreadfully cluttered at present, but we can certainly offer you a cup of tea."

Sarah blinked at the back of her mother's head. What in heaven's name was she thinking? The parlor was in no condition to host—

"I would be delighted, Mrs. Battersby."

Before Sarah could protest or even inquire as to where her mother had left her wits, Eleanor had escorted the gentleman into the room piled with their possessions—stacks of linens and clothing, books and dishes, keepsakes and silly mementos that should have been discarded years ago. The stuff littered every surface, interrupted only by wooden crates and two old trunks. He took it all in with a sweeping glance. She had the odd impression that he was calculating its value in his mind.

Her mother busied herself clearing space on the lone, threadbare sofa. Eleanor then patted the cushion and said, "There now, do have a seat if you like, Mr. Syder. It will only take a moment to pour the tea. Perhaps my daughter can tell you a bit about her skills as an instructor of curious young girls."

"I—I can?"

"Certainly, you can," Eleanor insisted, her inflection emphatic. "For, it sounds as though Mr. Syder's ward is in need of someone with your talents and experience. If not at a school, perhaps as a private tutor or governess." Her mother's eyebrows were bobbing up and down in a most peculiar way before she left the room, pausing only long enough to retrieve the china teapot she'd been packing.

Blast. Sarah had told her mother she would prefer a position at a school, where they could more easily settle in one place. How else could she provide a home for them both? Marriage, perhaps, but she had already rejected the idea. The only man who might have tempted her in that regard had left her behind nearly two months ago.

"Well," she said, now that her mother had given her no choice. "Perhaps we should sit." She picked her way across the room to remove a stack of bed linens from a chair then dropped them into an empty crate before sitting.

Mr. Syder's walking stick tapped on the plank floors, sounding sharp in the room before he sat on the sofa, leaning the thin cane against the rolled arm and placing his hat beside him on the cushion. Gray eyes leveled on her. "Keddlescombe is a lovely place. The villagers have been most helpful. They do seem to know everything of note that occurs in the area."

"The village is very small. It would be more difficult *not* to notice, I daresay."

"Indeed." He smiled at her, but his eyes had taken on a flat cast again. "I have a friend who passed through this way recently. He wrote to me, singing its praises. So green, he said. The air clean and smelling of the sea. Quite different from the coal dust of London. I felt I simply must see it myself." His hands rested beside his knees, perfectly still. The man did not fidget, scarcely blinked. "Perhaps you remember him. Tall chap."

Her heart kicked against her bones, suddenly turning and flopping and pounding in a frantic rhythm. A wash of cold, sick fever ran through her blood. "No, I ... I cannot say ..."

"His name is Colin Lacey."

The fine hairs on her forearms lifted away from her skin.

"*Lord* Colin Lacey, although he often prefers to dispense with the title, as it is a courtesy only. His brother is the Duke of Blackmore."

She could feel the blood leave the surface of her body. Perhaps it was fleeing from the man sitting across from her. The man who had sliced open Colin's ribs, blackened his face, and left him for dead.

For a full minute, she could not get enough air to speak. Finally, when she did, her words were faint. "I'm afraid I—I have not visited the village a great deal of late."

His eyes, gray as death, fell on the black band around her upper arm. "You are in mourning," he said, his voice soft.

"Yes."

Glancing around the room desultorily, he tilted his head. "Your father, I presume?" The way he said it, casually, easily, as though it were simply one more bit to add to her file, froze her in her seat. "My condolences to you. And your mother, of course."

Why, when her breathing had grown so shallow, did her heart suddenly feel squeezed by a vise?

"So, where did you say Lord Colin headed when he left here, Miss Battersby?"

She swallowed, nearly choking on the dryness in her throat. "I did not. I do not know a Lord Colin."

His head tilted again. "Oddly enough, the villagers seemed to think otherwise."

"They are wrong."

"Is that so?"

Eleanor entered, carrying a tray with her china teapot and three small cups, which clinked against their saucers. "It is freshly brewed. I simply cannot countenance tepid tea." She set the tray on one of the crates, then poured them each a cup. As she reached to hand Sarah hers, she froze, apparently noting her daughter's expression. "What is it?"

"I fear Mr. Syder is seeking that which we cannot provide."

His smile flattened, then disappeared. "Perhaps it is a matter of incentive." He took a sip of her mother's tea. "Come now, Miss Battersby. Your difficulties needn't continue in their current vein." The cup returned to its saucer without a sound. "You could live quite comfortably on what I am willing to offer for a rather inconsequential piece of information."

"Information?" Eleanor frowned. "I thought you were here about the school."

Sarah ignored her mother, unable to look away from the dead-eyed predator seated across from her. "I cannot sell what I do not possess, Mr. Syder."

Sighing, he leaned forward to return his cup to the tray. His nearness set her skin writhing with the need to run. "That is most unfortunate." He stood, returning his hat to his head and his walking stick jauntily to his hand. Head tilting the slightest bit, he again glanced around the cluttered parlor. "Perhaps a change of circumstances will persuade you otherwise." With that, he simply turned on his heel, walked calmly to their front door, and exited the cottage without another word.

"What in blazes was that?" Eleanor queried. She still hovered near the tea tray, her cup in hand, clearly bewildered.

Sarah sat in place, feeling ice crystallize inside her veins. "That was the reason you had to stitch a man's skin back together, Mama." Her voice was nearly soundless, but perhaps it only seemed so because her heart boomed loudly in her ears.

"That was ...?"

"Yes."

"Oh, my word."

Suddenly, Sarah could not bear to sit any longer. She stood and rushed to the front window, pulling back the curtain. He was gone. At least, from her house. "I must warn Colin," she mumbled, now pacing in the open space along the wall. Her hand covered her mouth, then dropped back to her side. "But I have no idea where he is. He did not tell me before he left, said only that it was safer if I did not know."

Her mother watched her pace, saying nothing. Which was unusual.

"Mama?"

"Yes?"

"I do not know what to do."

"I can see that."

"Please tell me what I should do."

Eleanor crossed her arms beneath her bosom. "Perhaps you should give Mr. Syder what he wants."

Sarah stopped pacing, looked at her mother's shuttered expression. "I just said I do not have what he wants."

Several heartbeats passed. "Perhaps I do."

"You."

Eleanor sniffed. "Yes."

Incredulity built like pressure behind a cork. "And you wish to sell it to someone who would beat and torture a man nearly to death?"

A slight flush entered her mother's cheeks. "I do not wish to, but ... Oh, *really*, Sarah. Do not look at me so. The chances of anyone still finding him there after all this time are quite remote."

"Mama."

"He said I should only contact him in case of a threat."

"This is a threat. It is the very definition of a threat!"

Eleanor shook her head. "To *you*, Sarah. Only if there is a threat to you."

Her heart began pounding again, this time not out of fear. "Tell me, Mama. I must find him, warn him. Please."

Her mother's eyes softened. "This Syder fellow will simply follow you straight to him, you realize."

"Not if I am careful."

Uncrossing her arms, Eleanor hissed out another sigh and closed the distance to Sarah. "*We* will be careful, because *we* will warn him together. I will not allow you to take such a chance on your own."

"Very well," Sarah said before her mother had even finished speaking. "Where is he?"

"First, we shall complete our packing. We will take our belongings with us, as we had planned."

Sarah frowned. "No, we must—"

"And then, daughter, we will formulate a strategy. One that avoids the circumstance in which either of us lies bleeding beside the road. Is that clear?"

Impatience thrummed and burned. She wanted to discard her mother's sensible warnings. Instead, she had no choice but to nod and obey.

Eleanor's hand settled on Sarah's shoulder. "Do not worry so. If he knew where Mr. Clyde had gone—"

"Lacey," Sarah said faintly. "Or, more appropriately, Lord Colin. He is the brother of a duke."

Her mother's long silence was filled with questions. Fortunately, she did not ask them, because Sarah had few answers. "Regardless. If Mr. Syder had the first inkling where Lord Colin was hiding, he would not have paid us a visit, nor would he have offered funds in exchange for the information."

The pressure around her heart began to ease just a bit. "You are right. But Syder is much too close to Colin's scent."

"Let us finish our work here."

Sarah started to protest again, then stopped when Eleanor held up a hand.

"We finish here," her mother repeated. "Then we shall see about saving your stranger once again."

Chapter Eleven

*"You wonder why I refuse to travel in such vehicles.
Now you have your answer."*

—THE DOWAGER MARCHIONESS OF WALLINGHAM to her son,
Charles, upon learning of his disastrous outing involving a certain
widow, an open barouche, and an unanticipated rainstorm.

FIVE CRATES AND TWO TRUNKS. SOMEHOW, THEY HAD
managed to winnow all their worldly possessions down to only
that, and still, the cart lent to them by Mr. Hubbard was
weighted and slow on the dusty, rutted road.

"We shall be fortunate to arrive before dawn," Eleanor
muttered, her focus on the rear end of the broad-backed farm
horse, which was all that was visible in the heavy dark.

Sarah held the lantern higher, her arm aching, her backside numb on the hard wooden seat. "You said it was less than twelve miles."

"Yes."

"We've been traveling for hours." They had left the Hubbard farm shortly after nightfall.

Eleanor was quiet, peering at the animal's back as though she could will it to move faster. "It feels longer," was her mother's only reply.

Sighing, Sarah watched her breath plume out into the chill air and absently rubbed her own shoulder, trying to ease the soreness. They had already spent three days packing up the cottage, saying their goodbyes, and laying a false trail toward Exeter. Urgency was like a fire licking at her feet, enervating and exhausting at once. She must get to him. She must make certain he was safe. That was all she knew.

Pulling the reins to slow the horse further, Eleanor said, "I think this is where we turn." Her voice did not ring with confidence.

Sarah squinted into the dark. "Are you certain?"

"Would you like to drive?"

"Happily," Sarah bit out. "Except that you refuse to reveal where we are going."

"Had I told you earlier, you would have left me behind and struck out on your own."

It was true, but it only rubbed harder against her blistering frustration. What was so wrong with wanting to confine the risk to herself? She had not even dared hire a boy to deliver the message to Colin, so fearful was she of anyone else being harmed.

Her mother scooted forward, perching on the edge of the wooden bench. "Hold the lantern higher, Sarah. I cannot see the sign."

"There is no sign."

"Of course there is. Just do as you are told. I am your mother."

Sighing loudly—again—Sarah complied.

"Ah, yes. This is it."

Peering past the dim ring of light cast along the horse's rump, Sarah could make out a low stone wall and a wooden post. "This is what, precisely?"

Eleanor began directing the horse forward, then to the right, where the wall gave way to a narrow lane. "The way to Yarnsby Manor."

"You mean Yardleigh Manor."

"Oh, yes. Yardleigh."

"He—he is hiding at Yardleigh ...?"

"Manor. Yes."

Sarah scarcely noticed the distant rumble of thunder, the two small droplets that struck her glove. He was a duke's brother. Naturally he would choose a manor house as his shelter, and that must have been his original destination when she had discovered him on the road to Littlewood. But why Yardleigh? She could only surmise he had a connection to the owners.

She had visited the place once before, at age ten, when her father had paid a visit to the ailing, elderly baron who lived there. Later, the baron and his title had both expired, leaving the house to fall into disrepair. Eventually, it was purchased by an unknown family of considerable means who, according to village gossip, was rarely in residence.

She did hope the new owners had properly maintained the property. She well recalled being charmed by the house, which was formed of two parts: a grand, square structure of violet-gray granite, and an older, half-timbered wing running perpendicular along one end. The whole of the house resembled a "T" that had toppled on its side, the two parts built in different eras, but oddly complementary. She had seen larger houses before—many along the road to Bath or London sprawled like great dragons across a wide, green landscape. But just one of Yardleigh Manor's wings would swallow every stone, window, and floorboard of her cottage and abbey. Perhaps more.

Cold drops landed on her cheek. She turned her gaze up toward the sky then examined the halo surrounding the lantern. "It is raining, Mama."

"Yes," Eleanor answered, clicking her tongue at the plodding horse. "If we do not wish to be drenched when we arrive, let us hope the house is closer than I remember it." She glanced over at Sarah. "Bad enough that we shall importune a wealthy household so late."

Unfortunately, they arrived well after the skies had torn open and released a deluge. As they pulled into the drive in front of the house, Sarah remarked, "Well, I suppose it will prove difficult to track us after all this. The rain will surely wash away any sign of our progress along the roads."

"If you are looking for good cheer," her mother grumbled, pulling the cart to a stop. "I suggest you seek it elsewhere, for I see little to applaud in our present circumstances."

They climbed down, both groaning at the stiffness in their joints and muscles. It had been an endless, frigid, wet ride. And they still must face the possibility that Colin had long ago moved on.

Three of the windows on the ground floor were lit, so the house was clearly occupied. Sarah set the lantern down next to the cart's wheel. "Should we ... should we knock?"

"Would you prefer to stand here until we are turned to mud?" Eleanor retorted.

Glancing at her mother, Sarah saw a thin, pale woman, drenched and shivering, hugging herself for warmth. Decision made, she nodded and clutched the skirt of her sodden, woolen pelisse, then strode to the door at the center of Yardleigh Manor's granite wing. Above the door, in the dim light from the windows, she could make out a date carved into the keystone: 1696.

Drawing a trembling breath, she lifted the heavy metal knocker on the paneled wooden door and knocked thrice. A minute or two passed. Her mother's jaw went tight as if to prevent her teeth chattering.

At last, the door opened to reveal a plump, rosy-cheeked woman in the apron and cap of a maid. The keys at her waist, however, revealed her for the housekeeper. "What's this?" the woman cried, extending her candle to view their faces. "Have you lost your way, then?"

"W-we are here with a m-message," Sarah said, her lips suddenly unresponsive to her commands. Perhaps it was the cold. "For Mr. Cl—that is, Lord Colin Lacey."

The housekeeper's brows lowered. "No one here by that name." Her bulk jiggled as she moved to grasp the edge of the door. "Appears you've braved the storm for naught. Now, I'll be bidding you good—"

Sarah leaned forward and grasped the woman's wrist. "Please," she said. "It is a most urgent matter. If by chance he is here, will you at least inform him that Miss Battersby desires to speak with him on a subject of utmost importance."

"I shall do no such thing." She yanked her arm out of Sarah's grasp. "For, there is no Lord Colin Lacey at this house. Furthermore, it is nigh on an hour past midnight. What sort of rabble would gad about at this wretched hour in the midst of a downpour, I ask you?" The round woman gripped the door once again, glancing over Sarah's shoulder to the humble cart still sitting in the drive, the wheel lit by her lantern. "Nobody a lord would grant an audience, I tell you that much. Now, be off with you."

With that, she slammed the door, leaving Sarah speechless, staring at paneled wood and dripping on her own boots.

"Knock again."

The words came from her mother, but took a moment to register.

"Go on, then," Eleanor said, clutching her elbows as she shivered, rain pouring from the brim of her bonnet. "We've come all this way. I'll not see my stubborn daughter give up so easily."

Slowly, Sarah turned back to the door and used the knocker thrice more.

Nothing.

"Again," her mother gritted. "Until she answers."

Lifting the heavy metal ring, she squawked as it was yanked from her grasp. She expected a round, red-faced woman in a white mobcap and striped apron. What she saw when the door opened, however, was a man. A tall, lean man in a silver silk waistcoat, white linen shirt, dark trousers, and gleaming boots. He was handsome—so very handsome, with refined, boyish features; hair of pale gold, the short-clipped strands barely resisting the urge to curl; and eyes as breathtakingly blue as a summer sky.

Was this, perhaps, a relation of Colin's? A cousin or brother? It was difficult to say, as she felt a bit stunned, her mind turning in circles. Did this mean he was here, after all? Her heart fluttered at the thought of seeing him again. She wondered if he could possibly be as handsome as the gentleman before her, then immediately dismissed the idea. The specimen before her was rare indeed, even with that scowl upon his face.

"... inside. Both of you are bloody well soaked to the skin. Apologies, Mrs. Battersby, but you bloody well are." He stepped back and waved them into a well-lit foyer with angled, oak-paneled walls.

Her mother nodded and entered ahead of her. But Sarah was preoccupied with the gentleman. His voice, *he* was so very—

"Sarah."

—familiar.

"Come inside, for pity's sake."

It was him. This was Colin. *Lord* Colin. Healed. Handsome. With a bit of a haircut and dressed in wealth's finery.

She could not breathe, and in fact, must have swayed a bit because he took her elbow and prodded her past the threshold.

"Sarah." Now, he sounded hoarse, staring down at her with heat and concern and visible agitation. "What is it, sweet?"

Blinking rapidly, she gathered her wits as best she could, under the circumstances. "L-lord Colin. I scarcely recognized you."

He released a breath, his frown easing. "I would imagine I

look different than the last time you saw me." He turned to the rosy-cheeked housekeeper and barked, "Wake the stable lad to take care of the horse and store the cart. I want bedchambers and baths prepared for each of our guests as soon as possible, do you understand? And tea, Mrs. Poole. In the drawing room. Now."

The woman bobbed her compliance and exited through one of four sets of doors. Colin led Sarah and Eleanor through another set into what was presumably the drawing room, a large, luxurious space with wood paneled walls and green-striped silk draperies. The same silk clothed two facing sofas and coordinated with dark velvet chairs rimmed in darker wood. The warm, elegant room was lit by the gentle glow of strategically placed tapers, along with the fire inside an oak-framed fireplace large enough to house Mr. Hubbard's cart.

Distantly, she heard Colin invite them to sit before he left the room with a promise to return. Sarah did not sit. Instead, she gazed at the green-striped silk on the sofas, then down at the puddle of rainwater gathering at her feet.

"You've gone awfully quiet of a sudden," observed Eleanor, who likewise maintained a standing-and-dripping posture just inside the doors.

She met her mother's eyes. They were tinged with worry. "I am well, Mama," she lied. "Simply chilled and spent from our journey." Glancing around the room again, she landed on the fireplace. Tugging at her bonnet's ribbon, she removed the soggy straw hat and waved it toward the fire. "Perhaps we should warm ourselves. It might make conversation easier if my teeth cease their chattering."

Following suit and removing her own bonnet, Eleanor led the way across the expanse of polished wood floors and thick, expensive carpet. Together they stood close to the hearth absorbing the heat of the flames.

The door opened. It was Colin, his arms piled high with what looked to be woolen blankets. His long strides, unimpeded by pain or weakness or injury, crossed the two-dozen feet between them in seconds. He was strong again, and it gladdened her heart.

"Here," he said, shoving a folded blanket beneath her nose. "Take two. And for the love of God, Sarah, sit down before you collapse. You are nearly blue."

Placing her bonnet on a low table, she shook out one of the blankets and wrapped it around her shoulders, only just finishing before those same shoulders were clasped in lean, masculine hands and she was nudged backward until she found the sofa's silk beneath her backside. "It will stain—"

"Hush," he said, his fingers lingering seconds longer than necessary before being removed. "Stay." He next turned to her mother, who had wrapped herself in two layers of clean, dry wool and plopped down in one of the velvet chairs. "Better, Mrs. Battersby?"

Eleanor nodded. "Better."

Colin seated himself on the sofa opposite Sarah, ran a weary hand down his face, and bent toward her, bracing his elbows on his knees. "Tell me what has happened."

This was it. The reason she had come here, the reason she had spent the last three days in a fevered state. And now that she faced him, this familiar stranger, words vanished like wisps of fog burned away by dawn's heat. Instead, her only thoughts were of how much she had missed him, how unexpected was the pain of it. How seeing him again destroyed her.

"Sarah," he whispered. "Tell me."

"A man came into the village," her mother answered, voice shivering as much as her small frame. "Claimed he had a young ward he wanted to send to St. Catherine's Academy. When we told him the school had closed—"

"Closed?" Colin asked sharply. "When?"

Sarah swallowed hard, wondering if the feeling would ever come back into her fingers. They felt frozen clear through.

"The last girl left a few days ago, but we've planned the

closure for the past six weeks," Eleanor said. "Since Mr. Battersby's ... passing."

Shifting her gaze to the flames dancing and crackling in the fireplace, Sarah squeezed the inside of her gloves. Perhaps there was a bit of sensation, but the leather was wet and clammy. Uncomfortable. The creases bit into her flesh. A little pain was better than numbness, she supposed.

"I am deeply sorry. Please accept my condolences."

"Thank you, my lord," said Eleanor. "His death was not unexpected, but it came with some changes of circumstance which have proved challenging for me and my daughter."

Sarah felt a tingling along her cheek. When she looked up, Colin's eyes were boring into her skin, blue and heated, almost accusatory.

"In any event," Eleanor continued. "This gentleman who called on us did not appear dissuaded by the news about the school. In fact, he seemed rather eager to further his acquaintance. I invited him in, as good manners would dictate, and while I was preparing tea, he—"

"He asked a great many questions," Sarah rasped, unable now to look away from his eyes, those haunting, sky-over-sea eyes. "About you."

Sitting straighter in his seat, Colin's jaw hardened, his nose flaring. "Me."

"Yes. He called you a friend. Called you by name." Sarah let her lips curl in a faint smile. "Your real name."

"Did he, now? What did you tell him?"

"Nothing. That I did not know anyone named Lord Colin Lacey."

This time, it was Colin's head that turned away as though he could not bear to look at her. When he turned back, his expression was hard and closed. "What did he look like? Did he say who he was?"

"Yes."

"And?"

Squeezing her gloves harder, she released a breath and felt the leather pinching her palms. The pain was reassuring. "Syder. His name was Horatio Syder."

Chapter Twelve

"The phrase 'courting disaster' was not meant
to be taken literally, Charles."

—The Dowager Marchioness of Wallingham to her son,
Charles, upon learning of a certain widow's strong aversion to
drenched gowns and ruined hats.

She was here. Hours after she and her mother had
disappeared upstairs to thaw and sleep, he still could scarcely
believe it. When he'd heard Mrs. Poole say her name, his
dormant heart had started beating again. It had twisted
inside him like a knife upon seeing her face, pale as blue-
tinged milk.

"We should depart for London as soon as the storm passes,"

said Harrison. "We've clearly waited too long already if he has tracked you this far." Colin's brother stood near one of the drawing room windows, his posture rigid beneath a dark tailcoat, his hands clasped behind his back.

In some ways, they resembled one another. The Duke of Blackmore was similarly blond and only an inch taller with the refined features from their mother's side of the family. He was a bit heavier about the shoulders, but still built along the same lean lines. In Colin's estimation, that was where the similarities ended. For years, they had been at odds, Harrison inheriting too much of their father's coldness and love of propriety for his liking, and Colin letting brandy and bitterness do most of his thinking. Only in the last four months had they begun to reconcile. Jane had seen to that.

"I cannot leave her behind," Colin replied, running a hand through his hair. It was shorter than he liked, but after his relapse with a bout of fever, he had needed the change. "Nor can she return to her village. Syder will use her against me."

Harrison stood silent and still for a long while, staring out at the sullen dawn drizzle. "She matters to you, then."

Presently, Colin sat in the same spot she had occupied last night. If it wouldn't have assaulted her mother's sense of propriety, he would have accompanied Sarah upstairs, watched her bathe, then slept on the cold floor of her bedchamber, just to hear her breathe. That was how much she "mattered" to him. He kept his answer to a simple "yes," however. No sense getting maudlin, particularly where Harrison was concerned.

"You wish to take her to London. What has she to say about this?"

Instantly, Colin's mood darkened. "It does not signify. She will come with us, and that is that."

Harrison merely hummed a neutral response, but otherwise remained quiet.

"Do you know what she had planned after delivering her message here?" Colin heard the outrage in his own voice. It was but a fraction of what he felt. "She and her mother were going to drive that rickety old cart all the way to Bath. Bath! With no man to protect her and little money to pay for food or shelter, not to mention the complete lack of assurances from some cousin ignorant of their impending arrival. The whole business is feather-brained nonsense!"

Turning away from the window to face Colin, Harrison lifted a brow. "Chancy, perhaps. However, from what you have described of their circumstances, it is not entirely without merit. Bath will offer many more opportunities for employment. Or marriage, should Miss Battersby desire—"

"No."

For a moment, Harrison appeared amused. But that was unlikely. His sense of humor was near nonexistent. "She does not desire marriage, then. That is surprising. It would be the most sensible—"

"It is not a subject for debate. She will not be going to Bath." Colin shoved himself up from the sofa and began to pace. "She will stay here until the storm passes. And she will bloody well eat enough to remove the hollow from her cheeks if I have to feed her like an infant." Perhaps this had turned into a bit of a rant, but she was driving him mad with her pert assurances and ridiculous plans. "Then, she will accompany us to London, where I will purchase her some proper gowns. Have you seen what she wears?"

Harrison murmured, "No, I can't say—"

"Rags, they are. What is not wash-worn is threadbare, and what is not threadbare has been mended so many times, it is little more than patches. Her father died six weeks ago. She is in full mourning but cannot afford more than a black band to signify her loss. It is untenable, Harrison."

Colin's brother said nothing. Colin took that as agreement.

"No, until Syder has been dealt with properly, she will remain in my care. And she will remain close, so that I may ensure her safety."

"Very well," Harrison said softly. "Whom shall we say she is? Others will wonder."

Halting in place next to one of the velvet chairs, Colin nodded his agreement. "I have given this a great deal of thought."

"I expected as much."

"We shall present her as my intended wife."

Silence.

"It is not as outrageous as it sounds."

More silence.

Colin resumed pacing. "This solution offers many advantages. As my betrothed, she would have every reason to accompany our family to London. But they are in mourning, so will not be expected to attend most society functions. Her mother must naturally act as her chaperone, which explains Mrs. Battersby's presence rather neatly."

"Your plan will require Miss Battersby and her mother to be complicit in an elaborate charade. Does this not concern you?"

Again, Colin halted, this time giving his brother a broad grin. "Ah, but there is the brilliance of it, Harrison. They have already done so." Briefly, he explained the deception he and Sarah had carried out in her village. "So, you see, she cannot possibly object."

Harrison took a moment to answer. "I would not be too sure. Women can be mercurial."

The drawing room doors opened to admit Harrison's wife, Jane. By all rights, most men would dismiss her upon first glance, as she was short, bespectacled, a bit on the generously rounded side, and plain. However, as Colin had seen while securing her friendship, she was also quite extraordinary.

"This, gentlemen, bears a dangerous resemblance to conspiracy." She grinned widely, her dimples flashing, her dark eyes sparkling. "I must insist on being included."

"No conspiracy, I assure you, Duchess," said Colin with a wink. "Merely the hatching of a devious plot. The differences are subtle, but worth noting."

She went to Harrison first, rising on her tiptoes for a kiss then crossing the room to squeeze Colin's hands and give him a smile to warm him through. "Agreed. I still would like to be included."

"You will be," Harrison replied sounding somewhat grim. "It cannot be helped."

"Excellent," she said brightly, turning back to Colin. "How are you feeling this morning? You look as though you haven't slept. I do worry, you know."

When Harrison and Jane had arrived weeks ago, he had been in the process of regaining his strength after a long fever and a struggle to heal fully. His ill health had delayed their trip to London, a fact for which he now was thankful. Otherwise, he might have missed Sarah.

"I am quite well," he reassured Jane. "Better than I can recall being in a long while, in fact. Perhaps Harrison will explain what has happened and inform you of our plans. If you will excuse me, I must speak with Mrs. Poole about breakfast."

He squeezed her fingers and kissed her cheek as she sputtered her surprise, then left the drawing room to search for the housekeeper. He found her in the morning room, conversing with the butler over the breakfast service. "Ah, Mrs. Poole. And Underwood, as well. Excellent."

The butler inclined his head and they both murmured, "My lord."

"I shall need a tray prepared for each of our guests. Do not scrimp—I want a full complement of Cook's offerings, everything hearty, understand?"

The servants appeared a bit startled, but nodded.

"Mrs. Poole, you may deliver one tray to Mrs. Battersby's chamber, but I shall deliver the other personally."

"Oh! Er—yes, my lord."

Underwood, more accustomed to disguising his discomfort, added smoothly, "I shall ask the footmen to prepare the trays at once, my lord."

"Very good. Bring it to me in my chamber when it is ready."

With that, he nearly sprinted up the main stairs to his dressing room, rushed through a quick shave and a change of clothes, and rehearsed in his mind what he would say to her. He must not let her gainsay him. Her stubborn pride might well prevent her accepting his plan. But he could not allow it. She must agree.

A knock signaled the delivery. He thanked the footman and admired the thoroughness of Underwood and Mrs. Poole—the tray was laden with bread, steaming eggs, ham, bacon, rolls, marmalade, and more. Much more. Grinning, he carried it down the long corridor to Sarah's door, knocked firmly twice, and listened for her response.

A soft, "Come in," widened his grin further. He swung the door wide, stepping through confidently. And stopped. He let the door drift closed behind him, his breath leaving him in the lurch.

She was seated at a dainty dressing table. As her back faced him, he was only allowed a glimpse of one feature—and it was magnificent. Spiraling strands of golden-brown honey, lush and profuse and wild, spilled down the length of her back. The curls she had long struggled to contain had been loosed upon his senses. He wanted to bury his face in them, to clutch them in his hands as he drove himself inside her body.

The cup of tea on the tray rattled against its saucer. Her head turned until her eyes—those honey eyes—met his and flared in surprise.

"What ...? My—my lord." She fussed with her white dressing gown, pulling it tighter across her bosom.

He wanted to unwrap her like a gift.

"To what do I owe this visit? Has something happened?"

Yes. Something had happened. Blood had surged into his cock and turned it to stone. Lust had filled his head like Devonshire fog, thick and impenetrable. He could not see his way out.

"Is that for me?"

Such an innocent question. Indeed, everything he had was for her. His cock and his lips and his hands and his tongue. All for her. Only for her.

"It smells heavenly." She rose and came to him, took the tray from his hands, placed it on a small, marble-topped table between two chairs. "So much food! It is far more than I will be able to eat, but I thank you for delivering it. Was Mrs. Poole too busy? Running a household can be very demanding, especially first thing in the morning."

Her chatter gave him time to let reason penetrate. Which was good. He needed his wits about him. "I brought it so that I may speak with you. Alone." He cleared his throat. "And you will eat all of it."

She sent a dubious look over her shoulder. "All? Lord Colin, this is more food than I customarily eat in three days, never mind one meal."

"Let us dispense with the 'lord.' I am Colin. Furthermore, you have illustrated my point precisely. You do not eat enough, and that will change here and now."

She huffed out a half-laugh. "Will it?"

"Yes. You are more waif than woman, dash it all, with nothing disguising your bones but a threadbare gown."

Sarah went still, her expression going from smiling to blank, her arms folding across her abdomen. "I see," she said quietly. "Is that all?"

"No, it is not. You and your mother will accompany us to London. We will leave after the storm breaks and the roads have dried a bit."

She said nothing, her finger now tapping her elbow rhythmically.

"Once in London, I will purchase new gowns for you, as yours are wretched. I have seen better in ragbags." Perhaps he could have phrased things more diplomatically, but he did not have time to backtrack. He must make her position clear in no uncertain terms. Her position was at his side, and that was final. "You will stay at my family's town house, where you will eat and rest and avoid labor of any sort."

Her face, so tiny and pale when surrounded by that spiraling nimbus of curls, took on a distinctly obstinate cast. Her chin raised a fraction, her lips tight and flat. If he did not know better, he would suspect she was about to gainsay him with significant force. Instead, the tapping finger increased its cadence.

He sallied onward. "After the threat to your safety has been eliminated, we can discuss where you and your mother will settle. Until then, you shall remain with me."

"Are you finished?"

"Aside from a few particulars, yes."

"Forgive me, my *lord*, but I fear you have misjudged the situation."

He folded his arms across his chest. "Oh?"

"Mmm. Remind me again whom Mr. Syder is pursuing. That would be you, would it not?"

"Well, yes, but—"

"Anyone in proximity to you must, therefore, be at greater risk, not lesser."

"You don't underst—"

"Besides which, I have gone to some lengths to prevent you from perishing at his hands. Not once, but twice."

"Sarah, you know I am grateful—"

"So, what gives you license to dictate my decisions? I owe you nothing, as I am neither your servant nor some poor relation that you can order about. If anything, *you* owe *me*."

He opened his mouth to argue that precise point—he did owe her—but she once again got there ahead of him.

"Furthermore, were I inclined to concede to your demands, what possible reason would your family have for hosting a country vicar's impoverished widow and daughter? Shall we claim I am auditioning for the role of governess? I suppose the Duke of Blackmore enjoys a much friendlier acquaintance with his servants and their kin than is customary. Or, perhaps we are long-lost cousins begging charity from our—"

"You will be my betrothed," he said calmly, wanting her to perceive his resolve. "And your mother our chaperone."

Her mouth fell open, her chest working on a breath.

He took the opportunity to offer the truth. Perhaps that would convince her. "We're headed to London so that I can assist in taking him and his empire apart. We intended my very public presence to draw Syder out, make him uneasy so that he might become ... careless. You are right—he is pursuing me, and I have run as far as I am willing to go. With my brother's help, I will take every precaution. I will surround myself with guards and family and the beau monde so that, should he grow so bold as to attack me, he will surely be penning his own ticket to the gallows." Colin took two steps toward her then stopped. "That was our plan. Before he found you. It is clear he now knows of your importance to me."

A tiny frown furrowed her brow. "You intend to act as bait? And what do you mean by importance?"

"Once he learned of our connection, he surmised that I would give you my location."

She sniffed. "Well, not me, precisely. You gave it to my mother."

Colin ignored her sarcasm and the charge, for it did not signify. He'd been trying to protect her from Syder while ensuring he would be informed if she ever needed him. "I am certain he intended to follow you to me. The storm obscured your trail. However, if you next travel to Bath or return to

Keddlescombe—go anywhere—on your own, he will find you. Hurt you."

Her mouth worked, her eyes searching and bewildered. "To what end? Now that I know your strategy, I would willingly tell him the truth—that you planned to travel to London."

Shaking his head, he answered, "A few days from now, he will know I am in London, and he will learn of the measures I have taken to put myself beyond his reach. He will seek leverage against me. I will not see you harmed."

The furrow above the bridge of her nose deepened and her lips pursed. "So, your solution is that we should feign an engagement. Again."

"Yes," he sighed, relieved she was at last seeing reason. "You have it." Then he gave her a half-grin, remembering another proposal, another agreement between him and Sarah Battersby. "As before, we shall be one another's intended. Temporarily, of course."

"You have utterly lost your senses." She breathed the words, her head shaking in denial.

"Where else can you go, Sarah? Forgive me, but you and your mother are quite destitute."

"I—I shall find a position. Once I am settled somewhere, it will only be a matter of time."

"Time you do not have. Purchased with funds you do not have."

Her eyes narrowed, her pride flaring. "A duke's brother cannot be promised to someone like me. It is simply not done."

He could see her will rising up against him, resisting past the last drop of reason. He understood, but he could not allow it.

She must not deny this. Fear collected in his gut, where it mingled with the desire he had felt from the beginning. *I shall convince her to stay with me, even if I must seduce her into agreement.*

Resolute, he closed the distance between them, crowded in until he smelled wildflowers in her hair, watched her eyes spark and melt. Pictured stripping dull white linen from her body and running his tongue ... everywhere. Over beaded nipples and velvety skin and shadowy hollows. He had dreamed of it. When fever had come upon him. When it had broken. Whenever he closed his eyes and, sometimes, when he stared up into the dark, unable to sleep for want of her.

He watched her throat ripple on a swallow, her sweet breasts rising faster with her breathing. "How easily you forget, Miss Battersby."

"No," she whispered, her eyes drowning him. "I've forgotten nothing. Not one moment."

He felt a slow, heating grin curl his lips. "Then you remember I care little for convention."

"No one will believe it. You and me. Preposterous." She sounded breathless.

Stepping into her, he expected her to retreat. She did not. He let his nose hover and nuzzle into the riotous curls at her temple, breathed more of her scent. It must be soap provided by Mrs. Poole. But on her, it was intoxicating, like lying in a spring meadow of bluebells and clover, green and wild and sweet.

"They will know it to be true," he murmured. Unable to fight the need any longer, he ran his cheek along hers, feeling her springy curls cushion his path. He kept his hands at his sides. Better not to court temptation.

"B-because you say so?"

His lips brushed hers as faintly as moonlight on a windowsill.

Her eyes drifted closed, her pixie chin tilting up for more.

"Because," he breathed against her parted mouth before slowly withdrawing, letting one of her curls catch on his cheek and spring away. "They will see the way I look at you." He stepped back carefully, clenching his fists behind his back, feeling every new inch of distance between him and the object of his desire. But he must leave before he gave in.

Before he made the mistake of thinking he could ever be good enough for her. "They will see, sweet. And they will know."

Chapter Thirteen

*"Just when I suppose you have exhausted every idiotic notion,
you pull an old relic down from the shelf and dust it off
for another go."*

—THE DOWAGER MARCHIONESS OF WALLINGHAM to her nephew
upon news of his third reprimand at Oxford.

"AN ENGAGEMENT?" MUMBLED SARAH'S MOTHER AN HOUR
later. Eleanor removed a hairpin from between her lips and
stabbed it into Sarah's coiffure. "Are you certain you did not
mistake his meaning?"

Sarah ran her hand over her mother's handiwork. *Tamed,* she
thought with relief. *For now.* "No mistake. I told him it was
preposterous. That was the word I used. Preposterous." She rose

from the small stool and set her borrowed brush on the borrowed dressing table. "You are to act as our chaperone, apparently."

Eleanor deliberately eyed the breakfast tray Colin had delivered earlier—still piled with food she'd been unable to finish—then looked back at Sarah. "It appears you need one."

Scoffing with perhaps too much enthusiasm, Sarah replied, "Gracious me, Mama. Nothing has happened." It was true. He had left her bedchamber after their almost-kiss. The disappointment had knocked the breath out of her. But, she supposed one did not form a habit of kissing the object of one's pity.

Her mother stared at her with a mother's eerie knowledge.

"Well, nothing alarming, in any event."

More silence and speculation.

Sarah cleared her throat. "The Duke and Duchess of Blackmore are waiting to make our acquaintance in the drawing room. Mrs. Poole should be here any moment to escort us downstairs."

"Sarah."

She smoothed her hands down the folds of her gown, cringing at the worn, checked fabric, the dull brown color. It was the same dress she had worn yesterday, for their trunks remained on their cart. Colin had mentioned new gowns. Shamefully, she found her will weakening, her pride crumbling beneath the onslaught of temptation. She mustn't give in. To accept his preposterous plan was to imply that a union between her and a man like Colin—handsome, wealthy, sensual, charming—was even possible. No, she knew precisely who she was. And who he was. And why he could never feel the same melting weakness for her as she did every time she glimpsed his lean hands or perfect chin or beautiful blue eyes.

Still, a new gown or two *would* be lovely. Her hand brushed over the black band on her arm. How dearly she wished to wear full black, to honor her father in that way.

"Sarah, look at me."

The demand came from her mother, so she obeyed.

As always, Eleanor was tidy and composed, her skin pale, showing only subtle signs of her age and hardships in fine creases at the corners of her eyes and lips. Now, concern wrinkled her brow. "You mustn't let him persuade you to actions which could result in ... well, in new burdens ... of a permanent nature."

Sarah felt heat rise and tingle in her cheeks. "Mama," she protested. "If I agree to his plan—and that is unlikely—we would be *pretending* to be engaged. It would be a drama, a stage play. And quite temporary, I assure you." She turned and busied herself tidying the few items on the dressing table. "You needn't worry so."

A knock at the door signaled Mrs. Poole's arrival. Sarah was grateful for the interruption, as her mother could be dogged when it came to protecting her daughter. Still, she dreaded meeting the duke and duchess.

As Mrs. Poole guided them through the lengthy corridors of Yardleigh Manor, Sarah cast surreptitious glances at her hem. Threads had come loose, damage from the last washing. The urge to turn back and hide in her bedchamber was strong. Instead, she followed the housekeeper to the paneled doors of the drawing room, drawing a breath just before Mrs. Poole knocked lightly and swung them open.

"Mrs. Battersby," a deep, quiet, masculine voice said calmly from beside the fireplace. "And Miss Battersby." He was tall, Sarah noticed. Even taller than Colin, and slightly wider about the shoulders, but with the same blond hair, trimmed severely short. His jaw was chiseled to a fine edge, his features refined and aristocratic. The Duke of Blackmore was an impressively handsome man, albeit in a more austere way than his brother.

"Your grace," murmured Eleanor, curtsying and inclining her head briefly.

Sarah followed suit, her heart thudding with trepidation.

"I trust you have found the accommodations to your liking."

His words were courteous enough, but his tone was pure frost.

"Indeed, your grace. We thank you for your kindness," Sarah said.

"It is not my house, and therefore not my kindness."

She blinked, uncertain how to respond. If not his, then whose? Colin's? Someone else's?

"Well," said Eleanor, blessedly entering the conversation. "Whoever has provided so generously for our accommodation has our sincere gratitude."

The duke simply stared at them from twenty feet away. A long silence stretched before a feminine throat was cleared.

Sarah had not even noticed the woman standing behind one of the velvet chairs. She was short, a bit plump, with dark-brown hair pulled back from a round face. Except for the fringe of hair along her forehead, it was a severe style on a rather plain woman whose spectacles made her eyes appear larger than normal. She slowly moved to stand beside the duke. *Who is she?* Sarah wondered. *Yet another guest, perhaps? Surely she is not the—*

"Ladies, may I present my wife, the Duchess of Blackmore."

Sarah looked to her mother. Eleanor blinked back at her. Together, they approached the unlikely couple, then gave this wren-like duchess her due courtesy. For all that she was a plain woman, Sarah could not help noticing the Duchess of Blackmore was exquisitely gowned in shining red silk. Along with the dress's hue, the square neckline and darker sash at a lowered waist were quite flattering. And obscenely costly. She could see it in every stitch.

Again, Sarah thought of the threads at her own hem, the stitches she had sewn herself rather than hiring a London modiste or even an Exeter seamstress. She longed to disappear.

"Truly," Eleanor ventured, "we are honored to make your acquaintance, your grace. And most grateful to have been recipients of such generosity." Sarah's mother gave them her best smile. They responded with taciturnity, the duke grim and unsmiling, the duchess's expression closed and tight.

Sarah could only conclude that they did not approve of her or her mother. Two shabbily dressed women from an obscure seaside village were poor company indeed for a powerful duke and his wife. Such a reaction was hardly unexpected, though quite uncomfortable.

It was yet another reminder of why Colin's plan was both preposterous—a most fitting word—and destined for failure. But she had tenuous ground from which to argue his folly, as she had perpetrated the same lie upon her village only two months ago. He would call her a hypocrite for her objections, and he'd be right.

"M-Mrs. Battersby, I—I am given to understand you were the granddaughter of Lord Chalsea," said the duchess, her voice husky and halting.

"Indeed," Eleanor replied. "My father was a third son. The title has since passed to a cousin, though I cannot claim a close acquaintance, I fear." She gave the duchess a warm, kind smile. "London and Keddlescombe are quite a long way from one another. In *many* respects."

A trembling smile, small and hesitant, preceded a warming of the duchess's dark eyes. She reached up to adjust her spectacles. "I have found Devonshire a delight. It is my first journey to this area. One can smell the sea on every breeze, here."

Watching the change in the duchess's demeanor with curiosity, Sarah almost missed hearing the duke's stark question. "Have you consented to my brother's proposal, Miss Battersby? Or may we assume you are in greater possession of your faculties than he?"

Well, she thought. *This one does not mince words.* His forbidding expression made her swallow against a dry throat. "I ... He ... That is, Lord Colin appears to be most committed to this course."

"He is. Precisely *why*, I have not yet determined." His eyes were blue, but a shade grayer than Colin's, like a lake that had frozen over.

"Were it not for his insistence, your grace, my mother and I would even now be on the road to Bath. I assure you of that."

He said nothing in response, merely stared down at her from his lofty height until his wife looped an arm around his elbow and gave him a subtle nudge. "Harrison," the spectacled woman murmured. "Be nice."

"Yes, Harrison," came Colin's voice from behind Sarah, at the entrance to the drawing room. "Do let's be civil." He was striding toward them, his gaze fixed on his brother, his brows lowered in a glare. "You are speaking to my future wife, after all."

"A false engagement," replied Blackmore dismissively. "And a preposterous plan."

Sarah blinked upon hearing her words echoed back to her from those aristocratic lips.

Colin came to stand beside her, causing a flush of warmth at his nearness. "Perhaps," he said softly. "But it is my plan, not hers. I will not countenance anyone treating her with less than proper respect. Even you."

Rather than responding directly to his brother, Blackmore turned his frost on her. "You are aware he has no funds of his own, but lives on an allowance over which I have complete control."

"Harrison," Colin gritted.

"Additionally," the duke continued, "my brother's present circumstances are entirely caused by his failure to repay debts incurred through profligate wagering at Mr. Syder's gaming hells."

Colin's voice deepened, sounding angrier by the second. "You are wrong. That is not the reason. I have already settled my debt, and well you know it."

Blackmore ignored him, holding Sarah's gaze with the force of his own. "So, you see, Miss Battersby, if your interest lies in securing a husband who can be relied upon to provide a home and income for you and your mother, I advise looking elsewhere."

"Harrison!" The Duchess of Blackmore's hiss and outraged expression finally turned him away from Sarah as he frowned down at his wife. "There is nothing to suggest Miss Battersby is of such mercenary character."

"She is not," growled Colin. "If anything, I have had a devil of a time persuading her to cooperate."

Carefully, Sarah cleared her throat. "May I say something?"

Blackmore turned his head toward her then, surprisingly, gave her a dignified nod.

"I am in agreement with his grace." Her simple statement seemed to stun everyone in the room, including the duke, as they all fell silent to await further explanation. "If I were searching for a man to support us, then I *would* look elsewhere. In fact, I would not have involved your brother in my life very much at all. He stayed in Keddlescombe for days longer than he'd planned in order to help me avoid such a marriage."

Blackmore appeared to consider her point, then countered with one of his own. "Perhaps you threw back a minnow in favor of a salmon."

The duchess stared at her husband, aghast. Eleanor gasped sharply. Colin was the first to speak. "Stop this, brother." His voice was low and deadly serious.

But it was the duchess who finally convinced Blackmore to relent, and her tone was surprisingly gentle. "If not for Miss Battersby, Colin would be dead, my love. Do you not think she is owed the benefit of the doubt?"

Blackmore's chin lowered a bit, his eyes softening on his wife. "Perhaps you are right. My apologies for any insult, Miss Battersby."

Sarah inclined her head in acknowledgment. But inside, she understood his concerns all too well. A vicar's daughter from a tiny village with only the barest trickle of noble blood should scarcely be in the same room with a duke's brother, much less pretending an engagement—for the second time. If she were the duke, she would take one look at the ragged, impoverished woman standing before him and draw the same obvious conclusion.

"He—my husband is quite protective of those he loves," said the duchess, her expression friendlier and her gaze more direct than when Sarah had first entered the room. "He is not as stodgy as he seems, I assure you."

Colin snorted. "He is precisely that stodgy. And I do not need protecting from a woman I could lift over my head if I so chose."

The duchess's mouth quirked and she stifled a giggle. "Now, there's an image."

The tension along the back of Sarah's neck eased, and she let herself smile at the woman across from her, whom she was beginning to think she had misjudged. The duchess now appeared shy rather than standoffish. Sarah had observed similar behavior in some of her students. Often it took a week or more for those girls to relax and feel comfortable around new acquaintances.

"We are here to discuss our plans for London," Blackmore interjected.

Colin nodded and invited everyone to sit. Sarah noted he took the spot beside her, on one of the sofas. He was close enough that she could feel his warmth and weight tugging at her senses, smell sandalwood and fresh air.

"The rain appears to be letting up, so we shall depart tomorrow morning," he began. "I have instructed Underwood and Mrs. Poole to see to the arrangements. With luck, we should arrive in three days." He glanced pointedly at Blackmore. "The engagement is not negotiable. Everyone must agree, and everyone must tell the same story. Miss Battersby and I met in Bath. She was there to visit her mother's cousin; I was there seeking a new horse for Blackmore's stable. We happened upon one another when that very horse went lame. She stopped to assist me, and we fell in love. A correspondence led to a proposal, and now I am bringing her to London to meet my family and prepare for the wedding. Questions?"

This was a side of Colin she had previously glimpsed in small doses but rarely observed in full force. He was commanding, assured, his words crisp and his tone resolute. He had thought through his plan and was determined to carry it out. Even his formidable brother would not deter him.

She wanted to kiss his beautiful mouth. Right there, in front of the duke and the duchess and even her mother. She wanted it so badly, her lips began to tingle, her palms to dampen, her breath to quicken.

"London is Syder's domain. What makes you think he will not come after her, once you have made your relationship with Miss Battersby so very public," Blackmore asked.

Colin glared darkly. "He may try. But he will not touch her. Ever."

The duke sighed. "Colin, we will do our utmost to guard against it, but even Jane was not safe from him on Blackmore lands."

"He will not touch her."

"Will you give him what he wants, then, if it comes to that?"

Colin was silent for a moment before answering. "I will not have to. My contact at the Home Office has a timeline for his raids, and soon, the knowledge I possess will be meaningless. Syder's empire is crumbling brick by brick. It is why he has grown desperate."

Blackmore's eyes narrowed on his brother. "You still have not told me who this contact is. Are you certain you can trust him? He did, after all, leave you to the mercies of that despicable butcher."

Sarah glanced at Colin, her heart twisting at the memory of his injuries. It was her first time hearing an explanation of their cause. He'd been aiding the Home Office somehow. Tortured to reveal vital information, he had refused to comply, allowing himself to be pummeled black and blue, sliced open like a piece of meat. She felt her overlarge breakfast churning to escape her stomach.

"I know you are vexed about that," Colin said. He was directing the statement at Blackmore, but he might as well be saying it to her.

She watched as the duke's face turned thunderous—dark and flashing white-hot. His voice, however, was eerily quiet. "I will have his head served to me on a platter."

"Which is why I insist on speaking with him before I tell you his name. Harrison," Colin said, silencing his brother's objection with a look. "This is how it must be."

"I beg your pardon, Lord Colin," said Eleanor, leaning forward a bit in her velvet chair, resting her hands on the wooden arms. "But if my daughter has agreed to any of this, I fear I must object in the most strenuous of terms."

Sarah had to give her mother credit for bravery. And Colin credit for maintaining his composure. He calmly nodded. "I would expect no less, Mrs. Battersby. If you will allow me to explain, I shall attempt to set your mind at ease." He then carefully did as he had promised, discussing his months spent alone, running from one end of England to the other to escape Syder's long reach. He described returning home to Blackmore Hall, hiding in a cottage on estate lands, and finding, even there, he had not been safe. "I was never safe, as long as I was hiding, running, alone. Syder operates in darkness. He is comfortable there. What he fears is exposure. By hiding and running, I have encouraged his pursuit. A man alone, anything can happen. Another wealthy chap set upon by thieves, a cottage catching fire. Not so unusual.

"However, if I am quite prominently in London, celebrating a new engagement, reuniting with my family, constantly surrounded by them and others within the beau monde, my disappearance would be noticed. He will be hard-pressed to spirit me away without drawing further attention to himself. Attention he does not want. That is also why the safest place for Sarah is at my side. If he cannot get to me, he cannot get to her."

Eleanor, patiently listening, finished his thought. "And if she and I travel to Bath together, as we had planned, you believe she will be in danger."

"I know it. Once I made my appearance in London, he would send his men after Sarah without hesitation. Easier target and all that."

Sighing, Eleanor looked to Sarah. "Do you agree to this?"

Everyone's eyes were suddenly upon her. She considered what had been said, what Colin had explained about Syder. She knew it to be true. Syder had pursued him to her village. He had all but threatened her in her cottage.

But, mostly, she remembered every time Colin had kissed her, and how she had felt watching him ride away. How achingly she had missed him after only a few days' acquaintance. How she had foolishly dreamed of him riding back into Keddlescombe upon Matilda's back, going to his knees at the sight of her and declaring that he could not stay away. She knew it was a fantasy. An impossible fantasy.

And yet, in the end, her choice was not really a choice at all.

"Yes," she said, knowing it might be the biggest mistake of her life. "I do."

Chapter Fourteen

"My traveling coach does not give a fig for sentimentality. Its wheels need only a taste of November mud to become gleefully mired—an opportunity I shall not provide."

—THE DOWAGER MARCHIONESS OF WALLINGHAM to Lady Atherbourne in response to said lady's inquiry about her possible attendance of Princess Charlotte's funeral.

LONDON WAS EVERY BIT AS FILTHY AS SHE REMEMBERED. Except here. Here was exquisite. Sarah brushed back the edge of the draperies in the parlor at the front of Clyde-Lacey House and gazed out upon Berkeley Square. The green at the center was like a quiet jewel, untainted by coal smoke and the muck left behind by too many horses. She had never cared for crowded, dirty London with its warren of narrow streets, clatter of carriage wheels, and smells of acrid smoke and excrement. But perhaps that was because she had never lived in a place like this.

Letting the silk slide against her fingers and fall back into a graceful curve along the window, Sarah turned back to the duchess, who was focused on her embroidery and laughing at something Eleanor had said. Over the past ten days, Sarah had grown quite fond of Jane, as the duchess insisted on being addressed. Her sparkling humor and frank intelligence made it clear how she had won her husband's obvious devotion.

"I sometimes wonder whether he has forgotten whom he married," Jane said to Eleanor. "Honestly, telling me I should exercise restraint whilst shopping for books. 'We have three libraries full,' he says, 'one here and two more at Blackmore Hall. Is that not enough?'" She chuckled and shook her head. "Silly man."

"Sarah was always the same about her fabrics," said Eleanor with indulgent humor. "Whenever she got a bit of pin money, I would invariably find her at Mr. Canfield's shop, mooning over the newest sprigged muslin."

Sarah glanced down at her plain, long-sleeved black gown, provided by a presumptuous Italian woman with a flair for the dramatic. It was beautifully sewn, exquisitely simple, and better than anything she had ever made or worn. More gowns had been promised. At least, that was what she assumed. Her Italian was quite poor.

"She does love to sew," her mother continued. "Sarah, do you recall the coverlets you made for those young men returning home after Waterloo?"

Grinning wryly, Sarah said, "I remember you thought I should spend less time on them and more time helping with the harvest fair."

"Well, they were extraordinary, I must say. Blue and white squares trimmed with velvet ribbon the precise shade of a soldier's uniform. You always were a fair hand with a needle."

Jane sighed and used her knuckle to nudge her spectacles higher on her nose. She then stabbed her needle through the stretched fabric in her embroidery hoop. "I do envy you, Sarah. While I admire excellence in that arena, I do not possess it."

The door opened and Colin's sister, Lady Atherbourne, entered. Sarah had met Victoria Wyatt and her husband, Lucien, the morning after arriving in London. Something about this golden-blond viscountess had instantly reminded her of Colin—a kind of earnest charm, she supposed. Notably, however, the couple was often present at Clyde-Lacey House when Colin was absent, as though they sought to avoid him. She had the sense from Jane that there was a rift between the siblings, but it had not been fully explained.

Presently, Victoria waggled a sealed letter in the air and sent them all a beaming smile. "It has come, my dears," she announced, her blue-green eyes sparkling. "The latest from Lady Wallingham. After last week's letter, this should be *most* illuminating."

Sarah had never met Lady Wallingham, and from all she had learned about the dowager marchioness, she did not want to. Victoria had dubbed her "the Dragon," while Jane spoke of her in sarcastic, yet fearful tones. However, as Victoria carried on a regular correspondence with the woman, she had taken to reading Lady Wallingham's letters aloud during her visits to Clyde-Lacey House. It had proved quite the entertainment.

"Listen to this," Victoria said, sinking gracefully onto a blue silk divan. *"When called upon to suffer through yet another tedious luncheon, offer commentary of a biting yet truthful sort. Perform ably, and the result will be fewer conversational demands and, happily, fewer luncheons."*

"This explains a great deal," said Jane with a quirk of her lips.

"Indeed," said Victoria, her eyes quickly scanning to the bottom of the letter. "Ah, she plans to remain at Grimsgate Castle until spring, rather than coming to town for the Princess's funeral. I expected as much."

Everyone in the room took on a solemn countenance. The death of Princess Charlotte—the Prince Regent's only legitimate child—and her infant son during childbirth had stunned the entirety of England, which grieved the loss of their beloved young royal most profoundly. Now, Sarah and her mother were not the only ones wearing black; all of London wore it as a sign of national mourning, including the other ladies in the room. In fact, the Italian modiste had complained bitterly about the shortage of black crepe. At least, that was what Sarah assumed she'd been saying. The blend of English and Italian had been dizzying.

Lady Wallingham took a more pragmatic view of the events, however. Victoria read the dowager's explanation aloud: "*The entire royal line could sink into the Thames and drown, and I still would not travel at this abhorrent time of year.*"

Sarah turned back to the window, listening to the other ladies chuckle and chatter. Her chest felt hollowed out. She missed her father. But, then, he had been gone in every way that mattered for two years.

Is it truly Papa that you miss, she asked herself, crossing her arms over her waist. *No. It is him. Colin. The man who can scarcely be bothered to wish you good morning.* She remembered him as he'd been in Keddlescombe, sitting with her in the orchard, smiling that rakish grin. Insisting on walking the road by himself because he was too proud to lean upon her. Waking with her in the night as she struggled to don her boots to search for Papa. Standing with her on the beach. Dancing with her in the abbey. Kissing her in the dark.

She squeezed her eyes closed, aching for a man who could never be hers.

Lord Colin had kept a careful distance since their departure from Yardleigh Manor. She saw him only at dinner each night, and they rarely spoke. Jane had explained that he was preoccupied with reestablishing his presence at the clubs and renewing his connections with old friends. All part of the plan,

Jane had assured her.

Perhaps what she needed was to cease moping and, instead, establish a plan of her own. Yes, that was it. A plan. She glanced down at her new gown, poked her toe out from beneath her skirts to admire her new slippers, which featured lovely jet beading in a swirling design.

"Victoria?" she queried, probably interrupting another Wallingham witticism. She did not care. All this knocking about in a large, luxurious house with nothing to do but miss Colin Lacey until she ached like a sore tooth—well, that was quite enough. "Do you know anyone in need of a governess?"

Large, blue-green eyes blinked back at her. "I am not certain. Why do you ask?"

Eleanor murmured her name with an edge of warning, but Sarah had begun to think this was just the solution she'd been looking for. She continued, "You know I have been an instructor for young ladies. I previously taught at St. Catherine's Academy for Girls of Impeccable Deportment, my father's school."

"My, that is a long name," murmured Jane, her expression intrigued. "Impressive."

"Unfortunately, my experience was not in a household, and so attaining a letter of reference has been challenging."

Victoria gave her a bright smile and a nod. "I believe I can help with that. And I shall send 'round some inquiries, as well. Who knows what will turn up?"

Sarah's relief warmed her skin. Finally, she'd found her answer. It was not ideal, for a position at a school would be more to her liking, but if she could find a post in a household, at least she would not be left destitute again when the Syder tangle was resolved. And perhaps looking for a position would distract her from this senseless melancholy.

"Thank you," Sarah sighed. "You are most generous. Oh, and in your inquiries, you may wish to ask after tutoring positions as well as those of governess."

As she was speaking, a cooler breeze wafted from behind

her, where the doors were. She'd been so pleased with her new plan and Victoria's ready agreement, she hadn't noticed. Now, however, she realized its cause.

"Governess? I think not." Given the frigid snap of the words from the man behind her, he might easily be mistaken for the duke. But instead, it was Colin. And he sounded furious.

She spun around to face him. He *looked* furious. His blue eyes flashed and burned through her. His shoulders sat square and rigid. Where was her devil-may-care scoundrel? Since Yardleigh, she seemed to have lost him entirely.

"You are to be my wife. My wife will have no need of a letter of reference."

Sarah blinked, frowning. "But, our engagement is a pretense." She glanced at the other ladies in the room, who looked similarly perplexed. "It cannot go on forever. I must plan for my future if I am to have any hope of—"

"Sarah," he bit out, his eyes falling briefly on his sister, then on Jane, then on Eleanor. "Let us speak privately."

"Perhaps I should accompany …" Her mother's protest came as expected from a chaperone, albeit one more lamb than lion.

"Privately," he repeated, then settled the matter by striding forward, clasping Sarah's arm above the elbow, and tugging her out of the parlor into the foyer, then down a corridor and into the duke's study.

She stared in wonder at the dark wood paneling on every wall, the enormous mahogany desk, and the window behind it looking out on a small garden. "I have not been in this room before. It is lovely."

"Sarah," he muttered as he released her arm to close the door. "You cannot seek employment. It will undermine our story."

Crossing her arms, she set to tapping one finger on her sleeve. "Victoria is simply going to make inquiries. She need not specify whom they are for."

Jaw flexing and lips tight and downturned, his face seemed so hard, so wracked by frustration. So different from how she remembered him. "The position of governess is a difficult and lonely proposition. Not quite family, not quite staff. You would be miserable inside of a week. Not to mention vulnerable to every sort of lustful impulse from men in the household. You cannot be a governess."

"Of course I can."

"I will not tolerate it."

"You have no say in the matter."

He released a hiss of pure exasperation. "Sarah, I am trying to protect you. Don't you understand that? Why can you not simply allow me to take care of you?"

"I have taken care of myself, my parents, and a school housing a dozen girls for two years now. I have done so on a mere portion of a country vicar's living, all while paying my father's debts and fending off the unwanted advances of Felix Foote." She gave him a tight, yet triumphant, smile. "I do believe that qualifies me to manage my own affairs, my lord."

"Why must you be so bloody obstinate? And stop 'my lord'-ing me. You only do it to dig under my skin."

Her finger tapped faster on her arm. "As you have been absent for much of our time in London, I fail to see where I have had the opportunity to dig under your skin. My lord."

His bristling agitation stilled, his hands settling on his hips. "You are complaining that I have been away from the house."

She scoffed. "Hardly complaining. Why should I?"

"You are! You are vexed that I have not—"

"That is ridiculous."

"—stayed here with you. And now you are punishing me."

Narrowing her eyes at him, she responded with the precision and care only an instructor of young girls could muster. "My desire to secure a position that can support me and my mother has absolutely nothing to do with you. You see, my lord, despite your frequent assertions to the contrary, I do enjoy eating. I also favor sufficient shelter and the occasional bath. I am not an ascetic, and therefore, I require funds. Which I must earn through em-ploy-ment." She smiled. "A foreign concept, perhaps. I can explain again more slowly if you like."

He came toward her, speaking as his long, slow strides ate up the ground between them. "Do you know what I would like?" His voice was soft now, his eyes smoldering with intent. He was so close now, the fine wool of his dark-blue tailcoat brushed against her bodice.

She swallowed hard and moved back, only to find him matching her step for step until the edge of the mahogany desk nudged her backside.

His face hung over hers, his breath hot and his gaze hotter as they flowed over her skin. "I would like to teach you pleasure. I would like to start by kissing you. Until you beg me. Never to stop."

Her eyelids fluttered as rapidly as her stomach. A low, warm ache settled between her thighs. "You only say these things to dig under my skin." She was not certain who had spoken those taunting words, but the voice sounded much like her own.

The slow-burning smile he gave her only made the fluttering and aching and weakness worse. "Does it bother you, then, when I do this?" Tracing a finger lightly down the slope of her throat, stroking tenderly over the small indentation at the base. "To your skin?"

This was her Colin. Scoundrel, indeed. Returned in full force. She could barely think.

"Sarah," he groaned, crowding closer and dipping his head to run his lips along the side of her neck. "Let me kiss you."

She clutched at his hair, frustrated by the too-short strands. She liked them longer, so she could feel them curling between her fingers. "You *are* kissing me," she panted.

"Mmm. Good point. No more arguing." With that final rebuke, he took her lips. Sliding his tongue along their seam, he made the entire earth stop spinning then start again with a shower of sparks. She moaned and invited him inside to play.

He did, grasping her waist and lifting her to sit on polished mahogany, fisting black crepe in his hands until his fingers wrapped around the bare skin just above her stockings. Just below her thighs.

His slick tongue, sliding and teasing against hers was only a part of her pleasure. In truth, everywhere he touched her was a source of glowing sensation—his hands on her thighs, squeezing and stroking; his hard chest rubbing against her hardened nipples through layers of fabric; his breath and his scent surrounding her in sandalwood and crisp autumn air and just a hint of coffee. The more he touched, the higher his hands climbed, the brighter the sparks grew until she was set afire with the pleasure of him.

Clutching at his shoulders, she instinctively spread her thighs wider to draw him close to her. Slowly, his fingers kneaded her skin until his thumb brushed against her core, pressing against her in a way that sent those sparks into an explosion. She gasped and jerked, feeling him touch her in a way no man ever had. Pleasure her in a way she had not previously imagined.

"Shh, sweet. Easy," he mumbled against her lips. "This tight little spring will take only the barest breath to release. But I do not wish to end our lesson so quickly."

His thumb slowed its entrancing circles at the center of her being, causing the spiraling tension to soften and lull. Meanwhile, his mouth resumed its heated trail down the length of her throat. "This," he murmured, nuzzling the skin at the juncture of her shoulder and neck. "Deserves pearls. Long, exquisite, luminous strands of pearls."

She breathed his name.

He used his second hand to stroke lightly over her breast, to caress and squeeze and shape the peaks that puckered the black crepe and sizzled to his touch.

She recaptured his mouth with her own, pressing and stroking and nibbling and coaxing, just as he had done to her.

His groan was her reward.

His thumb resuming a faster pace around and around and

around the sensitive nub at her core—that was her triumph. Her muscles in that secret place clenched and wept and rippled with their need.

Her nipple, tortured by his fingers, tingled and sparked, demanded he finish what he had started. A fire that would not be quenched by anything except ...

It broke. Suddenly, like a wave ripping through her lower body, the spring let loose and the sparks that had been gathering inside her breasts and her belly, between her thighs and everywhere his mouth had touched, burst outward in a brilliant explosion, cascading in rippling waves of pleasure.

She sobbed his name against the linen of his cravat. Colin, Colin, Colin. He had done this. He had given her paradise.

His chest heaved and worked, his hand stroking her inner thigh tenderly where she was curiously damp. He lay his forehead on her shoulder, as winded as a horse that had been run too hard. "You see, sweet," he panted, his voice guttural. "Letting me take care of you can be very, very satisfying."

Echoes of her pleasure still pulsed inside her, making her weak and warm and a little foggy. "Are you saying you did this ... to prove a point?"

"Of course not. Do you know nothing about me? This was my lust run amok. Pure and simple."

"I do not believe you."

He sighed, withdrawing one hand from her thigh with a gentle pat and the other from her bosom with a last, lingering stroke, as though he needed to smooth the silk.

"You have long maintained that I am not terribly attractive."

Pulling back to stare at her with stark incredulity, he burst out laughing, his head shaking in disbelief. "Sheer madness. The only explanation."

"You have!"

He continued laughing, seeming genuinely amused by her assertion.

She supposed she must catalog his observations for him. Perhaps then he would recall how many times he had let it be known that she was far from a beauty in his eyes. She ticked them off on her fingers. "First, you deemed me 'acceptable fare' for others, but not for yourself. Second, you have repeatedly insulted my gowns, calling them rags and worse. Third—"

"That is quite enough, thank you."

"—you have, on several occasions, stated rather bluntly that I am too thin."

His grin began to fade. "You are. You need to eat more. Is Digby providing the trays as I instructed?"

"You are the reason for those?" Every evening and every morning, regardless of whether she came downstairs for breakfast or dinner, she would find a tray piled ludicrously high with food—sliced ham and cheese, fresh-baked bread, and often several generous servings of whatever had been left from the previous meal. It was like she was an old, ailing hound being tempted with scraps, for pity's sake. "Colin, I cannot eat all that. It is preposterous to imagine I can."

"Humor me."

"I would need ten stomachs!"

"Someone must ensure you do not faint dead away from lack of nourishment."

"There is little chance of that with you and Digby conspiring—"

"Sarah," he said, his expression gone serious. "You have worn yourself out, sweet. Your father's illness, his death, the school, your mother. And me. There is little left of you but threads and determination."

Tears sprang into her eyes unbidden, unwanted, and entirely humiliating. She shoved at him. "Let me down."

He stepped back, his retreat slow and reluctant.

She slid from her perch and brushed at her skirts, then at her hair, then at her cheeks. Folding her arms and tilting her chin defiantly, she said, "I neither desire nor deserve your pity.

And were it not for the threat of Mr. Syder, I would not have accepted your charity, either."

"I do not pity you."

She attempted to brush past him, holding her skirts to the side so as to avoid touching his trousers, but he stopped her with a hand around her elbow. She felt the heat of his grip through her silken sleeve. "Colin."

He tugged her closer to him, his nose nuzzling her hair, breathing deeply. "Pity does not drive a man mad with thoughts of being inside you."

Her breath left her, gushing out and weakening her knees. Why did he have to be so irresistible?

"Neither does a man spend every night dreaming of bringing you torturous pleasure because he finds you less than attractive."

Suddenly, he yanked her flush against him, pressing his hips against her abdomen until she felt the hard, substantial bulge between his thighs, straining against his trousers.

"And this, sweet, certainly cannot be credited to charity. This knows only one thing. *Want.* It wants you. I want you. Think whatever you like about the rest of it—the food, the gowns, your search for employment. But never doubt the truth of this." He kissed her hard, his mouth insistent and swift.

Then, just as suddenly, he released her, his face flushed, his nose flaring, his hands raised out to his sides as though surrendering. Walking backward, he held her gaze until he arrived at the door. Then, without another word, he turned and left her standing alone in the duke's study, struggling for breath, needy and aching.

He wanted her, or so he'd said. He claimed he did not pity her. But she well understood his instinct for compassion. She had seen it in Keddlescombe, with her father and her students. And with her.

Now, she must decide how much she could accept in order to keep him in her life. *Just a little while longer,* her heart begged.

I shall let him go. Let me have that much.

Her head answered with what she knew to be true: *It will never be enough.*

Chapter Fifteen

"The appearance of harmlessness can be effective as a disguise. Thankfully, I am not easily fooled."

—THE DOWAGER MARCHIONESS OF WALLINGHAM to Lady Berne upon hearing said lady's despondence over damage caused by her new feline companion.

PLEASANT AND AFFABLE. IN COLIN'S ESTIMATION, THOSE words perfectly described Harrison's best friend, Henry Thorpe, the Earl of Dunston. The lean, brown-haired lord stood beside Harrison, a glass of sherry in hand, an expression of insouciance on his face. "So, this Mr. Simons—"

Colin lifted a brow at Dunston while lifting his teacup from its saucer. "Syder." He took a drink. It was not brandy, but at least it was strong.

"Ah, yes. Syder," continued Dunston. "He manages a number of these gaming hells, I presume. How many have been ... how would you put it? Shuttered, I suppose."

Sighing, Colin glanced at Harrison, noting how his brother examined his pocket watch and then peered across the Clyde-Lacey drawing room at Jane. "Four so far. More have been raided. But Syder owns more than the hells," Colin answered, though he was not sure why he bothered. "His empire stretches from one end of London to the other. He has interests in everything from slaughterhouses to houses of ill repute."

Dunston smiled his affable smile. "Nothing wrong with that last bit, I daresay."

Shaking his head, Colin focused on Sarah, who stood next to Jane near the fireplace. She was lovely, her slender form draped in smooth black silk, her hair softly glowing in the candlelight. Little honey curls had been left artfully loose to frame her face.

He wanted her badly. It was that simple. And he could not have her. Not if he wished to live with himself.

Once again, Dunston's voice intruded. "Harrison tells me you had a near miss this morning. A band of footpads made an attempt on you as you came out of White's?" He tsked. "A man should carry a knife to deal with just this sort of malefaction." Patting his own trim waist, he grinned at Colin. "The element of surprise, as it were."

"I would not require a knife or a pistol or a bloody battalion of footmen if Syder's holdings had been fully dispatched," Colin bit out. "An eventuality I await with great anticipation."

It was Dunston's turn to raise a brow. "Well, it is my understanding of Lord Sidmouth—not that I know the Home Secretary particularly well, mind you. Dreadful chess player. That is the extent of my acquaintance. In any event, I have heard Sidmouth is far more interested in stamping out seditious gatherings of impoverished upstarts than he is in dismantling London's criminal enterprises, however pernicious they may be." Dunston took a sip of sherry. "I suppose, given the limited resources of the Home Office, it would take a very determined individual to press for raids and such on the timetable you seem to prefer."

Colin glared at the earl. "Such an individual would do well to accelerate his efforts, as it is his skin I am protecting."

Harrison looked at his watch for the second time in three minutes. Dunston released an exasperated sigh. "What is your obsession with that thing?"

Giving Dunston a glare of his own, Harrison replied, "It is no concern of yours." Then, the duke's attention drifted again to his wife. He swallowed visibly.

"Your brother is hopeless, you understand," Dunston observed, addressing his comment to Colin and tipping his sherry glass in Harrison's direction. "Besotted. Counting the minutes—literally. He has turned his preoccupation with timepieces into a preoccupation with—"

"Why exactly are you in London?" Harrison grumbled. "Plaguing me with your unsolicited observations cannot be the only reason."

"Hunting has been dreadful this year. Too much rain." Dunston took another sip and shrugged. "I heard you had gone up to London, and I decided it could not possibly be as tedious as Fairfield Park, where a quarter-hour of riding means a drenching down to one's ballocks." He shuddered and brushed at an invisible speck on his sleeve. "Besides, I was in need of some new waistcoats."

"You have more waistcoats than any man I have ever met," Harrison retorted. "That includes the Prince Regent. And Beau Brummell."

Dunston scoffed. "One can never have too many waistcoats."

Hearing a distinctive laugh from across the room, Colin turned his attention again to Sarah. She was smiling, listening intently to Jane.

So, she wished to plan for her future, did she? Become a

governess in some unknown household where any male with an itch to scratch could corner her in an empty room or shadowed corridor? Hike her skirts up and have his lecherous way with her? Like bloody hell. She would become a governess over his rotting corpse.

"Oh, dear," said Dunston. "Now it appears we have *two* besotted brothers."

Colin's head swiveled back in his direction. Seeing his subtle grin, Colin muttered, "Hardly that. We are friends. She and her mother were left with nothing upon her father's death. She needs my protection."

"Mmm. If that is true, then get thee to a church, old chap."

Giving Dunston a sharp frown, Colin repeated, "A church."

"Well, you are already putting it about that she is your beloved intended, yes?"

"Yes."

"Then marry the girl."

Colin blinked several times before answering with great acuity, "What ... I ... What's that you say?"

"Marry. Her."

Harrison looked as flummoxed as Colin felt. The duke stared at Dunston for a long while, then at the glass in Dunston's hand. "I do believe you've had enough sherry, Henry."

The earl chuckled. "Do not say you haven't contemplated it yourself."

Colin had, but not for any unselfish reason. He was not good enough for Sarah. She had more strength and honor inside her dainty foot than he had in his body.

"It sounds to me as if there is some unfortunate, unavoidable delay in the process of abrogating Mr. Syder's nefarious activities. Which has resulted in greater risk of death or maiming for you." Dunston took another sip and smiled blandly. "Who will protect her when you are gone? Or, worse yet, missing some critical appendage?"

"Good God, man," Harrison said. "This is my brother you

are talking about."

"Indeed," Dunston replied calmly. "*Your* brother. If he expects the lovely Miss Battersby to be reliably provided for, particularly in the event of extreme misfortune on his part, he can do no better than offering her the position of his widow. Or wife. Makes no difference, really." He met Colin's eyes. "If she belongs to Harrison's family, she will want for nothing. Unless she becomes a drunkard and attempts to sully the family name by behaving in a scandalous manner. Then he may cut off her funds for a time. Frankly, she doesn't seem the sort."

Colin could not speak. He simply could not. It was almost perfect. The perfect answer to his appallingly imperfect predicament.

"That is patently ridiculous," snapped Harrison, now glowering at his friend. "If Colin wishes me to provide for Miss Battersby, I will happily do so. He needn't marry her. Bloody hell."

Shaking his head, Colin felt strangely relieved that he could rebut Harrison's argument. "She would never allow it. She refuses to accept what she considers charity. The only reason she's accepted anything I have offered thus far is that she knows the danger to her is real."

"But if you marry her, what's yours will be hers," concluded Dunston, who lifted his glass in a mocking toast. "One of the many benefits of matrimony. Well, perhaps 'benefit' is overstating it a bit. Bedding rights. Now there is a benefit I can endorse."

Colin's libido heartily agreed. He imagined having Sarah in his bed every night, being able to make love to her whenever he desired, to teach her pleasure and "benefit" each other until they both collapsed from exhaustion.

Marriage. To Sarah. He did not deserve her. But if it would offer her much-needed protection, perhaps it was the right and honorable course.

"Dunston," he murmured.

"Yes?"

"You are brilliant."

The earl smiled and sipped his sherry. "I know."

It was genius. In the short term, he could take care of her and ensure she ate in sufficient quantity and buy her dozens of gowns. Since Harrison had reinstated his funds, he could buy a house for them to live in and a decent pianoforte for the music room and perhaps even help her reopen her school. Never had he heard a better idea.

There was only one small flaw.

It had been hard enough persuading her to participate in a pretense. To actually marry him? Knowing Sarah's stubborn pride, she would see it as elaborate charity. He must convince her otherwise. But how?

"Colin, you do not have to do this," said Harrison, sounding vaguely alarmed. "If you are concerned about her welfare, I will offer her a position as a paid companion to Jane, then compensate her extravagantly. She will be earning her living, and so cannot object."

Shaking his head, Colin held up a hand. "There will always be men like Felix Foote."

"Who?"

"It doesn't matter. Suffice it to say an unmarried woman is particularly vulnerable. No, this is precisely what must happen."

What he needed was sound advice from someone who might understand how he should approach her with his proposal. Glancing around the room, he saw James Kilbrenner, the Earl of Tannenbrook, a giant of a man who, as near as Colin could determine, communicated primarily through grunting. Tannenbrook was a friend of Atherbourne's, and had agreed to add his massive height and impressive breadth to the wall of lords surrounding Colin. He was unmarried and likely to remain so, as his overgrown size, blunt-featured face, and taciturn demeanor kept him off the prospect lists for most matchmaking mamas.

Not much help there, he thought.

Next came Lucien Wyatt, Viscount Atherbourne. Under normal circumstances, Colin would strongly consider seeking the advice of the absurdly handsome lord, as he'd had quite a reputation as a charming rake before marrying Victoria. But there was that small matter of the all-consuming hatred Lucien bore him for his very real transgressions against the Wyatt family. Colin was still sickened by his own actions. He could not imagine how Atherbourne felt or how he had resisted taking revenge.

Another unlikely source of assistance.

Traveling around the room, he lit on Eleanor. Sarah's mother sipped her tea and craned her neck to view the book Jane was holding. She looked relaxed and content for the first time since he had known her. She was finally eating and sleeping properly, resulting in better color in her cheeks and more sparkle in her green eyes.

She will simply tell you to speak to Sarah.

There was always Jane, he supposed. She was a great friend and had given him valuable counsel in the past. She'd grown close with Sarah and so might be able to offer insight into what would work best.

Considering you are the reason she was forced to marry Harrison, asking her advice on pushing Sarah toward marriage might not be the wisest course.

Finally, he came to Victoria. His sister. She had been his friend since they were children. And she had stopped speaking to him for over a year after discovering the things he had done. Only recently had she broken her silence, and that merely to offer polite courtesies. But he had sensed her softening toward him. The fact that she was here at all spoke volumes. Perhaps she was ready to forgive the past.

His mind made up, he set his cup on a low table, left Dunston and Harrison to their devices, and crossed the room to where the ladies were clustered admiring Jane's latest acquisition.

"Victoria." When she raised her eyes to meet his, he cleared his throat. "May I speak with you?"

Giving a reluctant nod, she rose from her settee and followed him to the area between a potted plant and the center window, away from the others in the room. As she stood before him, her brow slightly furrowed, her familiar, blue-green eyes filled with questions and caution, he felt a tug in the region of his heart. He had missed his gentle, sweet sister.

"What is it you wished to speak to me about?" She was more reserved than before his fall from grace. Colder. As always, the guilt and regret that lived inside him rose up to coil inside his chest. For that very reason, he had avoided pressing her for reconciliation. But perhaps he could use his predicament with Sarah to open a gate in the wall between them.

He drew a deep breath and dropped his gaze to the floor before meeting her eyes again. "I have a bit of a ... a quandary. And I could use some advice."

She blinked, her gloved hands twisting at her waist. "From me."

"It is a delicate matter involving a lady for whom I have developed a certain fondness."

Suddenly, she paled, her hands strangling each other. "Colin," she breathed. "Not again."

"Er—again?"

"Tell me you have not"—her eyes darted around the room to ensure their privacy before continuing in a whisper—"compromised another young lady."

Reeling back, his breath left him in a whoosh. "No!"

"I was so sure you had changed." He watched in horror as tears began to fill her eyes. "Who is it this time?"

"Tori, you misunderstand—"

"You must marry her. You cannot abdicate your responsibility as you did before."

"That is what I'm trying to—"

She stiffened as she glimpsed something over his shoulder. The dark presence resounded with wrath. He felt the force like breath on his neck. Before he even turned around, he knew who stood there.

"Atherbourne."

His brother-in-law came around to his wife's side looking every bit as menacing as he had envisioned. "When Victoria is distressed, I find my murderous tendencies emerging, Lacey. You may wish to avoid further provocation."

Jaw clenching, Colin answered, "It was not my intention to cause distress. She is my sister. I would not seek to upset her."

"You'll forgive me if I find your protestations unconvincing after all you have done."

He did not know how to answer. His guilt was choking him.

"Lucien," Victoria said softly, running her hand down her husband's arm. "Perhaps we should—"

"Nothing to say, Lacey?" The other man's posture took on an aggressive tilt. His dark eyes flashed a warning. A storm was about to be unleashed. "No quips or clever deflections?"

He noted the room had gone silent. "What is there to say?" he said quietly. "I have begged Victoria's forgiveness. I would beg yours as well, but I know for you it is impossible."

Atherbourne's head snapped back, his storm expanding until Colin imagined him surrounded by bolts of lightning, a wrathful archangel come to exact justice. "My sister is dead because of you!" he roared.

Colin swallowed, feeling the dinner he'd eaten earlier roiling in his stomach, rising in his throat. "I know," he whispered.

His acknowledgment was lost amidst the gale of Atherbourne's righteous fury. "You seduced her. You compromised her. Abandoned her. You ignored her pleas when she carried your child in her belly as easily as you would brush aside a bothersome insect. Now, you stand here and speak of forgiveness. You are still breathing, Lacey, only by the grace of my wife's kind and loving heart."

They all stood silently for a full minute. Colin looked to Victoria. Her tears had been released and now streamed down her cheeks. "I cannot change what happened, what I did," he said hoarsely. "It is my greatest shame. Please believe I would not repeat the same mistake. To even contemplate it is abhorrent to me." Returning his gaze to Atherbourne, whose temper began to recede when he, too, noted Victoria's tears, Colin addressed the man he had damaged the most. "I do not ask your forgiveness because to do so presumes I am deserving of it. I am not. Some wounds are too grievous to be forgiven."

Breathing heavily and seemingly stunned by Colin's statement, Atherbourne swallowed visibly, his nostrils flaring. "You expect me to believe this."

"I expect nothing. I deserve nothing."

His eyes narrowed on Colin, heated by skepticism. "What has changed?"

Colin wished he could simply laugh and shrug Atherbourne's question aside. But he owed the man a debt that could never be repaid. Not with words. Not with blood. Nothing could balance the scales. He could, however, answer truthfully.

"I did not know she was with child when she ..." He stopped. Cleared his throat. "Regardless, it is the worst thing I have ever done, Atherbourne, and that is saying something, for I have made many, many mistakes before and since. When Harrison discovered the truth, he cut off my funds. No more brandy. No more hiding." His mouth quirked humorlessly. "The world looks different without that pleasant glow. One's regrets tend to creep forth and take over like thorny vines. Being viciously pursued across England and nearly dying several times also puts matters in perspective." *And Sarah*, he thought but couldn't say. *Sarah changed me, too.*

Victoria, her eyes shimmering and luminous, sniffed and ventured softly, "What you wrote to me—of your desire to do better, to be different than before—you were sincere? Jane said as much. I—I was afraid to believe it, Colin."

He gave her a gentle smile. "You should know that my efforts in that regard have been far from perfect, Tori. But, yes, I am sincere."

The Earl of Tannenbrook came quietly to Atherbourne's side and placed a massive paw on his shoulder. "Everyone is listening, Luc," he said in a deep rumble. "This might be a good time to bring the evening to a close."

A flush of alarm burned through Colin's mind. Immediately, his head swiveled as he scanned the room, assessing the damage. Harrison looked grim and torn. Dunston looked riveted. Eleanor looked appalled. Jane looked sad and sympathetic and hopeful. But there was only one face that mattered to him. One face that would point to either heaven or hell. Reluctantly, he found her.

And felt his heart sink into darkness.

Chapter Sixteen

*"Bah! Regrets do not interest me. Make better decisions
and cease nattering about it."*

—THE DOWAGER MARCHIONESS OF WALLINGHAM to Lady Berne
upon learning of a certain feline companion's abrupt dismissal.

LYING IN THE SHADOWY DARK OF HER BEDCHAMBER, SARAH
let her head loll to the side so she could look up through the
window. No stars were there. Or perhaps they were simply
disguised by clouds and coal smoke. A bit of moonlight played
throughout the room. She sighed and rolled over to tuck her
hand beneath her cheek.

He was different than she had thought. Stronger. Darker.
With her in Keddlescombe, he had been gentle and kind,

teasing and sensual, amusing and full of charm. While he had hinted at a past filled with regret, she had not supposed the scars to be so deep, nor their cause so reprehensible.

Sleep was a dream now, as elusive as those shadows along the draperies and floor. Her mind restlessly reviewed all that had been said between Colin, Victoria, and Atherbourne.

Seduction. Abandonment. A child and a woman lost. Colin the reason for it all.

Tossing aside her blankets, she rose and moved to the fireplace, where low coals still smoldered. Using the cinders to light the tip of a long, wooden spill, she cupped her hand in front of the flame and walked to the dressing table near the window where, during the day, one could enjoy the best light. She felt around for a candle and lowered the flame to light the wick. Carefully, she blew out the spill and watched a curl of smoke rise and dissipate before setting the thin piece of wood aside.

She breathed, deeply and rhythmically, resting her hands on the cool surface of the dressing table, watching the candle's flame dance and flicker with every exhalation.

I thought he was a good man. A bit of a scoundrel, yes, but not wicked. Not really.

Her hands clenched into tight fists, her fingernails digging into her palms. She'd been wrong about him. She had let him sleep in her bed. Let him kiss and touch and pleasure her. Now she felt as though she'd never known him at all.

The quiet settled in to smother her. No wind battered the windows. No fire crackled its warmth. No footsteps signaled the busyness of servants. The silence roared and pressed and suffocated.

Almost of its own volition, her hand opened a small drawer and sought the comfort of worn, wrinkled paper. There. The corner of it clasped between her fingers. She pulled out the folded letter and carefully peeled it open. Then, in the silence, she could hear her father's mellow, comforting voice.

Dear Sarah, he said. *On the day you were born, the apples had just come ripe. Your mother did not want me to take you to the orchard, but I insisted—you know how I can be sometimes. With you in my arms and the harvest scenting the air and the sea keeping time in the distance, I found it impossible to imagine a moment when I might willingly let you go.*

She stopped, clenching her empty fist and squeezing her aching eyes closed. She gave herself three heartbeats then resumed reading.

Now the decision is being stolen by time, my darling. Every day, I look at you and see a babe enchanted by green leaves and red apples, a babe small enough to rest in my two hands. Every day, I see the woman you will be. And I try to envision the man worthy of receiving you into his care.

Sheer impossibility, I must tell you. For in this Papa's eyes, no such man exists. Still, time cares not. Ever forward it travels. And so, I write this letter in the fond hope that, one day, an impossible man will come along and you will find him as familiar, as beloved, as the trees in our orchard and the sea on our shore.

This man will seek to deserve you and when he falls short, he will seek your forgiveness. (Do not be too forgiving too quickly. As a servant of God, I can attest that a little humility is good for a man's soul.) His mind will be strong so that he may attempt to equal yours. His heart will be fierce and true for the same reason. He will see your life as the only reason for his, and he will guard it accordingly. You will see yourself in the mirror of his eyes, and you will be more beautiful, more precious than you were to me that early September morning.

You see, my darling girl? Impossible.

I will forever be,

Your loving Papa

Tears streamed down her cheeks, swelled around her heart. She laid her head down upon her folded arms and wept for her Papa. For Colin. For what she had secretly begun to hope.

A draft of air whispered past her cheek. Warm fingers

threaded through her hair and stroked her temple. Strong, gentle, familiar fingers.

"Colin," she croaked, her voice strained. "What are you doing in here?"

He knelt next to her and continued stroking her hair, the pleasure of it both soothing and mesmerizing. "I could not sleep. I wanted to see you, to know how you are."

That was when she crumpled. Sliding her arms around his neck, she drew him close, let his arms come around her like two unyielding bands. And she let him comfort her as the sobs choked and gathered and spilled out in staggering bursts.

"Ah, Sarah. I am so sorry, sweet. I did not wish for you to hear these things in such a way."

She shook her head, her damp face wetting his linen shirt. "That is not ... I mean, it is, but ... I was reading a letter. From my father."

His hands, stroking down the center of her back then up to her shoulders then cradling her head, paused. "He wrote to you before he ...?"

Sniffing through a clogged nose, Sarah nodded. "He knew he was losing his memories, and so he wrote letters. I managed to find five. He tucked them away in the oddest places." She gave a watery chuckle. "As if he hoped I would come across them by chance." Pulling back until Colin's arms fell to her waist and his hands settled on her hips, she turned and smoothed the paper on the dressing table with her palms. "This one was inside a boot. I discovered it last year. I have read it so many times, I think the ink is wearing off."

His finger brushed her cheek, carrying away a drop of her grief. "He loved you."

She smiled. "Yes."

Colin nodded, his thumbs turning little circles on her hipbones. "Sarah, what you heard this evening—"

"About your past."

"Yes. About that. I—I want to explain."

"Why?"

He seemed startled by the question. "You need to know what happened."

She sniffed, longing for a handkerchief. Before she could search one out, Colin offered his. She took it, rubbing the linen between her fingers. "Thank you," she rasped.

"It is important that you understand the truth. About me. I have done things I deeply regret. Things which brought harm to innocents."

Wiping her nose and then the underside of her chin, where tears had somehow managed to gather, she replied, "I know. Lord Atherbourne's sister."

"Yes. Mary Sophia Wyatt. Her brothers called her Marissa. She and I ... we were lovers, and I ... I shudder to think of how selfish I was. Our liaison meant nothing to me. A lark. A way to thwart Harrison's sense of propriety. I assumed when I was finished with her, she would move on to another chap. But she was far more fragile than I knew."

He swallowed before continuing. "She professed to be in love with me. Wrote to me so incessantly, I began tossing her letters in the fire. By the time she took her life, I thought her half mad. Then, her oldest brother accused Harrison of being the man who abandoned her." He huffed out a dry chuckle. "Harrison, of all people. Patently absurd. But, they fought a duel over the matter. Harrison shot him. And Lucien inherited the title."

Bracing his hands on his thighs, he pushed himself to his feet and turned his back for a moment before facing her again. "All the while, I said nothing. I let Harrison kill a man over what I had done. I let Atherbourne marry Victoria when I knew very well he might have revenge in mind. I discarded a woman who, I later discovered, was carrying my child."

His voice had gone raspy and raw. "I was in my cups more often than not in those days. Worse, afterward. I could not live with it, what I had done. Every day since I learned of the babe, I have known I must either change or die. I have tried to change.

Along the way, I have managed to cause further damage. To Jane. To Harrison. To myself. But I am determined to keep trying. And to never repeat my mistakes."

Silence settled in again. When she failed to respond to his confession, he shook his head. "Surely you must have questions."

"It is none of my concern."

"We are engaged to be married."

"No, we are *pretending* to be engaged. Why does that always seem to get lost in our discussions?"

He released an exasperated sigh. "Are you not curious about—"

"No."

Running a hand through his hair, he paced to the bed then back to her. "I wish for you to understand who I am now. To do that, you must understand who I was then."

He stood above her, his handsome face wreathed in consternation, lit by candlelight and darkened by shadows. She did understand him, she realized. Better than she had supposed. The man she'd met in Keddlescombe was not the same man who had done those dreadfully selfish things. He was the man who had stood with her father in the frigid waters of the English Channel. The man who had threatened Felix Foote in defense of her. Still, it was not as though they would live together when this was over. Their relationship was one of circumstance. And when that circumstance came to an end, so would any tie between them.

"Why should it matter?" she asked. "Once Syder is no longer a threat, I will move on. And so will you."

This seemed to disturb him greatly, as he resumed pacing, his breathing agitated. "I have been thinking. Differently. About everything."

"Differently." She sniffed, the sound embarrassingly loud in the room.

On his return trip to the dressing table, he paused a few feet from her. "Yes. That is, I ... I believe we should ... oh, bloody hell. Sarah, I believe the proper course is for us to marry."

She waited, but he did not finish his thought. Or, perhaps he had. "Each other?"

"What the bloody hell do you think I'm trying to—yes. We should marry each other. A false engagement is not enough. You must be protected in the event of my death. As my widow, you will be well provided for; so will your mother. Harrison will see to it."

The room spun. His *death?* No. No, no, no. He could not die. She could not bear even the thought of it.

"What has happened?" she asked sharply, scarcely aware of uttering the words. "Why would you even speak of dying? Has Syder tried to hurt you? What did he do?" Heart kicking in her chest, she could not stop the frantic flow of questions. Even as he came to kneel again before her, placing his hands over hers in her lap, the urgency in her mind sounded like bells tolling a funeral dirge, deep and ominous. "Answer me!" she snapped.

"You knew there was some danger, Sarah."

She could not catch her breath, could not stop picturing him as he had been the day she had hauled him into a wagon on the road to Littlewood, limp and bloody. "Promised. You promised London would be safer."

"I did not promise, but yes, it is safer. Nothing is certain, sweet. I am still here, yes?"

Unable to stop herself touching him, she cupped his lightly bristled cheeks in her hands, and pulled his face closer so he could not mistake her words. "And here you shall remain, do you understand? Breathing and laughing and ordering me about as if I don't have the sense to eat a proper meal."

"Ever at your service."

"I did not save your life—twice—to hear you speak so cavalierly about its end."

"Yes, Miss Battersby."

Tears she thought had stopped started up again. "Dash it all, Colin. This is not a jest."

He sighed and laid a tender kiss on her lips. "Don't cry, sweet. Just say yes."

She tried to sniff, but her nose was now entirely plugged. Blast. She must be *terribly* attractive to him in her present state. "How will that prevent you from being attacked?"

"I am not the one who matters."

"Of course you matter! To your family. To me."

"Then say yes. Marry me, Sarah."

She wanted to. The yearning swarmed inside her, buzzing and bursting and needing and gnawing. Demanding a yes. It would be so easy, just one syllable. Yes.

But her eyes searched his, then dropped to her father's letter, then to her lap. She had relied upon a man to provide for her. A man she'd thought would never abandon her, never leave her alone to claw and scrape and fight for every blasted inch of her existence. And then he had. Left her. Drifted away bit by bit. Not because he wanted to, but because he'd had no choice. The result was the same. She was alone. And she must provide for herself. To rely upon a man for that purpose merely made one complacent and vulnerable. Even when the man in question loved her with all his heart. Colin, of course, did not. And he never would.

Saying yes was what she wanted. Her heart whispered it in her ear. *Yes.*

But, in the end, her lips did the only sensible thing. "No, Colin," they said. "I cannot marry you."

Chapter Seventeen

"Gifts are never the wrong answer. And when the question is what kind of gift, jewels are always the right one."

—THE DOWAGER MARCHIONESS OF WALLINGHAM to her son, Charles, upon his lamentations about a certain widow's unforgiving nature.

FIRST, HE HAD SENT FLOWERS. IT HAD TAKEN FOUR TRIES TO determine her favorite—roses—since so few plants were available this time of year. Second, he had attempted reason, pointing out that he would gladly consent to whatever conditions she wished to set if she would only say yes. It had felt a bit like begging, which had been bloody humiliating, but he'd been at his wit's end.

Sarah Battersby was the most deucedly stubborn, frustrating, confounding female he had ever encountered.

Beneath him, Matilda snorted as though in agreement, her equine breath blowing white in the frigid air of Hyde Park. He patted her neck. "Thank heaven you are much more agreeable, love. For that reason alone, I shall search out an apple when we get home."

"You realize your horse does not speak English."

Colin glanced to his left, where Lord Tannenbrook rode a stout gelding from Clyde-Lacey's stable. The man made the horse look like a child's pony. "She comprehends me better than some other females I could mention."

Perhaps his complaint was ill-humored. He did not care.

She had declined his proposal with nary a word of explanation, saying only that his past had nothing to do with her decision. Then, she had used his kerchief to wipe her cheeks and ushered him out of her bedchamber with the admonition to return to his own.

But in the week since that night, he had refused to give up. He was now employing his third strategy: gifts. He patted the pocket of his greatcoat, feeling the shape of the pearls inside with satisfaction. No woman could fail to be dazzled by jewels. It was some kind of universal law, surely.

He'd been struck by the idea when they had attended a soiree given by Lady Bramstoke the night before last. Watching Sarah laugh and talk and dance in her beaded black gown, he imagined pearls—his pearls—gracing her delicate white neck. He imagined placing them there, the soft glow of their sheen a poor neighbor for her skin. He imagined them as a signal to other men. Perhaps once she wore his pearls, for example, the odiferous, corpulent, licentious Sir Barnabus Malby would realize that she belonged to Colin, and if the toad wished to keep his bulging eyes in his head, he would remove them from her décolletage with all due haste. He had grumbled something foul about Sir Barnabus to Atherbourne, who had happened to be standing nearby. It had been a rare moment of solidarity with his brother-in-law, who had said only, "I could not agree more."

In truth, if the pearls did not cause Sarah to soften toward his proposal, he feared he would be at a loss. His last remaining device was seduction, and there was a problem with deploying it: He could scarcely be in the same room as his honey-eyed temptress without the need to drive himself inside her overwhelming his will.

He refused to repeat his mistakes. Seduction, therefore, must be kissing and a bit of touching, nothing more. And there was simply no way he could kiss or touch her without taking her. Not now.

Tannenbrook grunted, nodding toward the two men riding ahead of them, Atherbourne and Harrison, who seemed to have spotted some commotion in the distance, along the bank of the Serpentine. November's early penchant for downpours had transformed in the past week to a fondness for freezing. The result was thick, slick ice beneath a fine dusting of snow. Given the shrieks of alarm and laughter echoing from a footpath winding near the lake, he deduced someone had taken a tumble.

Harrison said something to Atherbourne, and together, the two men trotted to an opening in the wooden fence bordering Rotten Row. There, they dismounted and tied their horses before crossing the field to investigate.

Meanwhile, Colin and Tannenbrook rode to the low rail fence and peered across the expanse of grass and shrubbery to where a small gathering of gawkers stood guffawing. Some were bent double with their mirth. A few of the ladies covered their mouths in apparent shock. When one of them moved aside, Colin saw why.

"Good God. The lass has lost her skirts." Tannenbrook's muttered observation was correct, but only in part. The "lass," a very tall, long-limbed redhead, lay sprawled on her back, booted feet inches from the water's edge, her skirts hiked up around her waist. It looked as if she had slipped on the ice and fallen on her backside. Then, given the marks in the fresh snow, her momentum had carried her feet-first down a small slope, peeling her skirts up along the way. Beneath, she wore nothing but what nature had given her, of course, which was now visible to all.

Harrison reached her first, barking at the onlookers, and lifted the young woman up by her arms. Atherbourne, meanwhile, shoved the shoulder of one of the mirthfully bent gents and used his superior height to intimidate. The young woman's modesty was restored within seconds, but the damage had been done.

Behind him, he sensed other riders crowding close, probably to get a better look. He turned to encourage them to move on. And saw the knife a half-second too late.

Shouting, he dug his heels into Matilda's flank, driving her to spin toward Tannenbrook's mount. The knife glanced off the thick leather of his boot. Short, dark, and meaty, the attacker raised his arm for another swipe but by then, Colin had managed to release his foot from the stirrup and reeled back to drive his heel into the man's nose. A sickening crunch was followed by a gush of red and a cry of agony.

Something—Tannenbrook's horse, likely—jarred against Matilda's other side, jostling him hard and sending her sidestepping into his attacker, who held his nose and moaned loudly. Tannenbrook was being assaulted by two rangy men in dark, heavy coats. They, too, held knives, but the oversized earl merely gave them an oddly anticipatory grin and reached down to grab one of them by his hair. Then, his other massive paw grasped the second man's collar, and he slammed their heads together like one would do with a rod and a rug. The crack of the collision rang out across the Row.

Matilda danced and sidled, nearly unseating Colin as he struggled to regain control of her. He worked the reins, sucking cold air into his lungs as the muscles in his legs strained to keep him on her back. Suddenly, she screamed in pain, rearing up for a breathless moment before hitting the ground hard with all four hooves already digging into Rotten Row's gravel and tan. The momentum of her fear thrust them both forward at a terrifying gallop. Sprinting and heaving and laboring to escape whatever had startled her, she ignored his commands, the pulling of the reins.

With no sign of slowing, he bent low over her neck, reaching down to stroke her and speak soothing nonsense. He was fortunate to still be mounted. She was normally the most obedient of horses, but something had hurt her. Craning his neck around, he saw blood on her flank where the attacker had laid his cut.

Fury turned the white-dusted world around him red. He wanted to kill the man who had attacked him so brazenly. But first, he must get Matilda to slow.

Eventually, he did, but by the time she stopped, the wound was weeping profusely. He dismounted quickly, then stroked her tense, trembling muscles as he moved back to examine the deep cut. "Ah, love," he said, gently. "I am sorry they hurt you."

There was no help for it. Unless he wanted the wound to worsen, he must lead her back to Clyde-Lacey House. Repositioning the reins, he moved to her side, and together they headed toward where he had left Tannenbrook. Matilda's shuddering breaths and pained whinnies tore at him.

She had carried him across England, from Richmond to Liverpool, from Yorkshire to London. She had carried him away from Syder's butchery, carried him—feverish and delirious—all the way to Devonshire. She had carried him to Sarah.

And that bloody butcher's paid men had sliced her open. He wanted to tear them apart with his bare hands. He wanted to slice *them* open and let their insides fall out onto Rotten Row.

Something of his thoughts must have been evident on his face, because when he finally reached Tannenbrook, the bruising lord lifted a brow and shook his head. "I tried to keep them for you," he said. "My horse bolted. They escaped in a carriage that drove by moments after the attack. I assume it was meant to transport you."

Harrison approached on his horse, red-faced from cold and exertion. Both he and his horse were breathing heavily. "No luck. Disappeared off Piccadilly. The coach was black, unmarked. Looked like a hack."

Colin frowned. "Where is Atherbourne?"

"Headed to Clyde-Lacey House," Tannenbrook answered. "He wanted to ensure Syder did not seek two targets at once."

Alarm flared through Colin.

"I have Drayton's men guarding the house," said Harrison, "along with fourteen additional footmen hired specifically for their military experience. The safest place in London is there."

It was a small comfort, but Colin would take it. "Come," he said, nudging Matilda forward. "We have to get her back to the stable. She will need stitching and rest."

Then he would find a way to persuade Sarah Battersby to marry him. Syder was growing bolder, attacking him during the day in the middle of Rotten Row. If he was killed, she would be left alone and unprotected. He could not allow her to delay any longer.

She must be provided for, he thought. *Come what may, she must be protected, for nothing else matters.*

SARAH'S MOTHER HAD ONCE DESCRIBED SHOPPING ON BOND Street as an experience of "painful exhaustion and budgetary trepidation." Sarah could now see why.

As they emerged from Mrs. Bowman's shop, Sarah felt dazed. Depleted. The elegant Italian woman and her numerous assistants had swarmed Sarah like a hive, measuring, pinning, assessing with a calculating eye. After the buzzing had ceased, she had glimpsed the appalling total on the dressmaker's bill and nearly collapsed. Her protests to Victoria had been met with a raised palm and a calm, "I will hear no more of it. Neither will Colin." She now understood why Jane spoke of these excursions with dread.

"Next, I believe we must purchase proper gloves for you, Sarah." Victoria's innocent statement was met with simultaneous groans from Sarah and Jane.

"Come now." Victoria grinned at them over her shoulder as she pushed open the door onto Bond Street. "Don't be such fainthearted ninnies. It is only one more shop."

Jane snorted and pushed her spectacles higher on her nose. "I would rather collect the muck out of Blackmore's stable. Or attend one of Lady Wallingham's luncheons."

Eleanor chuckled. "You know, I simply must meet this Lady Wallingham one day."

As six strapping footmen followed them out onto the street, Victoria and Jane simply looked at each other and shook their heads.

"What? She sounds rather amusing."

"Clearly you haven't met her."

"That is my point," Eleanor replied. "I would like to judge for myself."

Victoria cleared her throat delicately. "Well, you may have that opportunity. If certain ... events come to pass."

Eleanor gave the viscountess a blinking frown. "I'm not sure what you mean."

"Er—only that Sarah might find a position with a household that will travel to London for the season."

Sarah's mother inquired, "Have you any news in that regard?"

"I'm afraid not. It is early yet. If need be, I shall query Lady Wallingham," Victoria replied. "She is acquainted with all the best families."

Jane added, "And she can list their servants from memory. Truly, it is astonishing. I do not know how she keeps track."

Sighing, Victoria rose up on her toes to get a glimpse past one of the very tall footmen surrounding them. "Thomas, would you mind moving to your right? I cannot see down the street."

The footman apologized and immediately complied. That was when Sarah spotted a familiar, dark-haired girl coming toward them wearing a black pelisse and plumed hat. She carried a package wrapped in brown paper and spoke animatedly with her companion, a forbearing older woman in a matching hat.

"Miss Thurgood," she breathed, feeling a bit disoriented. The girl's thick-lashed eyes brushed past Sarah at first, then came back to her and widened.

"Miss *Battersby?*" Breaking into a wide, beaming grin, Caroline Thurgood approached through the thicket of footmen. "How delightful to see you. So unexpected! And Mrs. Battersby! You both are looking wonderfully well. I cannot tell you how pleased I am to see you here in London."

Sarah quickly introduced Caroline to her companions, watching Caroline's eyes widen at the lofty titles. "Doing a bit of shopping, I gather?" Sarah inquired.

Caroline nodded, her eyes still lingering on the two titled ladies. "Purchasing an item or two for next season. Papa wished to wait another year, but Mama insists I shall have my debut this spring."

"How lovely for you," Sarah said, genuinely pleased. Caroline was mature for her age and quite pretty, a combination which Sarah had little doubt would meet with success on the marriage mart.

"You know, it is such a coincidence seeing you here on Bond Street," Caroline exclaimed, her eyes smiling and keen.

"Indeed, especially as London is quiet this time of year."

"Oh, but that's precisely what I mean. You are the second acquaintance from Keddlescombe I have encountered in the past week." The girl shook her head in disbelief. "I had no idea the road from Devonshire was so well traveled."

Frowning, Sarah asked, "Really? Who else have you met here, Miss Thurgood?"

The girl's thick-lashed eyes blinked slowly then flared. "Why, Mr. Foote, of course."

Sarah's stomach dropped into her feet. Cold seeped rapidly through her thick wool pelisse.

"He asked after you. Then he inquired about Mr. Clyde." Caroline smiled, oblivious to Sarah's distress. "Naturally, I told him you were as well as could be expected. How *is* Mr. Clyde faring? I do hope he has recovered from his injuries."

Giving Caroline a trembling smile, she nodded. "He—he is well."

"Splendid!" Caroline glanced over her shoulder to her companion, who waited impatiently outside one of the shops. "I should go. Oh, Miss Battersby we simply must have a visit while we are both in London. I will be most pleased to have your company."

After they said their goodbyes and Sarah was seated inside the Atherbourne carriage, it took several minutes for her heart to calm, for her stomach to cease threatening to rebel. Felix Foote. That hated man was in London, inquiring about her. And about Colin. The very thought made her twist her fingers together in her lap, made her fists curl and release, curl and release.

It was a reminder; that was all. A reminder of what she must do—secure a new position so that she and her mother had some way to survive when this transitory dream ended.

But she did not want to do it. Although she had refused Colin's offer of marriage, that decision felt less certain, more wrong, every day. She could sense herself weakening for him, wanting him, wanting what he promised. Over the past week, the argument played in her mind, repeating like her students' rote recitations.

He said he will help reestablish St. Catherine's Academy, her heart argued.

But I had the school before and was forced to close it when Papa died, her mind refuted.

He said he will ensure I have a home, that Mama will have a home, and he will secure it with funds in our name.

His funds are controlled by his brother. What if he displeases Blackmore again? Where would that leave Mama and me?

He has changed. I know he has. He would not risk such a thing.

I cannot risk such a thing. The only one I can be certain of is myself.

He is granting you the moon, Sarah.

Only out of pity.

True or not, can you not simply swallow your pride and take the gift he is offering?

The alluring thought stayed with her day and night, pulsing inside each second as though it were linked to her heartbeat. She feared if she did not soon set a different course, the next time she saw his handsome, tempting face, his firm, tempting lips, his tall, lean, tempting body, she would not only say yes, she would fall to her knees and plead with him to touch her the way he had before. And then she would beg him never to stop.

Chapter Eighteen

"Marriage is your duty, much like sitting in Parliament.
Perhaps you do not wish to be trapped inside an echoing
chamber, listening to someone disparage your ideas for hours
on end. Perhaps you would prefer to be riding. However,
that is marriage. And that is what must be done."

—The Dowager Marchioness of Wallingham to her son,
Charles, upon many occasions.

"I SWEAR, WHEN I GET MY HANDS AROUND HIS BLOODY NECK, I will crush the life out of him."

Tannenbrook's heavy brows lowered at the duke, who was seated on his horse, riding beside Colin and a limping Matilda.

They were on Park Lane, returning to Berkeley Square. Two of the three men were afoot, so their pace was much slower than it had been when they'd ventured out for a ride that morning. "Syder, do you mean?"

"No," Harrison answered Colin. "The blackguard who lured my brother into danger without a whit of concern for his life. He shall answer to me when this is done. That I promise."

Listening to a man known for his coldness and adherence to propriety describe choking the life out of someone was almost amusing. Colin had rarely heard him speak with such heat, particularly in Colin's defense. However, there could be no doubt Harrison's instincts had always been protective toward those he loved, even at his harshest and most judgmental. It had taken a great deal of hardship for Colin to see it. Now he wondered what had blinded him for so many years—possibly the similarities to their father's demeanor, a superficial resemblance at best.

Richard Lacey had been cold through and through. If he had ever loved his children, he'd seemed driven to prove otherwise. Harrison, on the other hand, had taught Colin to fish, to ride, to lace his boots. He'd taken him swimming and read to him from his favorite books. He had secretly thwarted their father's punishments and taken many upon himself. As bloody insufferable as Harrison could sometimes be, Colin was grateful he was his brother.

"Why you cannot see fit to tell me the man's name is beyond my comprehension," Harrison now groused, his face grim, his eyes flashing ice.

"Perhaps because you have repeatedly threatened his life," Colin replied, reaching out to gently stroke between Matilda's ears as they walked. He wished they could move faster, but he wanted to keep the wound from bleeding too heavily.

"That is a poor excuse."

"Harrison, I endured torture for this information. Do you suppose I would surrender it to you now? Here. In the middle of Park Lane."

The duke scoffed. "I am hardly Syder."

Tannenbrook shot Colin a speculative glance before asking, "Incidentally, why does Syder want this man's name so badly? Doubtless you have proved an expensive and troublesome quarry."

Considering his answer carefully, Colin pondered how much to reveal. Too much, and his contact's identity might be forfeit. "When Harrison cut off my funds last year, I turned to gaming. Had a bit of luck at first. Then I went to the Gallows Club."

"One of Syder's places."

He nodded. "I won rather substantially the first time. Lost substantially thereafter. Even deep in my cups, I had never lost so much. After the fourth visit, I became suspicious that the outcomes had been predetermined."

"Damn me," Tannenbrook grunted. "They fixed the games?"

"Mmm. Fleeced a great many green gulls, I venture. I complained a bit, but things went on as things do. A fortnight later, I received a note from a ..." He glanced at Harrison who glowered down at him. "An acquaintance who works with the Home Office on certain ... projects. He'd heard I had been frequenting the Gallows Club, and he wanted information about it. So, I returned, gathered what he needed, and delivered it to him. Aside from my debt, there was nothing more to the matter. He had his information; I'd done my bit.

"It wasn't until Syder chased me all the way to Liverpool and then to Blackmore that I began to suspect he was after more than repayment. Somehow, when the Home Office began to show an interest, he must have traced it back to me." Colin shrugged. "I didn't learn what he truly wanted until he asked me for the name. By then, I knew enough about Syder to understand that the Gallows Club was the least of what he'd done. The rest of his holdings ..." Colin had to swallow down his gorge. "Let us say there are things you'd rather believe do not exist."

"You refused to give him the name," said Tannenbrook. "What did he want with it?"

"The Home Secretary concerns himself almost exclusively with threats to the Crown."

Harrison grunted his agreement. "That is putting it mildly. Sidmouth is convinced the rebellions will burn out of control, and we will all end in guillotines."

Colin continued, "My contact has different priorities. He believes criminality among England's populace is equally a threat and deserving of investigation by more than feckless magistrates. Because of his unusual position, if he were removed, the resources of the Home Office would be redirected. As it stands, he must choose his projects carefully. In his view, dismantling Syder's empire is a prize worthy of sacrifice, but he must remain hidden if he wishes to complete the task."

"A man of rank, I take it."

Tannenbrook's observation was a bit too close to the truth for Colin's liking. "Who he is matters less than what he intends to do."

"And *when*," Harrison snapped. "This must be finished. I cannot have you or Jane or any of the others at risk any longer."

"He has said it will be done by Christmas."

"A month away. That is not soon enough."

Colin clenched his jaw and rubbed Matilda's neck. "I have told him as much."

The hush that followed was broken only by the soft crunch of snow, the clop of hooves, the rough breath of Matilda. New flakes began to fall, melting on the mare's steaming coat.

Mayfair was quiet, but that was to be expected. Most ton families remained in the country until January, when Parliament came into session, leaving only a smattering in London to host fetes and dinners and soirees. The mourning period for Princess Charlotte put a further damper on entertainments. On the whole, remaining visible within society had proven difficult, as there was little society in which to be seen.

He tried to be glad that this evening was another of Lady Rutherford's routs. The wife of the aged Marquess of Rutherford favored inviting both the objects and the purveyors of salacious gossip to the same gatherings, so he certainly would be noticed.

However, the only thought that buoyed his spirits was the anticipation of placing pearls around Sarah's lovely, slender neck before they departed. Perhaps he could lay a kiss just at the top of her spine, then nibble his way around to her earlobe.

Drawing crisp, snowy air into his lungs, he tried to breathe away the longing. First he must take care of Matilda. Then he must pen a note to his contact to inform him of the attack—and demand an end to this interminable danger. Not for his sake, but for Sarah's. Harrison was quite right. It must be brought to an end.

As they approached Berkeley Square, his sigh of relief plumed out before him. *Thank God. Almost there.*

The sound of carriage wheels came from a distance. As they drew closer, Colin could see it was one of Atherbourne's, returning to the square from the opposite end, the direction of Bond Street.

"It looks as though the ladies have returned from shopping," Harrison murmured, his voice hard. "I shall have to speak to Jane about that."

"The carriage is covered in footmen," Tannenbrook remarked. "They seem to have ample protection."

"Not enough." The words should have come from Harrison. Instead, they'd been pulled from the center of Colin's chest, where a lump of stone had settled when he realized she was not safely ensconced in Clyde-Lacey House. She'd been out on Bond Street where anyone could have taken her.

He wanted to shake her senseless. He wanted to kiss her and stroke her honey curls until he could breathe again.

Suddenly, the carriage halted two houses away from its destination. Frowning, he watched as the vehicle jostled from side to side. He could hear faint cries of alarm coming from inside. Then the door was shoved open with a crack, and out scrambled Miss Sarah Battersby. She leapt to the snow-dusted ground, her dark skirts gathered in her hands.

He stopped walking to stare as she bolted toward him from fifty feet away, her face nearly the color of the snow, her breathing frantic, her honey eyes huge and round and fearful in her pixie face. He dropped the reins. "Sarah," he breathed, his voice as weak as he suddenly felt. Was she hurt? Had someone tried to attack her as well?

"Colin!" she cried, slipping the last few steps and crashing into his chest, sending him stumbling backward. Her hands were everywhere at once. On his face, on his neck, on his chest and arms and hands. "What has happened?" she demanded. "Where are you injured?"

"Nowhere, sweet."

She turned to shout back toward the carriage, "We need a physician!" Then, she immediately resumed her frenzied examination of his person, her gloved hands reaching up to brush his hair and press against his scalp. "What in blazes were you thinking? Out for a ride as if you have not a care in the world! Let me tell you something, Colin Lacey, if you live through this, I will kill you for your recklessness. Mark my ..." Her breath shuddered alarmingly. "... words, you ..." A small sob. "... foolish man." The tears were coursing now.

And all he could do was wrap his arms around her delicate back, draw her in tight, and whisper in her ear, "It's all right, Sarah. I am unharmed. Everything is fine."

Her little gloved fist struck his shoulder as she gave another small sob. With her words muffled against the wool of his coat, she muttered, "If ... if you are not injured, then where did all this blood come from?"

Glancing behind him, he saw the trail of red, stark and bright where it soaked the white snow. "Blast. It is Matilda, sweet. She was cut."

Tannenbrook stepped forward to take the horse's lead. "I'll take her to the stable and make certain her wound is tended."

"And I shall inform the ladies that a physician is unnecessary," Harrison said, turning his horse toward the carriage, which was now stopped in front of Clyde-Lacey House.

Colin nodded his thanks and continued stroking Sarah's back.

But soon, she was pushing away from him, sniffing and swiping at her cheeks. "How?" she demanded.

"Do you mean how was she cut?"

She nodded, her chin taking on a distinctly pugnacious tilt.

"There was a bit of a scuffle on Rotten Row."

"A scuffle."

"Yes. Nothing to worry about. Matilda was the only one injured, and she should heal well if we stitch her properly."

Her arms crossed beneath her bosom, her finger tapping the side of her elbow in a rapid rhythm. "This was Syder, was it not?"

"Well, I do hope I have only one such enemy." The moment after he said it, he realized sarcasm was likely not the best way to calm Sarah's obvious, mounting fury.

Her delicate jaw clenched. Her upturned nose flared. She looked like an angry sprite. "You could have been killed, Colin Lacey! Or taken away and sliced to ribbons. Have you any idea how I felt when I saw that trail of blood behind you?" She gestured wildly toward the long, red stain. "What if that had been yours? What am I supposed to do if you go and get yourself murdered? Answer me that!" Raw and hoarse by the end, her voice was full of tears, full of something less definable.

"That is precisely why we should marry," he replied, unable to suppress his exasperation. "I have been telling you for the past week. For the love of God, all you must do is say yes, Sarah."

This time, her hands landed on her hips defiantly, her eyes flashing gold. "Perhaps I *should* marry you. It would serve you right to have to answer to me for the remainder of your days. Gracious me, *someone* in your life should be helping you make decisions, as it is clear you cannot make sensible ones of your own!"

Fully two heartbeats went by before he absorbed the staggering nature of what she had said. Granted, his heart was thundering rather briskly, so two heartbeats was not a very long time. But when it finally sank in, he could not stop the slow-growing but deeply satisfying smile he was certain she was seeing on his face.

"Then, we are agreed, sweet."

"We are?"

"That was a uniquely insulting way to say yes."

"Er—Colin. I did not precisely say—"

"Nevertheless, I accept. We are none of us perfect."

"Oh, but I—"

He cupped her pixie face in his hands and laid a lingering kiss on her sweet, bowed mouth. Then, he stayed for another. He stroked her cheeks with his thumbs, then breathed another soft, heart-starting kiss upon her honeyed lips.

"Colin," she whispered, her breath warm against his chin. Her eyes were closed, her upturned face dreamy. "I am so thankful you are not dead."

He kissed each eyelid, letting his lips brush tenderly against her temple before he answered, "As am I." Tucking her beneath his arm, he steered her in the direction of the house. "Now, let us go inside and warm ourselves a bit. If we are to be married this week, I have a few tasks to attend. The license. The church. St. George's will do. Victoria will insist on a breakfast with cake, of course."

"This week?" she squeaked.

"The sooner the better, sweet." He dipped his head to capture her lips again as they walked. She was more addictive than brandy. More intoxicating. "The sooner the better."

Chapter Nineteen

*"I say, Lady Rutherford, your punch explains a great deal
about your lack of inhibition."*

—THE DOWAGER MARCHIONESS OF WALLINGHAM to Lady
Rutherford upon attending one of said lady's routs for the first
(and last) time.

WHAT HAD SHE AGREED TO? SARAH'S HEAD WAS SPINNING,
her skin warm and flushed. She could not decide if it was the
rum punch in her hand—she took a sip to test her theory—or the
pearls around her neck.

Or, more to the point, *how* she had obtained the pearls.

Her eyes searched for Colin through throngs of Lady
Rutherford's guests, most of whom were vapid and vain. Of

course, Lady Rutherford was both, in addition to being overly fond of young men, so perhaps it was appropriate.

Her hand went to her neck for perhaps the seventh time that evening, feeling the smooth, round pearls through the silk of her gloves. Her eyes lit on Colin, looking so dashing in his black tailcoat and white cravat, his golden-blond hair finally beginning to curl again. Just a bit. Just enough for her fingers to find satisfaction.

She was to marry him. Within the week.

Her knees turned to water. He was gloriously handsome, and her head was swimming.

Perhaps it was the punch after all.

An elbow bumped hers, sloshing a bit of the stuff onto her glove.

"Oh, I am terribly sorry."

Sarah glanced to her right—and then up. And up a bit more. One of the tallest women she had ever seen stood there, looking abashed and flustered. Flame-red hair reminded Sarah of Lydia Cresswell. And a layer of light freckles brought to mind Ann Porter. A dark-blue silk gown with swirling streams of embroidery and glittering spangles at the neckline and hemline was also familiar.

"Mrs. Bowman?" Sarah guessed.

The woman, an intriguing blend of unfashionable coloring, unusual height, and exquisite gown, gave her a queer look from intelligent eyes.

"Your gown, not you." Yes, it was definitely the punch.

"How did you know?"

"I do not particularly like her, but her creations are magnificent. I do a bit of sewing myself. Recognized the skilled hand."

The long-limbed redhead smiled, her eyes lighting up like a green sunset. That was rather fanciful. Green sunset. Sarah took another sip of punch.

"I am Charlotte Lancaster."

Blinking up at her, Sarah nodded slowly. "I am very pleased to make your acquainance—er, acquaintance, Miss Lancaster. I am Miss Battersby. Sarah Battersby. Call me Sarah. I shall call you Charlotte, won't that be lovely?"

The woman's laugh had the most winsome tone to it, like a church bell, but lighter, more delicate. "I would be delighted, Sarah." She waved to the throng of vain, vapid, very tedious people crowding the overwrought décor of Lady Rutherford's ballroom. "What do you think of the crush?"

"I think I would rather be somewhere else."

Again, the laugh. It really was quite nice. "I am pleased to know I am not the only one."

Sarah stared down into her cup, closing first one eye then the other. "What is in this?"

"A substantial amount of rum, I believe. I might suggest employing caution."

"I am about to be married."

Green-sunset eyes lit above freckled cheekbones. "What wonderful news."

"This week."

"Quite soon, then. Just in time for Christmas. I adore Christmas."

"To him." She swung her glass in Colin's direction, sloshing more liquid on her white glove.

Charlotte leaned down to follow the direction of Sarah's gaze. "Lord Chatham?" she squeaked, sounding horrified. "To whom did you lose a wager?"

"No," she snorted. "Not Lord Chatham. Though, he is oddly attractive, isn't he?"

With a choking sound, Charlotte shook her head. "I suppose one might say so. If one were entirely foxed."

Sarah considered the dark-haired man standing next to Colin. She had met him earlier and found him charming, even magnetic. He was quite thin, though, and not as handsome as her Colin. There was no curl to his hair, for example. And his eyes were a curious shade of turquoise that had been almost unnerving when he'd locked them upon her, hooded and assessing. "I suspect he believes himself quite seductive," Sarah pondered aloud. "Perhaps he is. But, to me, there is only Colin."

More choking sounds from her right. "Lord Colin. As in, Lord Colin Lacey." Charlotte chuckled and shook her bright-red head. "My, you do have an eye for the scoundrels."

"Have you seen him?"

"Of course I have. He is standing right there."

"Then you know. Or perhaps you don't. He is also a wondrous kisser."

"Oh, dear."

Sarah sent her a frown. "You should not seek to discover that on your own. I would be forced to do you great bodily harm, and that would be most distressing. I like you very much."

Charlotte chuckled. "I like you, too, Sarah. You needn't worry. I haven't the faintest interest in kissing a scoundrel."

Sighing, Sarah smiled. "Pity," she said. "It is supremely pleasurable."

That was the simple truth, as he had proven yet again earlier that evening, when he had slipped into her bedchamber to give her the pearls. She had just finished donning her gown—black, embroidered silk net paired with a crimson silk underdress—but had not yet tamed her hair. The wild curls had tumbled around her shoulders as she'd sat at the dressing table, contemplating the vagaries of making life-altering decisions under severe duress.

He had entered quietly, leaning back against the door. She caught a glimpse of him—still in his riding clothes—in the dressing table mirror. His smile was wicked and slow. His steps toward her were the same.

"I have been dreaming of this moment," he said.

Nervously, she stood and paced to a cream-colored divan before turning to face him. "I—Colin, I must speak to you about this morning ... I mean to say, do you think it advisable ...?"

He moved closer. So close, she breathed in sandalwood and the clean-air scent of his skin. "Yes. Highly advisable. Now, stop fretting and relax. I have a gift for you."

Still in his riding clothes, he had discarded his coat so that his strong shoulders and lean torso were covered only in a linen shirt and pale silk waistcoat. She let her eyes linger on his throat, then lovingly trace his firm jaw and firm lips and firm, muscular shoulders. Warmth settled low in her belly, gradually connecting to the ache between her thighs. The two together bloomed outward until she wanted to reach for him like a flower toward the sky.

Plunging two fingers into his waistcoat pocket, he withdrew a double strand of creamy white pearls, sliding them out in a long, seemingly endless stream. "I meant these as a point of persuasion," he murmured, his blue eyes heating with intensity. "Turn around."

Breath quickening, heart beginning to pound, Sarah slowly complied, giving him her back. Long, strong fingers gently sifted through her hair, stroking and sending unbearable shivers of pleasure across her scalp and down beneath her skin. She felt her nipples tighten beneath layers of corset and gown.

Taking his time, he swept her curls over her shoulder. It took several passes, as her rebellious hair seemed not to want to leave his fingers. On his final pass, he smoothed his hand down over the riotous tumble, his palm streaking over a nipple as hard as the pearls he held. She gasped and jerked at the sharp streak of pleasure, her back colliding with his hard, warm chest.

"Easy, sweet," he said, his voice a hoarse rumble. Then, she felt the cool pearls sliding sinuously against the skin of her neck, catching and curving and winding around her throat. "I dreamed of seeing these against your skin. When I purchased them this morning, I thought they might soften your resistance to my proposal." Gentle, heated lips touched her nape, just above the line of pearls. "Now that you have said yes, I view them differently." His breath warmed her, his fingers stroking her throat and her hair and her nipple. "They will mark you as mine."

She groaned, the heat and need inside her thrumming to be quenched. Of its own volition, her backside searched out his hips and met with fascinating hardness.

"A bit primitive, perhaps," he whispered in her ear, nuzzling there before giving her lobe a tiny, pleasurable nip. "But the notion will not leave my head." His breath grew rougher and faster, his chest pumping. She fancied she could feel his pulse racing as fast to her own. "Say you will wear them for me, Sarah."

"Colin." His name was a question, a plea. She closed her eyes and reached back to cradle his head. The slight curl of his hair settled between her fingers.

"We shall marry as soon as possible. Only days now. And then you will wear my ring upon your hand, and you will take me inside your body, and you will be mine in truth." His tongue traced beneath her jaw, leaving a cooling trail of moisture from his hot mouth. "Until then, promise me you will wear my pearls and let the world see to whom you belong."

She had, of course, said yes. Repeatedly and demandingly. He had rewarded her answer by cupping both breasts and stroking her nipples through her gown until she begged him to stop the unbearable motions, begged him for more. Then, he had gathered up her skirt and stroked her delicately with his fingers until that pleasure had burst and flooded her vision with light, flooded her body with rippling waves of indescribable pleasure.

Even now, standing amidst titled ladies and dark-clad lords, hearing the strains of a waltz, and watching the golden glow of Lady Rutherford's numerous candles play with Colin Lacey's hair the way she longed to do, the need for him made her weak.

If she did not know better, she would suspect he had sensed her doubts about agreeing to marry him and had deliberately seduced her to prevent her changing her mind. Her eyes narrowed on the man she could not bear to resist. He was giving his companion a hard stare. Then, he turned that stare on her. And it was not hard. It was ablaze.

He wanted her. Perhaps as much as she wanted him. She could see it from across the room as though he held a sign in his hands.

"I must say, you may have a point," said Charlotte, glancing from Sarah to where Colin stood. She had almost forgotten the redhead existed. "When he looks at you just so, it is quite ... affecting."

Sarah nodded. "He is remarkably good at it. I have not quite determined how much is deliberate technique and how much the result of genuine feeling. But the effect is the same."

Charlotte wielded a lace fan in a vain effort to cool her cheeks. Sarah could have told her it was fruitless. The man was potent, indeed.

"Still, he is a walking scandal," Charlotte continued. "If this were not his mother's rout, I suspect he would not have been invited at all."

It took long minutes of sorting through what she had said before Sarah realized to whom Charlotte was referring. "Oooh, you are speaking of Lord Chatham." Dratted rum punch. How was a lady expected to think clearly after imbibing such a drink? "Yes, as I said, oddly attractive in a devilish sort of way."

"Mmm." The fan worked faster. "I wonder if he will attempt to reform after he inherits. A marquisate carries responsibilities of some significance. There is the estate, of course, and one's tenants to consider. Add to that his role in Parliament, and ..."

Sarah's newest friend continued debating the matter, but Sarah was only half-listening. Colin was still gazing at her, his eyes now sensually tracing the line of the pearls around her neck. As though he, too, remembered her promise and the moments after she had given it. She sighed with longing and gave in to the desire to trace the little gems with her fingers.

A gentleman—short of stature and bearing an unfortunate

resemblance to a carp—sidled up next to Charlotte. He
appeared to be deep in his cups, as his gait was stumbling, his
motions slow and uncoordinated as he craned his neck to
examine her face. Without explanation, the man snorted out a
loud burst of laughter, bending double and holding his
thickened middle. Tightening his lips and puffing out his
cheeks, he waved his hand as though to sweep aside his
transgression. "How do you find"—he hiccupped—"London's
first taste of winter, Miss Lancaster?"

Sarah watched Charlotte's face go from freckle-dappled
white to furious red within seconds. Bewildered, Sarah watched
as the man once again doubled over, unable to contain his
guffaws. He kept sputtering words that sounded like
"Longshanks Lancaster," but it was difficult for Sarah to
understand him because he could not control his gasping,
obscene mirth.

An enormous shadow came from Sarah's left, moving into
her view moments before its owner walked in front of her and
Charlotte, then calmly grasped the carp's cravat in a large,
powerful fist.

"Lord Tannenbrook," Sarah breathed, disoriented by the
punch and confused by the incongruity of his actions in their
current setting.

The earl, who made Charlotte look petite by comparison,
calmly forced his ugly captive upright, then lifted until the
man's toes dangled in the air above Lady Rutherford's marble
floor. He lifted him with seemingly no more effort than he
would a fish on a line.

Charlotte covered her mouth with one hand and crowded
against Sarah, attempting to give Lord Tannenbrook the space
to do ... whatever it was he intended to do.

"Gracious me," Sarah murmured, stunned by the dark-blond
lord's sheer physical power. "That is most ... impressive."

"Apologize," Tannenbrook said, his voice grim but calm.

The man choked and squirmed, clutching Tannenbrook's arm.

Beside her, Charlotte lowered her fingers from her lips long enough to whisper, "I do hope he refuses."

Seeing the fish-faced man's writhing attempts to escape and recalling Charlotte's unexplained humiliation, Sarah looped her arm through her friend's and squeezed. "I must confess, so do I."

For Colin, the evening had been nothing short of torture. Lady Rutherford's ballroom was stifling and crowded, her only beverages designed to get everyone cup-shot. And a bloody set of pearls was driving him stark staring mad.

Beside him, Benedict Chatham, Viscount Chatham, threw back half a cup of his mother's rum punch in a single swallow and followed Colin's gaze to Sarah. She stood alone in the corner near the bowl of rum punch he'd earlier refused.

"She seems a trifle spindly," said his former friend.

Colin eyed Chatham's pale, thin frame and raised a brow.

Chatham gave him a casual half-smile. "I cede your point. Well done."

"Why are you here speaking to me?"

Turquoise eyes blinked but, as always, remained cynical and assessing. "Were we not speaking?"

"You sold Reaver's betting book to my brother."

Chatham shrugged. "A minor transaction."

"It ensured I could not possibly pay my debt, which meant Syder would kill me. You knew. And yet, you did it anyway."

The future Marquess of Rutherford turned to the marble statue of Poseidon behind him and set his empty cup next to the god's feet. He was likely quite drunk, but one never knew with Chatham. "And yet," he said mockingly, "you are still alive. Huzzah."

With a snort of disgust, Colin wondered how he could have admired Chatham for so long. Granted, the man was devilishly clever. A genius, in many ways. But recalling how he had attempted to ape the viscount's cynicism and debauchery made him cringe. In part, he blamed his own drunkenness, the catalyst of many disastrous decisions.

Dismissing Chatham from his mind, he returned his gaze to Sarah, who now conversed with a tall, freckled, red-haired woman. He frowned, wondering if it could possibly be the same woman who had lost her skirts in Hyde Park. It seemed unlikely that she would make an appearance at Lady Rutherford's rout on the same day. Perhaps there were two such red-haired, abnormally tall women. In Mayfair. In November.

"If it is funds you seek, I suggest the Long Meg. Half American, sadly. But the American half is obscenely flush."

Colin shot the other man a scathing glance. "Using women to fill one's pockets is your game, not mine."

A sardonic smile curled Chatham's lips. "My, how swiftly the bitter grape becomes the sweet wine of righteousness. May I assume the fair Miss Battersby is the cause of this newfound moral purity?"

"Miss Battersby is none of your concern."

Watching the two women, Chatham's hooded eyes took on the peculiar cast that had always made Colin uneasy. He likened it to being measured by a predator—dangerous, calculating, and volatile.

"No," the viscount said softly. "She is yours." That gaze came back to Colin. "More's the pity."

His mood growing darker by the second, Colin stepped close to Chatham. They were of a height, so he was able to meet those eerie turquoise eyes directly. "Your meaning?" he gritted.

A single dark eyebrow elevated. "Those who have enemies should seek to avoid acquiring weaknesses."

"What do you know of my enemy?"

Something flashed behind Chatham's hooded gaze, but it was gone by the next blink. "I know this: If you continue to tempt the devil, no amount of blunt will loose you from his butchery. Eventually, his minions will grow too skittish to be purchased."

Colin's head reared back. *Purchased*. He'd told no one about Benning. The only one who would know, aside from Benning, was ...

A loud burst of shrieks and shouts was followed by a reverberating crash, pulling Colin's attention toward the sounds. The refreshment table had broken in half, glass and silver scattered across the marble floor, the silver punch bowl overturned several feet away. And in the center of the broken refreshments, a prone figure, red, gasping, clawing at his cravat as though it had choked him. Lord Tannenbrook stood over the ugly man, intimidation radiating from every line of his body.

"What the deuce?" Colin murmured, wondering who had been bloody stupid enough to draw the ire of the Earl of Tannenbrook. The man was the size of a horse and surly besides.

Without a moment's thought, he searched for Sarah and spotted her almost immediately, standing off to one side of the chaotic scene, clinging to the arm of Chatham's "Long Meg." She appeared to be well, even grinning at the prone man's calamity. He sighed with relief. She was safe.

Glancing to the spot where Chatham had been standing, Colin frowned, then looked back at Poseidon. Blast. He was gone. There would be no more answers from that quarter.

"Looks as though Tannenbrook has taken exception to the punch," said Harrison, approaching from the direction of the doors. "Perhaps we should depart before Atherbourne decides to enter the fray."

Colin nodded his agreement. More than anything, he wanted Sarah as far away from chaos and harm as he could manage, no matter the source. Chatham's words echoed in his mind, repeating until they resembled an ominous warning. *She is yours*. Colin could not help adding what he knew to be true. *She is yours. Yours to protect.*

And yours to lose.

Chapter Twenty

"Like a dance, every courtship has steps which must be carried out to their conclusion. But the dance must conclude eventually, Charles. You realize this, don't you?"

—THE DOWAGER MARCHIONESS OF WALLINGHAM to her son, Charles, upon his expressed desire to give a certain widow time to recover her previous affection.

MARRIED. HE WAS MARRIED. TO SARAH.

Colin shook his head and took a sip of tea, letting his eyes rest where they invariably settled—on her. She stood chatting with Jane near the windows of Clyde-Lacey House's drawing room. Honey hair laced with pearls and a silver gown rich with white embroidery shimmered in the waning daylight. The snow outside cast a glow the same color as her gown.

For most of his existence, Colin had believed he would never willingly don leg shackles. He'd thought marriage a trap, or at least inadvisable for a man who savored being the sovereign in his own life. Even hours after the ceremony, he had difficulty reconciling his prior view with his current thrumming satisfaction.

"I am pleased for you, Colin. You and Sarah will find much happiness together; I am certain of it."

He turned to his sister, who sat beside him on the dark-blue velvet sofa.

Victoria, who had been warming to him increasingly since their confrontation, gave him an affectionate smile. "Providing you do not place worms in her slippers, of course."

He chuckled. "It was only one time, Tori."

"Mmm. But memorable."

Laughing, he set his cup on the low table in front of them and then reached over to squeeze her hand. "Thank you for your advice. In the end, she was persuaded by an injured horse, but I suspect the flowers and reassurances laid the foundation for her consent."

"A proper courtship is always an excellent start. My own experience notwithstanding."

Atherbourne approached and held out his hand for his wife, saying they should make their way to Wyatt House before the snow grew much deeper. Victoria rose to her feet and Colin followed suit before she turned to him, braced a hand on his arm, and kissed his cheek. "I wish you both every happiness, brother," she said, her blue-green eyes shimmering suspiciously.

Colin nodded. "Thank you, Tori. Now, do be a love and try not to turn into a watering pot."

She sniffed, laughed, and gave him a playful swipe before moving away to say her farewells to Jane and Sarah. Atherbourne remained in place, giving Colin a hard stare. Then, the dark viscount extended his hand, shocking Colin down to his boots. Colin accepted the gesture, feeling a strong pressure inside his chest, feeling a hollow place of unmitigated darkness receive the tiniest flicker of light.

"This is not forgiveness, Lacey," the other man uttered in a low voice. "I want you to know that. It is doubtful I can ever fully forgive what you did."

Colin swallowed hard and nodded, releasing Atherbourne's hand. "I underst—"

"However, I do see a change in you, and for that reason, I wish you well in your marriage." He turned away before throwing his final thought over his shoulder. "Try not to make a muck of it."

Atherbourne and Victoria departed soon thereafter, and Eleanor retired early to her bedchamber to write her friends in Keddlescombe with details of the wedding, leaving only Harrison and Jane remaining in the room with Colin and Sarah.

"Harrison," said Jane pertly, "I believe it is time for us to retire. It was a lovely day, but I am quite weary."

The duke frowned and flicked open his pocket watch. "It is not yet five o'clock."

Jane glanced at Colin, then at Sarah, who stood watching the snow fall on Berkeley Square, then finally narrowed her eyes on her husband. "Do you know I received a delivery yesterday?"

Harrison blinked. "Of what?"

"Gloves. Several pairs. I was thinking I should try them on. Ensure that they fit perfectly, that they are the ideal tightness and a pleasure to wear upon my hands."

The conversation, along with Harrison's sudden ruddy color and accelerated breathing, was beginning to make Colin dreadfully uncomfortable.

"We should retire," Harrison said abruptly, placing his hand at Jane's waist to push her toward the drawing room doors. "At once."

Without another word, the couple left Colin and Sarah alone, closing the doors behind them. In the hush, the fire crackled, the gentle sound of wind whooshed beyond the glass, and Colin's pulse drummed a faster rhythm in his ears.

My wife, he thought, looking at Sarah's dainty white neck. His pearls lay there like an invitation. *She is finally mine.*

All the lust and anticipation he had been suppressing for weeks gathered like storm clouds, heavy and thick, roiling inside him. His groin tightened, hardened, and pulsed warning peals of thunder.

His reasons for marriage were as nothing to that iron-hard part of him. All it wanted was her. And, for the moment, his mind was similarly consumed.

"It is beautiful," she murmured, watching delicate white flakes fall and gather in a curve along the base of the window. "We never saw much snow in the village. I quite like it."

Pulled toward her by an irresistible force, he came to stand at her back, letting his nose settle along her temple. Breathing her in, he stroked his hands down her smooth arms and laced his fingers with hers. Wildflowers and honey filled his senses until he forgot entirely where he was. All he knew was her. Her scent, her soft, soft skin. That was when he felt it—the trembling. She was nervous.

"Don't be worried, sweet."

She stiffened in his arms. "I am not. I am fine."

He grinned. "As compared to what? You are shaking apart."

"It is the chill."

He nuzzled her neck, just above her pearls. "Perhaps you need something to warm you."

"Yes," she said before clearing her throat of its huskiness. "A bath. I have asked for one to be prepared."

"For us? Your cleverness is your most attractive quality, sweet. Apart from your hair. And your skin. And your—"

"For me. I ... You must give me a moment, Colin. To prepare."

He wanted to groan. He wanted to lift her into his arms and take her to bed. No bath, no delay. Just a headlong rush to possession. But he would control himself, damn it all. He would. She deserved his every consideration after all she had endured for his sake.

"Very well," he said, withdrawing from her temptation. "Go. Enjoy your bath. I shall come to you in an hour or so."

Nodding, refusing to meet his eyes, she hurried from the room, leaving him alone with his thoughts and unabated lust. He ran a hand through his hair, pacing the length of the large room. Barely seeing anything, his gaze wandered over his mother's favorite red chair, then her portrait above the fireplace, then the windows where snow continued to fall amidst the early dark. As his long, impatient strides ate up the floor, thoughts of Sarah pervaded his muscles and his mind.

She was his. Soon, she would belong to him in all ways.

Yours to protect. That thought, too, refused to leave him. *Try not to make a muck of it.* His pace slowed as he approached the end of the room opposite the fireplace. She was his responsibility now. He felt the weight of it settle upon his shoulders, a burden for which he had been eager. *What if something happens to her?* His hand came to rest on polished, golden-brown wood. It was the color of her hair. *What if I fail? As a husband. As a man.* His heart twisted at the thought.

He remembered the look in Victoria's eyes last year, when she had discovered what he had done. It had been here, in Clyde-Lacey House. Atherbourne and Harrison had forced his confession, and his sister had heard every word, her heart breaking in front of him. Seeing such anguish and disappointment in Sarah's eyes was unthinkable. But worse was the thought that she might be harmed. Because of him.

His hands fisted on the rich honey wood. He blinked, realizing what it was. The pianoforte. It was the same color as her hair. Smoothing the wood with his fingers, he slowly made his way to the bench and seated himself at the keys. Then, the compulsion seized him. His thoughts became notes, notes became chords, and chords the music that would be contained no longer.

AN HOUR, HE'D SAID. IT HAD BEEN TWO. SARAH CLUTCHED THE shawl around her shoulders tighter and sighed, watching her breath fog the glass of her bedchamber window. *Their* bedchamber window. At least, it would be theirs if he ever arrived.

Drat the man. What is keeping him?

There was no help for it. She must seek him out. Briefly, she examined her attire, a peignoir of apricot-hued silk and cream lace. Her serviceable woolen shawl was only for warmth, but it gave her an added degree of modesty. Debating only a moment, she quickly donned a pair of slippers and poked her head out into the corridor. It was quiet, except ... she could hear music. Wondrous music.

She found him where she had left him, in the drawing room. Closing the white-paneled doors behind her, she stood gazing at her improbable husband, hunched over the keys of a beautiful pianoforte, his eyes closed either in agony or ecstasy.

His song was lush, complex, the lowest chords turbulent and twisting, the upper notes heartrendingly sweet. Her own heart pounded as she listened, knowing there was no sheet music, no other composer. Emerging from Colin wholly formed, the song billowed into the air like a storm, a cascade of dark notes, tumbling and deep. Gradually, it gentled like the pattern of rain upon a wagon's canvas. When it grew as sensual as autumn sunlight, as rhythmic as waves upon a shore, she found herself moving toward him as though tied by a long, lustrous line tugging, pulling, propelling her forward.

She scarcely recalled crossing the room, did not remember deciding to wrap her arms around his neck from behind, to close her eyes and thread her fingers through curling golden hair. The song stuttered at her first touch, his body jerking in surprise at her boldness. She laid her lips along his hard jaw, rubbed her breasts against his back to quench a need that only heightened more. Her hair fell forward to brush her face and his, surrounding them both in the scent of her soap.

His shoulders heaved on labored breaths, his notes ceasing until only their echo remained. "Sarah," he groaned. Finally, he twisted around on the small bench, grasping her waist and pulling her between his thighs. He yanked her shawl from her shoulders, tossing it away impatiently. Locking heated blue eyes on her begging nipples, he tightened his grip on her waist, his fingers digging a bit before easing and drawing her closer. The skin on his forehead and cheekbones grew tight, flushed.

Head falling forward as though he did not have the strength to keep it upright, his face came to rest between her breasts. His breath heated the apricot silk. His hands began a sensual slide over her hips and her buttocks, pressing and squeezing, forcing her hips closer to his body. His lips nuzzled a hard, aching nipple through the silk, forcing a gasp from her throat at the fiery surge. Then, his mouth opened over the nub, drawing deep and making her writhe. She arched into him and moaned his name. He suckled for long minutes before pulling back to strip away the silk. She thought she heard the delicate fabric tear, but by then, she did not care a whit. Not with his mouth, as hot as a coal fire, sucking and working upon her bare nipples. First one. Then the other.

Her legs weakened until the only thing keeping her from collapsing at his feet was his hard grip on her waist. He clutched at her, wrapped his strong, unyielding arms around her, suckled and nibbled and pleasured her breasts. His hands dropped to the skirt of her peignoir, pulling the silk up her legs until he could grasp her thighs in his lean, strong hands.

One of those hands disappeared briefly to unfasten his trousers. The other slid between her thighs, urging her to widen them, stroking the tender flesh between and making her gasp.

"Colin, please," she begged, bracing her hands on his

shoulders, staring into his blue-fired eyes, feeling his fingers stroke and intrude and slip inside, where no man had touched.

He said nothing. Swollen from his ministrations to her breasts, his lips parted to accommodate panting breaths. He slowly withdrew one finger from inside her, only to return with two. Then he hooked those two fingers forward, pressuring the wall of her core and using them to draw her closer. A powerful, aching burst of need exploded from a point inside her body, robbing her of breath, of any ability to resist.

He could have whatever he wanted if he would only do that again.

She fell against him, sobbing, her arms wrapping around his neck, her lungs filling with sandalwood and the delicious scent of his skin.

When he withdrew his fingers, she protested, but he shook his head and gripped her thighs again, forcing first one of her knees and then the other to bend, placing them beside his hips on the bench. She straddled his lap now, her lips brushing his, her hands stroking his cheeks.

His tongue slid into her mouth, the salt and lingering flavor of tea as intoxicating to her as rum punch. Between her thighs, she felt a hot, blunt *something* stroking against her folds. The smooth tip wet itself in her juices before pushing, parting, seeking a place inside her.

Strong hands gripped her hips. Firm, sensual lips ate at hers. A pressured burning built where her folds gave way to allow him entry. Gasping, she held her breath as he pushed inside, then released it in a whimper as the stinging grew into a pinching pain. His hands on her hips lowered her steadily. His firm upward thrust stole every bit of air in her lungs. He sank inside her fully, the blunt pressure both unbearable pleasure and foreign pain.

His hand tangled in her hair, pulled her into his kiss. His arm around her waist controlled a new rhythm as he slowly slid out and in, the heat and tight friction unfamiliar yet somehow resplendent. Her nipples pressed and rubbed against his shirt, sending shocking thrills of sensation across her body.

Her gasps of pleasure turned to a grin as she realized he'd not removed his clothing. Not even his cravat.

Thrusting hard enough to jar, he drove any thoughts of amusement from her head. Any thoughts at all, really. There was only him inside of her. Driving and pumping and moving and sliding in the slick interior. He was stirring up a thunderstorm that wanted desperately to release upon him, to burst forth and wash him in a deluge. The intensity grew and gathered, roiling and rolling, her hips now catching his tempo, now losing it because he moved faster, drove harder.

"Please, Colin," she begged again, clawing at his woolen coat, gripping the linen over his muscular neck. "I need ..."

Still, he said nothing, letting his actions communicate his desires. One hand tore the silk away from where they were joined and brushed his knuckles over her folds before letting his thumb settle in. There, at the center of every pleasurable sensation, he stroked her with a light, sliding touch.

Circling. Circling. Circling.

Pressing and teasing.

And her body was seized by lightning, great waves of white-hot implosion. She sobbed his name, felt his mouth open and suckle where her neck met her shoulder. Felt him stroking and thrusting and circling until lightning sizzled out across her every nerve and fiber. Until the waves of it coalesced and turned the entire world into a brilliant, pulsating flash.

His thrusts grew deeper and sharper. His hands frantically clutched her hips. He pumped and drove himself home until she heard him groan her name. Once. Twice. Then, he gave a hard, final thrust, and she felt the muscles of his neck stiffen to stone beneath her biting fingernails, his voice grinding in agonized pleasure. Shouting her name, he squeezed her tighter, his fingers digging, his body pulsing inside her, releasing inside her, until together, they rejoiced in the culmination of the storm.

Chapter Twenty-One

*"My dearest Humphrey, you are the only one
who understands me."*

—THE DOWAGER MARCHIONESS OF WALLINGHAM to her
boon companion.

"SHE IS POSITIVELY MAD FOR HIM." JANE'S VOICE WAS AMUSED
and not at all mocking. Well, maybe just a little. "She speaks of
nothing but how handsome he is, how clever he is, how well-
mannered. They go for long walks together in the snow and
spend hours cuddling next to the fire. Cuddling!" She snorted
and shook her head. "Can you imagine?"

With a hand over her belly, Victoria giggled helplessly. "Oh,
you must stop. I cannot—oh, it is too much!"

"I think it quite lovely that she has found a companion she enjoys," said Eleanor from one of the parlor's green velvet chairs. She smiled at the two women but seemed bemused by their mirth.

Jane held up a finger. "Listen to this: *'His ears are not as pendulous as I would prefer. However, I find that small flaw endearing. Perfection is, after all, a form of banality. Nothing is so tedious as banality.'*"

Tears streaming down her cheeks, Victoria struggled to control her laughter, which caused Eleanor and Sarah to join in.

Sarah, Colin thought, finding his attention fixed upon her, as it was almost constantly. Seated beside him on the rosewood-and-silk settee, his wife chuckled along with the other ladies before returning to her stitching. With Christmas two weeks away, she had begun crafting a small quilt for Victoria's infant son, Gregory. He suspected that was merely one of several planned projects, as she spent much of her spare time with a needle in her hand. The rest was, naturally, spent in his bed.

He took a deep breath and tried once again to focus on the note he had received earlier that morning. But his eyes did not wish to see the words. They wished to see honey curls spread out over a pillow, a lambent honey gaze clinging to his as he thrust inside her tight, wet sheath. They wished to watch her bowed lips part in surprise as ecstasy took her.

"To be clear, we are speaking of a dog, yes?" That was Harrison, emerging briefly from *The Times*.

"Do not let Lady Wallingham hear you refer to Humphrey in such a way," said Jane. "In her eyes, he is her boon companion."

Still recovering from her fit of chortles, Victoria retrieved a handkerchief from inside her sleeve and dabbed her cheeks. "After all her lofty protestations about the worthlessness of the flea-ridden hound."

Colin let the chatter fade around him and silently absorbed the message from his Home Office contact. The unsigned note wrinkled with the pressure from his fingers. *Five targets taken since last week. The mission nears completion. Syder grows desperate and has escalated the game. Increase your vigilance accordingly.*

His vigilance. Chest tight and burning, he looked to Sarah. They had been married such a short time, but already, he could not envision his life without her. The calm, sensible Sarah. The stubborn, maddening Sarah. The ripe, sensual Sarah. The kind, selfless Sarah. His beautiful honey girl.

If she were ever taken from him, his life would end. It was that simple.

He sighed and ran a hand through his hair. *She is all that matters*, he thought. *I cannot allow anyone to harm her. Especially me.*

"Colin," Sarah said quietly. "What is it? You look distressed."

Dropping his gaze briefly to the note crumpled in his hand then eyeing the colorful quilt, he wondered how he was to protect her when she stubbornly insisted on venturing outside of Clyde-Lacey House. She argued that *he* did not choose to confine himself, but that was immaterial. He had *important* matters to attend, not excursions to the linen-draper on Pall Mall.

Perhaps if he occupied her more thoroughly, she would be too exhausted to defy his wishes. He noted her soft, pale throat rippling on a swallow. The thought had merit. If she was in his bed, panting and writhing beneath him, then she could not very well be in danger.

"Come with me," he murmured, standing and waiting for her to rise.

She glanced down at her sewing, then back up at him, her wide, golden eyes blinking with consternation. "Why?"

He sighed. "Must you question everything? I have something to discuss. Privately."

Reluctantly, she gathered up her sewing and followed him out of the parlor, up the stairs, and into their bedchamber. She placed the quilt inside the basket near her reading chair and turned a frown upon him. "Very well, out with it. What is wrong? You have been decidedly morose this morning."

"I do not want you venturing out again without my particular permission, do you understand?"

Slender arms crossed beneath tidy, delicious breasts encased in black bombazine. "No, I'm afraid I do not."

"Of course you do. You are simply being obstinate."

A finger began tapping against her elbow. "Currently, whenever I step beyond the front door, I am surrounded by an army of tall, strapping footmen."

His stomach burned, his hands curling by his sides. "What do you mean by 'strapping'?"

She ignored his question in favor of her own. "Did you learn something alarming? Has Syder—?"

"I am your husband."

She lifted a brow and tapped faster. "Yes. I do seem to recall something to that effect. Promises in a church or some such."

He did not appreciate her sarcasm, but nevertheless nodded. "Just so." She should cease noticing how "strapping" the footmen were and obey her husband. It was in the vows they had said to one another. Surely that meant something.

Her eyes narrowed on him, her bowed lips tightening. "You know, long before we married, I managed my life with some skill and competence. I even made my own decisions about where I went and with whom." Her eyes flared with more sarcasm. "Quite shocking, when you consider it. Sarah Battersby, a humble woman with no husband, using her tiny, pigeon-like mind to get from one place to another without mishap!"

"Believe me, I am well aware of your penchant for taking charge and ordering others to your liking."

Something akin to hurt flashed across her face, but it was gone before he could decide whether he'd actually seen it. "I only ever did what I had to do."

He started toward her, pausing a foot away. He wanted to

take her in his arms, but at the moment, she did not appear receptive to his affection. "I know," he said quietly. "But now you have me to care for you. Can you not accept that I am concerned for your welfare and wish to keep you from harm?"

That finger beat a fast rhythm against her black-clad elbow. "You are in just as much danger as I. More, really." Her eyes took on a calculating glint. "If you believe the risk to me is too great, I shall accede to your wishes. Providing you follow suit."

He crowded closer. "Damn it all, Sarah, I married you to protect you. I bloody well wish you would let me."

The earlier flash of hurt returned, this time settling in and making her pale. His insides twisted at the sight. Bloody hell. What had he said? Only that he wished to protect her. Causing her pain was precisely the opposite of his aims.

"My offer stands," she said softly. "You may prove the seriousness of your admonition by adhering to it yourself." Her posture was stiff, her chin raised in defiance.

How had he bungled this so badly? Running one hand through his hair and propping the other on his hip, he muttered, "I am a dreadful husband."

Some of the starch left her shoulders and a frown furrowed her brow. "No, you are not."

He snorted. "Yes, I am."

"No."

"Yes."

"Colin."

"I have already made you unhappy. After a week."

Her folded arms unfolded. "On the contrary, I am most content."

"Content."

"Satisfied."

"Are you, by chance, referring to all the times I made you—"

She cleared her throat pointedly and arched her brows in warning. "I am speaking generally."

Inching closer until nothing separated them but a breath of

her wildflower scent, Colin lowered his head and his voice. "Are you certain of that?"

Her only answer was several panting breaths, a parting of lips, and a flush of skin.

He ran a knuckle lightly from her jaw down to the small indentation at the base of her throat. "Because, if I knew your contentment rested in that quarter, I would not cease my efforts until every inch of you was saturated in ... satisfaction."

She gave a little moan in the back of her throat. Then she grasped his face between her hands and pulled him down into her kiss. Her honeyed mouth opened against his, seeking his tongue. He happily obliged, enfolding her in his arms and taking control.

He'd had a great deal of practice stripping her of her clothing over the past week. Swiftly, he put his skills to work, unfastening, unlacing, uncovering his beautiful wife. Then he lifted her, loving the feel of her arms clinging to his neck, and set her gently upon the bed. Before he pulled away entirely, he let his hands linger on her skin, stroking over creamy flesh and hard, cinnamon-hued nipples.

Her panting moan stoked blistering need, hardening his cock so intensely and swiftly, he worried he would not have the patience to tend her properly, as he wished to do. *I will control it*, he vowed silently. *I must.*

It was becoming a familiar pattern. Their first time making love, he'd not been able to say anything other than her name. The fire between them had literally rendered him speechless, like an animal in thrall. With other women, he had always been playful and teasing. With Sarah, his obsessive lust crowded out everything other than itself. But if he wished to occupy her mind to the exclusion of all else—including thoughts of defying his wishes—then he must focus on her pleasure alone.

Breathing deeply and slowly to calm his body, he carefully stripped away his clothing, then backed slowly toward her dressing table.

"Colin," she protested, squirming against the bed to prop herself up on her elbows. The move thrust her round, beautiful breasts forward. "You cannot leave." Her voice was stern. Demanding.

He dropped his gaze to his fully erect cock, flying high and flushed with need, then grinned at her. "Does it look as though I am going anywhere, sweet?" He retrieved what he'd been seeking from her dressing table and returned to her side. Trailing the end of the strand of pearls from her throat's hollow down across her chest and belly, he let the gems tease the thatch of honey curls at her core. "Other than here, of course."

Breathing labored, eyes dilated, she collapsed back onto the pillow and panted, "Well, do be quick about it."

"Hmm," he uttered as he lay down next to her, settling one of his legs between hers and leaning his elbow next to her head. Immediately, she spread her thighs, anticipating that he would accede to her demand. "Perhaps not too quick, Governess."

She frowned up at him as he plucked the pins from her hair and spread the delicious curls out where his hands could grasp them properly. "Governess?" she asked huskily.

He took the strand of pearls and stretched it along her thighs. "I have long wondered what it would be like to take instruction from you." Leading with one end of the long strand, he gently pressed pearls between her glistening folds, ensuring they nestled against her firm, swollen nub. Then, with small, steady tugs, he drew the pearls up over her mound, crossing the plains of her belly like an explorer, letting the gems drag and pulse against the tiny center of her pleasure. A long, keening cry choked from her throat. Her hips writhed against the mattress. Her hands clawed at the coverlet then at the pillow beneath her head.

"We shall soon discover how much I have to learn," he continued, dragging the pearls upward until they touched her nipple. He continued pulling, pleasuring those tight, puckered tips, as well. First one, then the other, curling the pearls along their curves. Finally, the trailing end of the strand left her folds, releasing with a small tug, and he drew the necklace up to drape twice across her throat. "Tell me, Governess. Tell me what you want."

A blaze of honey met his eyes. "You."

He gave her a wicked grin. "Is that all?"

"Inside me. Now," she growled.

"Yes, Mrs. Lacey."

Ever the obedient student, he moved atop her and thrust into her slick heat, driving hard and high. She wailed and clutched his hair, her sheath quivering around him, adjusting to his swift invasion. "Is that better? Have I got it right, do you think?"

"Oh, Colin," she groaned. "More. Please."

He gave her what she asked, driving his hips against hers, burying his face against her neck, where the pearls lay scented with her wildflower honey. He tasted them and her skin, running his tongue along two lustrous surfaces until he was drunk. Drunk on her.

He felt the gathering of his release build with each hard thrust. Where her legs wrapped around him and her heels dug into the small of his back, it coiled and spread, centered in his cock. Suddenly, she seized upon him, clawing his shoulders with little stinging bites and screaming his name in a voice nearly gone. He pumped harder through her spasms, maintaining their intensity as long as possible before his own climax could be contained no longer. With three final thrusts, he let go and lost every thread of himself in her depths.

Chapter Twenty-Two

"Obviously, a wife must obey her husband in all important matters. If he continues believing his admonitions are his own ideas, so much the better."

—The Dowager Marchioness of Wallingham to Lady Atherbourne in a letter filled with wifely wisdom.

Watching Caroline Thurgood serve tea in Mr. Thurgood's red-draped drawing room, Sarah felt a twinge of foreboding. She swallowed and accepted the cup from her former student. Perhaps more than a twinge.

He will be incensed, she chastised herself. *Only a day after he requested—very well, commanded—you to remain at home, you simply had to pay a visit to Miss Thurgood.*

The girl had invited her for tea at her home on Grosvenor Street, two houses away from where Jane's family resided during the season. As it was a quiet street minutes from Berkeley Square, she had reasoned the minor outing was the equivalent of remaining within Clyde-Lacey House's walls. Near enough, at any rate.

Additionally, Colin himself had gone to White's only this morning, saying he had an important matter to attend. And the other ladies in the household had gone shopping for books, taking numerous footmen with them. If they were permitted to venture beyond the gates of Colin's designated fortress, then surely she should be as well.

Sarah sighed. Her logic was sound, but she was quite certain she would endure a good deal of displeasure from her husband upon her return, particularly since she had only taken two footmen and the coachman with her. They had been all that were available.

Be certain to tell your husband that during your next argument. Which should be coming shortly.

"The school is in Bath," said Caroline, a glint of excitement in her eye. "*Very* respectable. I thought of you immediately, Miss Battersby."

Sarah would have told Caroline she was no longer Miss Battersby, but the girl had not ceased chattering since Sarah's arrival. *Perhaps I should have spent a bit more time explaining the virtues of conversational restraint.*

"The headmaster is a vicar like your father. He wrote to Papa of his simply desperate need for an instructor in deportment and household management, and Papa mentioned it over breakfast, and, well, here we are!" The girl took a sip of her tea, her lashes forming shadows on her cheeks. Then she grinned widely. "I have a letter in which Mr. Lawson describes the requirements and compensation. It is a marvelous position for someone of your talents. That is, if you have not already found a post."

It *was* a marvelous position. Ideal for her in every respect. In fact, she felt a peculiar kind of regret that it had not been available two months ago. It certainly would have made her choices simpler. She could have moved to Bath with her mother. Perhaps rented a small cottage. Colin Lacey would have been merely a wistful autumn memory. Instead, he was now her husband. And she his wife. It was odd how fate led one down certain roads and forever closed others.

Clearing her throat delicately, Sarah set her cup in its saucer and opened her mouth to answer.

"Oh! Silly me, I almost forgot," Caroline continued. "It is the very school Lydia—Miss Cresswell—will be attending in the spring. Wouldn't that be lovely? Lydia is most fond of you, Miss Battersby."

"Lady Colin Lacey."

Long lashes swept down and up in a rapid blink. "I beg your pardon?"

Sarah gave Caroline a gentle smile and repeated, "I am now Lady Colin Lacey. No longer Miss Battersby. I have married since you saw me last. Forgive me for not saying so upon my arrival."

"Oh!" Surprise turned to confusion. "But I thought—I was certain his name was Mr. Colin Clyde. Am I misremembering?"

She shook her head. The necessity of explaining why she had participated in a deception was one of the reasons for her reticence. "Lord Colin's injuries were not caused by being thrown from his horse. He had been attacked by a dangerous criminal. When he arrived in Keddlescombe, he was fearful the villain might hear of his presence and perhaps follow him with intent to do further harm. To protect me and all those in the village, he used a false name."

Caroline gasped and covered her lips with her fingers. "How very shocking. And gallant. Oh, you are so fortunate, Miss—I mean, Lady Colin. He really is quite dashing. I'm certain even more so now that he has healed properly."

"Dashing." Sarah smiled, recalling the previous day and night when he had pleasured her so diligently she had forgotten her own name. "Yes. Quite."

A half-hour later, she and Caroline were saying their goodbyes in the foyer. Tying the ribbon on her bonnet, Sarah said, "You shall be a wonderful success in your debut, Miss Thurgood. I haven't a single doubt."

"Thank you for saying so, Lady Colin. Perhaps we shall see one another during the season."

Sarah smiled and murmured a neutral, "Mmm." In truth, she did not know where she would be come spring. Colin had stated explicitly that he had only married her to give her his protection. She, on the other hand, had married him because she could not bear to be parted from him. What would happen when the crisis with Syder was over? Would Colin's interest fade? Pity and charity could last only so long, after all.

Caroline picked up an unsealed letter from the tray of calling cards on a mahogany table beside the door. "I intended to give this to you. Mr. Lawson's letter. You are most welcome to take it, of course. I certainly won't be needing it." The girl laughed. "I don't imagine you will either. You are a lady now. I feel as though I should curtsy."

Sarah looked at the folded paper in her hand. A part of her wanted to accept it, to tuck it away just in case. Another wanted to decline, to believe in him, in her marriage. She watched as Caroline placed it back on the tray. "No curtsy necessary, I assure you. Thank you for a lovely visit, Miss Thurgood."

"It was my pleasure, Lady Colin."

Outside, waiting for the carriage to pull around from the mews, Sarah breathed in the wintery air and wondered if perhaps she was making a mistake. Surely it would do no harm to take the letter with her. She looked to her left. "Thomas," she said quietly to the tall, brown-haired footman. "I—I seem to have forgotten something. Would you be so kind as to retrieve it for me?"

He argued for a moment, claiming his duty was to be her shadow, but she explained that she would be alone for less than a minute. Reluctantly, he complied, warning her to "stay put until the coach arrives, if you please."

In the seconds he was gone, the coachman at last pulled the carriage onto the street. It came to a stop directly in front of her. She frowned as she focused on the door, noting the Duke of Blackmore's crest was not present. Most peculiar.

Then, it flew open. A hard band circled her waist and squeezed until all the air was forced from her lungs, lifted upward until her feet left the ground and her ribs were crushed under the pressure.

She couldn't breath. Could not understand. Her lungs burned and her legs kicked, meeting only hard leather boots. She was half-thrown, half-shoved into the carriage, landing painfully on her knees. Her head collided with the opposite wall. Sharp pain exploded in her skull. Dazed and beginning to see spots, she struggled to gather enough air to scream. Distantly, she heard a shout, but by then, the coach was moving, the wheels clacking and rolling, carrying her away from safety. Blood pounded in her ears. Pain pulsed inside her skull.

"Why, Miss Battersby. A happy coincidence, indeed," came the vile voice of a snake.

The shock of it sent nausea into her throat. She thought he had slithered away, no longer her concern. She'd been wrong.

"I must say, I do enjoy seeing you in that position. A female on her knees. Holds a great many ... intriguing possibilities."

Her need for air warred with her need to retch. With gasping, wheezing breaths, she struggled to rise, bracing a hand on the wall. Her bonnet had slid forward so the brim kept him from her view as she scrambled to rise. Finally, she sat on the seat opposite the man she despised more than anyone else—with the possible exception of Horatio Syder.

"Wh—What do you think ... you are doing, Mr. Foote?"

Felix Foote's pomade-slicked hair gleamed in the light from the window. His brown-toothed grin was both gleeful and grotesque. "I am earning my prize, my dear Miss Battersby."

"I am married now. My husband will kill you for this." She did not know if it was true, but it did seem like the thing to say in this situation.

His laugh was nasal and high. "Your *husband?* Your engagement was a fraud, Miss Battersby. I knew." He tapped a finger against his temple, his too-small eyes shining with triumph. "I came to London to find proof. His name is not Clyde. You scraped up his remains after Mr. Syder finished with him and dressed him in your father's clothes."

Dizzy and yet hearing everything with preternatural sharpness, she blinked and pulled air into her aching lungs. "It does not matter how it started," she said. "We are married now. Colin Lacey will not allow his wife to be taken." She hoped it was true. Prayed it was true.

His smile turned into a snarl. "He is a corpse. Mr. Syder will simply give the matter some finality."

As though the snow outside had found a way inside her veins, Sarah shivered and froze. "You are in league with Syder. That is how he learned Colin was in Keddlescombe."

He leaned forward. "We have mutual interests." His eyes slowly traveled from her throat to her bosom to her legs and back, lingering and lighting until it felt like worms were eating her from the inside out. "Mine is you."

It was all the warning she had before he was upon her, tearing at her skirts, sliding his disgusting mouth across her throat. She clawed his face, shoved his bony chest, screamed until her throat was ravaged. But he was so strong. He merely grasped one of her wrists and squeezed until she whimpered at the pain. His breath drifted across her face, smelling of rotting meat. Clutching and groping, his other hand tightened on one of her breasts, the pinching agony causing her to shriek.

"For every moment you resisted me, Miss Battersby, I will repay with—"

Scrambling for purchase, her boot landed forcefully between his legs, eliciting a high-pitched cry reminiscent of a strangled cat. Foote crumpled away from her, at last releasing her from his hold and his revolting touch.

Get away. Must get away.

She scrambled to the door. Wrenched at the handle. Clawed the leather lining with nails containing Felix Foote's skin. *Open the blasted thing.* She must open it so she could get free. Get back to Colin.

The carriage stopped. The door popped open. And there, in the gap, was Horatio Syder wearing a top hat on his ruddy blond hair.

And smiling his welcome.

THE FEAR HAD ITS OWN WEIGHT. IT PULSED AND HUMMED AND shook and pressed in upon him until every nerve was screaming. It wanted to kill.

"Sh-she insisted, my lord. I were only gone a minute. Mayhap less."

Colin did not wish to hear any more from Thomas. "Get out of my sight," he said softly, leaning forward and bracing his hands on his brother's desk.

Thomas hesitated, worrying his hat in his hands.

"Now!" Colin roared.

A snuffling sound from the girl beside Thomas's vacated position drew his attention. "Miss Thurgood." Colin tried very hard to keep his voice even. It was difficult with the fear pulsating in every heartbeat. "What can you tell me?"

"I—I don't really ... She was there for a visit, Lord Colin. We had a pleasant time. I served tea."

"She was taken."

The girl's face scrunched and her long-lashed eyes welled. She nodded, apparently unable to speak.

His fists slammed the desk and he hung his head between his shoulders. "Did you see anything? When it happened?"

When she finally spoke, her voice was strangled with her distress. "I thought—I was standing in the morning room. It looks out on the street. When I glanced outside, I thought I saw a man I recognized. But I must have been mistaken."

His eyes flew up to hers. "Who?"

"F-Felix Foote."

Nostrils flaring, Colin reared back. "Are you certain?"

"Well, no. That is why I—"

"Is he in London?"

She bit her lip and nodded. "But why would Mr. Foote do Miss B—I mean, Lady Colin harm? He has always been quite fond of her. He even intimated that they were engaged. Of course, he did not know that you and she—"

Quickly, Colin took up a quill pen and scratched out a note.

"Do you know where he's been staying? Did he tell you?" he barked.

Her fingers twisted together, her lower lip trembling. "Knightsbridge. H-he rented a house." She gave the address, saying that Mr. Foote had sent her a letter previously containing his direction.

Coming around the desk at a swift pace, he brushed past Miss Thurgood and threw open the door to the study. "Digby!"

He strode into the foyer, shouting again for the sandy-haired butler. "Digby!" He did not have to wait long. Digby was ever efficient.

"Yes, my lord?"

He handed him the note. "See that this is delivered will all haste. The urgency cannot be overstated, do you understand?"

"Straight away, my lord."

"And have a horse saddled immediately."

His heart was pounding, but his vision was sharp, almost too bright. Taking the stairs two at a time, he hurried to his bedchamber—their bedchamber—and dug through the wardrobe to find ...

Ah, yes. There it was. The knife slid neatly into the waist of his trousers, just at the small of his back. He threw on his greatcoat and rushed back down to the foyer.

Harrison entered, doffing his hat and shaking the moisture from the brim. He took one look at Colin's face and paled. "Who?" he asked.

"Sarah. Not an hour past."

"I shall come with you."

"No. Harrison, I cannot have anyone else—"

His brother gave him a stark, tormented stare. "I will not allow you to face this alone."

Feeling like he'd been rammed in the chest by a bull, he nodded. "Best tell the groom to bring your horse 'round again. We leave now."

Chapter Twenty-Three

"Some men deserve to die."

—THE DOWAGER MARCHIONESS OF WALLINGHAM to Lady
Atherbourne in a letter of exceptional gravity.

FELIX FOOTE SAT ACROSS FROM HER IN HIS KNIGHTSBRIDGE parlor, legs crossed and posture hunched. "You intend to kill him, do you not? I must have assurances."

Syder twirled his walking stick between two fingers, twisting it in place on the wood plank floor. "He will die," he confirmed softly. "After a time."

Sarah's head continued to throb, making her vision blurry, her stomach precarious. They had removed her bonnet, so the firelight disturbed her sight, causing odd shadows and flickers.

Both men spoke as if she weren't there sitting between them, her wrists bound at her back, her ankles bound together. She sat on the floor, her back resting against the sofa where Syder lounged, twisting his black cane as though trying to erode a single point in the plank.

Foote's toe stretched out to nudge one of her boots. "I want her. I will have her. That was our agreement." His nasal voice made his words into a whine. It was difficult to read Syder, and she was afraid to look at either man for fear of drawing attention, but from the change in the pace of Syder's turning fingers, she suspected Foote was beginning to outlive his usefulness.

"You may have her after our business is concluded, Mr. Foote." The precise, toneless words should have warned the snake it was inching dangerously close to a much more lethal predator, but Felix Foote had never been the intellectual sort.

"I've gone to a great deal of trouble," he whined. "Courted the whore for more than a year. Traveled all the way to London to hunt down her lies."

The walking stick spun faster. Back and forth. Back and forth.

"To be sure, you had the dealings with Lacey. And recognized his mother's name when you heard I had made inquiries—"

"Mr. Foote," said Syder. "We are at the culmination of our agreement. Now is hardly the time to lose one's confidence."

Foote shifted gingerly in his seat, still pained from his collision with her knee. "My point is that, were it not for my persistence in discovering the truth about Miss Battersby's supposed engagement, you could not have followed his trail to—"

The cane's tip tapped twice. Tap-tap. Then, it was gently set aside. She watched Syder's polished shoes walk casually to the other man's chair.

Foote's legs uncrossed and splayed wider. "What are you—"

Wet gurgle. Legs kicking. Jerking. Flailing.

A spray of warm, metallic liquid.

On her face. In her hair.

Her eyes were closed. It was not real.

Someone was wheezing, whimpering. Weeping. She wished they would stop.

It was not real.

"Calm yourself, Lady Colin."

It was not real.

"Oh, I do like that title. Lady Colin." Polished shoes strolled back to the sofa. The cane resumed its twisting motions. "It will be like killing him twice."

Penetrating deep, the ice turned everything numb. She opened her eyes. Pressed her lips together until her teeth dug into the soft inner flesh, stifling her distressed keening. Blood dripped from her hair onto the bodice of her gown, soaking the white trim at the neckline. Her shoulders ached from her awkward position. Her teeth began to chatter.

A finger drew one of her curls away from her forehead, the sodden lock of hair dragging against her skin. "You know, you remind me of someone. She, too, has a curious strength. Resilience." Another stroke, then the finger was gone. "Lovely, curling hair."

She sat, shaking in the silence, wondering when he would kill her. Wondering if Colin would come. Whether she wanted him to.

No. She could not bear for him to be destroyed because of her. She would rather die.

"You would have liked her, I think," Syder continued in his soft, even voice. "Quite brilliant." He chuckled, the sound almost normal. "I fancy she takes after me a bit."

That was when she remembered. He had talked of a ward. A girl. She had assumed it to be a lie, but perhaps it wasn't.

"I considered keeping you alive to act as her governess. She must be constantly challenged or she grows bored." He tsked and gave another small laugh. She could almost believe she was hearing the father of one of her students ramble fondly. "Alas, I have many demands upon my time and cannot devote the attention to her studies that I once did. I have attempted to explain I am building a kingdom for her, ensuring she will never again want for a single thing her heart desires. She can sometimes be ... resistant."

The walking stick stopped its spinning. The finger came back to stroke her hair, cooling now as the blood slowed its drizzle against her skin.

"It is comforting to speak of her with someone who understands these things." The finger withdrew, leaving only the blood and her horror behind. "A pity you must die."

THE HOUSE WAS NOTHING—A PLAIN, BRICK STRUCTURE similar to many along Sloane Street. Colin handed his reins to Thomas and nodded to Harrison. "Wait for Atherbourne and the others."

"I am coming with you."

He shook his head. "Syder is clever. We will need the element of surprise. I shall delay as long as possible." Indicating Harrison's waistcoat, he said, "Mind the time. Ten minutes, come all, others or no. Enter through the garden. Thomas."

"M'lord?"

"Find somewhere to tie the horses. His grace will need your assistance."

Skin crawling, urgency coursing through his blood, he glanced in each direction, looking for signs of Syder's men. The long street was quiet. Snow began to fall, joining that which was already melting and muddying into a slushy soup. Gritting his teeth, he loped across the street to the painted black door. He did not bother to knock. Inching the door open a crack, he listened.

A voice. Syder's.

A muffled, feminine whimper. His heart and lungs and bones and blood roared, recognizing the sound.

Sarah. It was Sarah.

Shoving the door open wide, he charged inside and followed the voice to a room on the right. The rank, metallic smell reached him first. His feet staggered to a stop. His heart twisted and jerked hard within its cage, strangling his air, squeezing until he felt it crack.

Red. Everywhere. Soaking the area around the fireplace, the tight cluster of furniture where Syder sat, spinning a thin cane negligently between his finger and thumb. Opposite him, Felix Foote sprawled, his body slumped and staring blankly upward in a chair, a hideous, unnatural gape in the flesh of his throat.

Frantically, Colin searched. And found her on the floor, head hung forward, frightfully still. Stumbling several steps further into the room, he saw blood dripping down her face, coating her hair and skin. So much blood.

Light turned to darkness. Sound went silent. He could feel himself swaying, all strength draining out through his feet.

She could not be ... Not Sarah. *Please, for the love of God, no.*

Syder's voice emerged across a valley of fog. "She is yet alive, my lord. Fear not. We have been chatting while we awaited your arrival."

He thought perhaps Syder rose from the sofa to stand next to Sarah's hunched form, but he could not take his eyes from her. The knowledge that she lived was slowly expanding his vision, returning his hearing. Even now, he could see the fine trembling of her skin. She would not look at him, however. Her eyes remained downcast to a point on the floor near her bound ankles.

Swallowing his need to vomit, he prepared to move, his only thought to take her in his arms. But those arms were grasped and wrenched painfully upward behind his back.

"Are you acquainted with Mr. Lyle?" said Syder, giving Colin a polite grin. "He is no Benning, to be sure. He is, however, still above ground, which gives him a bit of an advantage over my former employee."

Colin could sense the size of the man from the strength and angle of his grip. He was every bit as large as Benning. "If you touch her, I will kill you." The guttural words emerged without Colin's permission, a vow he would make to God himself. He wanted to scream and roar those words into dimming eyes as his knife plunged through the butcher's heart. But it was unwise to grant Syder any further weapon. He knew with sickening certainty Chatham had been right on that score.

"Tut tut, Lord Colin. Ever the impulsive sort, aren't you? These needless threats achieve nothing. Give me the name, and I shall consider our association concluded."

"It will do you little good. He has reduced your monstrous empire to rubble."

"Ah, but he has not taken my treasury, has he? With ample resources, and with time, even a humble solicitor such as I may rebuild what has been lost."

He was not wrong. Syder had begun as a "humble solicitor," just as he said. Using his knowledge of the law, he had slowly spread his poisonous arms outward into all quarters of London's filthy underbelly. None of the businesses had been in his name, of course. He'd maintained a rather hidden existence, posing as a solicitor for the true "owner." Then, to solidify his holdings and skirt prosecution, he had hired others to bribe highborn gentlemen of influence and to brutalize or slaughter anyone else who stood in his way.

It was why Colin's contact had been forced to take things slowly, to plan and outmaneuver and untangle with excruciating care. To eliminate Syder for good, one could leave no remnant behind, lest he reemerge like a foul, pernicious vine.

"I refused to give you the name before," Colin said. "What makes you think I would surrender it now?"

Syder stroked red fingers through the blood-soaked curls of Colin's wife. "This."

Feeling his stomach bind and lurch, Colin nearly retched.

"It is a simple matter, my lord. The name. It cannot be more dear to you than your beloved's precious skin."

"No." The trembling word came not from him, but from her.

"Sarah," he breathed.

"D-do not, Colin. Mustn't ... let him win."

"He will kill you, sweet."

Devastating honey eyes finally rose to meet his. "He will regardless. Y-you have braved too much in recovering your honor. Please do not let me be the reason you sacrifice it."

"How affecting," said Syder. "The name, my lord." He removed a long, familiar blade from a pocket sewn into his coat. "If you please."

Colin weighed the decision, knowing she was correct. The moment Syder had the information, he would slice her throat. And then Colin's. How much longer could he delay? "Surely you do not expect to escape the consequences of what you have done," Colin said, nodding toward Foote's corpse. "This will see you hanged, Syder, if nothing else. And I shall relish watching your neck snap inside a noose."

"Unlikely." His voice was soft. Chilling. Certain. He pressed the knife's tip just beneath Sarah's delicate jaw. "If I were you, I would concern myself with *her* lovely neck."

Colin's breath sawed in and out. The man behind him had slackened his grip, apparently distracted by the conversation. Just a few moments more.

Sarah whimpered as the knife twisted and gouged. A trickle of her blood slid down to mingle with Foote's.

"Stop! It is Dunston."

Syder's lifted the blade, turning surprised, faintly amused gray eyes to him. "The Earl of Dunston." He chuckled. "Pleasant fribble. Impeccable dandy. You mean that Dunston?"

"Yes."

Gray eyes lost their false amusement. "I do not believe you."

The soft words were spoken a half second before his world was torn asunder.

A half second before the silver blade streaked across his wife's throat.

Two seconds before the room exploded in chaos.

And three seconds before every good thing he had been or wanted to be died along with her.

Chapter Twenty-Four

"I have told you the Lacey men are not to be trifled with.
You did not suppose I meant only Blackmore, did you?"

—The Dowager Marchioness of Wallingham to the
Home Secretary, Lord Sidmouth.

He did not remember shoving, heaving against the
brute behind him, nor slamming the man against the
doorframe. Did not recall grabbing the knife from the back of
his waist. Nor driving that knife into the brute's arm and
shoulder and throat. He scarcely remembered crossing the
room to Syder, ignoring the others who had crowded inside,
dismissing the shouts and deafening blasts of gunfire.

One moment, he was watching his wife's blood ooze from

Syder's cut. The next, he was dodging a slicing swing from Syder. He caught the man's arm with his own blade. Felt something strike his shoulder and neck from the right. The cane. It was in Syder's other hand.

It was nothing. The knife was nothing. Syder could beat him. Cut him. Kill him. It meant nothing.

Colin had already died.

Syder's flat eyes flared as Colin calmly grabbed his wrist on the next swing. Calmly smiled. And then calmly sank his own blade between the butcher's ribs. Pulled back and sank again, hearing a satisfying grunt. Sank again. And again. Watched blood drain until skin was ashen and eyes were dull.

"Lacey!" The sharp bark from behind him was as nothing.

He pulled back and felt the blade puncture again, a small resistance then a gratifying slide.

"Lacey! Stop, man. You must stop."

Other hands pulled at him. He did not want to stop. He liked seeing Syder's eyes fade, the faint surprise dimming until they were flat for another reason.

"She is still alive, brother," Harrison murmured in his ear after wrapping unyielding arms around his shoulders and neck, struggling to move him away from the butcher. "Do you hear? She is still breathing."

Someone was panting, harsh breaths loud in his ears. "S-Sarah?"

"She needs you."

He let the arms pull him away from Syder's body, now limp and collapsing in a heap on the floor. The cane, too, clacked onto the wooden planks, released from Syder's slackened hand.

Colin's eyes moved to her. Sarah.

Beneath smeared blood, she was white and still, her honey eyes closed, her soft mouth parted. But breathing. Atherbourne knelt beside her, pressing his cravat hard against her throat.

Behind him, Dunston questioned one of Syder's men, his affable voice hardened to steel. Tannenbrook grunted as he tied another one's hands.

But all he saw was his wife. Like a cannon had been shot into his chest, he felt both devastation and unimaginable fire. He must get her to a surgeon. Now.

"Harrison," he rasped, falling to his knees before her, stroking her pale, precious cheek. "A physician. A surgeon. Please, God. She cannot die. She cannot."

"Dunston has a man. He is on his way to Clyde-Lacey House. We must move her outside. Dunston's coach is waiting."

Atherbourne turned dark, sympathetic eyes on Colin. "The cut is not as deep as it first appeared," the viscount said quietly. "He probably meant it as a warning, intending to keep her alive a while longer to gain your cooperation. She will need stitching, but—"

"I will not let her die." Colin noted someone had already cut her hands loose. He quickly sliced through the rope binding her ankles and let his knife fall to the floor with a thud. "I will carry her. We will take her home, and she will not die." He slipped his arms behind her back and beneath her knees then looked to Atherbourne. "Hold her wound."

He stood with Sarah in his arms while Atherbourne pressed the now red linen against her neck. She was so light, so small. When she was conscious and standing before him in quiet defiance, arms folded, chin thrust into the air, she seemed indomitable. A great, towering goddess of honey and stubbornness. Now, she was only delicate bone and too little flesh.

While they waited for Thomas to open the door of the coach, Colin whispered in her ear, ignoring the snowflakes falling and clinging to her lashes. Ignoring the blood that smeared onto his cheek. "Don't leave me, sweet. Please don't leave me."

They climbed into the coach, Atherbourne using his long arms to maintain the pressure on her neck while Colin settled her gently on his lap.

He read Atherbourne's grieving sympathy on his face. He

wanted to shout at the other man that she would live. Because she must. Because he had already died once today, and he could never bear it again.

Instead, he rested his lips against her temple, where her curls could tickle his chin. He rocked her with the motion of the speeding coach.

And he begged in repeating whispers, "Please don't go, my love. Please don't go."

SARAH WAS HAVING THE MOST PECULIAR DREAM. HER MOTHER was singing to her, a country tune from her childhood, perhaps. Her father was whispering to her that he loved her, telling her he wished to see her hold her children someday. Then he joined in the song. She lay beneath her quilt in her bedchamber at the cottage. It was bright. Probably midday. But she felt so weak she could scarcely keep her eyes open. She tried to ask her mother for the name of the song. Something about it was so familiar. Comforting.

Her throat hurt. The searing pain was distracting. Frustrating. She wished to speak, to tell her father that she had missed him terribly.

Something brushed her lips, brushed her eyes, brushed her hair away from her forehead. A warm, strong hand enfolded hers.

At last, she was able to open her eyes a bit. Her father was there, smiling down at her. But it was not his hand. Not his voice she had heard. It was Colin, holding her wrist to his lips, rocking back and forth in the chair beside her bed.

She sighed, relieved and happy. He was here. Her husband. She let her eyes close and drifted off to sleep, hearing a tender lullaby.

When next she awakened, she was alone. This time, she lay

in her bedchamber at Clyde-Lacey House. She recognized the red draperies and the cream divan beneath the window. Snow swirled outside.

Blinking, she reached up to rid herself of whatever was causing that horrible pain in her neck. Her fingers found linen bindings.

"Sarah?"

It was her mother, entering with a tea tray. She tried to say, "Mama," but it came out as a croak.

"Oh, my darling. Do not try to speak. Lord Dunston's surgeon said there would be a bit of swelling that would make you uncomfortable for a few days. Blackmore's physician has given you laudanum for the pain." Her mother's fingers brushed her forehead, then her cheek. "Let us see if you can manage to drink some tea."

After a bit of maneuvering, Sarah was able to sit up and take small sips. It hurt quite terribly to swallow, but she was painfully thirsty. The two discomforts warred, and the thirst won. She finished an entire cup before her eyes began to flag, her need for sleep intruding.

"Mama," she mouthed.

"Yes?"

"Colin?"

Worried green eyes met hers. A subtle frown. A downcast gaze. Sarah grasped her mother's wrist. "Colin?"

Eleanor sighed, brushing wispy curls along the side of her coiffure. She looked exhausted. Sitting on the edge of the bed, she took Sarah's hand. "He is sleeping. He was awake for three days. We gave him a bit of your laudanum." She read the stirrings of alarm in Sarah's expression and tightening grip. "He is well, aside from not eating or sleeping. He has been mad with worry for you, daughter. Simply mad. He would not leave your side. His brother had to pick him up and drag him bodily from the room so the surgeon could work in peace."

Again, Sarah's hand drifted to the bandage at her throat.

"Yes, you were cut, I'm afraid. A few stitches were necessary, but both the surgeon and physician assure us you should heal very well. Perhaps a small scar, that is all."

Lethargy was taking over now, warm weight and a floating sensation. Her eyelids listed. Her mother's lips brushed her forehead.

"Sleep now, my sweet babe. Let Mama care for you."

The third time she awakened, the room was dark. Only the fire and a single candle served as illumination. At the window stood a man, broad shoulders covered in white linen, blond hair boasting of its curl. His back was to her, head tilted forward, one hand on his hip.

Her heart squeezed. She loved this man. Loved his humor and wit, generosity and sensuality. She even loved his poor attempts at being stern. It filled her like music, soaring and booming and lilting and singing. If only he could love her in the same way. For a brief moment, when he had entered a parlor in Knightsbridge, she had thought he just might. But that had been a desperate moment. And sometimes desperation looked a good deal like love.

She shifted, feeling the aches in every part of her body—her head, her throat, her back and arms and knees. Drawing a deep breath, she stretched her neck to see him more clearly. "Colin." This time, his name was more rasp than croak.

He turned, gazing at her with blue, tormented eyes. He held a letter in his hands, which he quickly folded and tucked away. "How are you feeling?"

"Hurts."

Striding to the bed, he sank down next to her and lifted her hand in his. "I know, sweet. Let me give you a bit more laudanum."

She shook her head. "How are you?"

He laid a tender kiss on her wrist, then a few more on her fingertips. Turning aside briefly, he measured liquid from a bottle and poured it into a cup of tea, then added a teaspoon of sugar. "Here," he said, lightly tapping the spoon against the rim. "Drink."

Sighing again, she complied, letting him help her by holding her head up. When she had finished the brew, which tasted bitter and sweet, she grasped his wrist. "Not your fault."

He refused to meet her eyes, setting the cup and spoon on the table with a quiet clink. "It is entirely my fault. And I shall never forgive myself." He grinned, the gesture breaking her heart. "A new one to add to the list, I fear."

"No, Colin. Mine."

"It was my duty to protect you. I failed in that most fundamental of tasks."

His duty. His task. It was as she had feared. To him, she was an obligation, another act of contrition and charity on his road to redemption. Swallowing hard, she winced at the pain. Nevertheless, she could not countenance his blaming himself for what Felix Foote and Horatio Syder had done. Once again, she grasped his arm, digging with her fingers until he looked at her. "I left." She placed her free hand over her heart. "Me. I went to Miss Thurgood's."

"I should have known you would not adhere to my wishes. I should have been here with you."

Sighing her impatience, she shook her head on the pillow. "My fault. Not yours." Lassitude seeped into her muscles. Pain began to lessen. The laudanum was taking effect. She wanted to argue further, but she could scarcely think, sleep beckoning like an old friend.

Warm, tender lips traced her forehead, then settled for a breath against her mouth. The sweetness of the kiss made her want to weep.

"Every day for the rest of my life, I will remember the moment when I failed you, Sarah." His warm breath flowed over her as his forehead rested against hers. "You knew of my weakness." Lifting his head, he whispered his final words seconds before sleep took her. "Is it any wonder you contemplated leaving me?"

"Miss?" The housekeeper entered the library where Hannah sat, practicing chess. First moves were sometimes the hardest. "There is a man to see you. Says he has news about your father."

Hannah's fingers froze above her knight. If someone else was here with word about Horatio Syder, that could only mean he was dead. He never allowed others to see her. Not in ten long years.

"Show him in," she said softly.

Loud, heavy footsteps approached the library door. Clomp-clomp-clomp. Regular rhythm, no tapping.

"Miss Syder."

Without glancing up, she held up a single finger in his direction. "That is not my name."

"I—I beg your pardon?"

Finally, she made her decision. The knight. Definitely. It was the right move for this game.

"My name," she said, turning to the big, rough-looking man in the doorway of the library. "It is not Miss Syder."

The ugly man appeared confused, his worn, floppy hat twisting in his grip.

"What is it you wished to tell me?"

His discomfort seemed to grow. He tugged at the collar of his brown woolen coat as though it itched. "I regret to say your father—that is, Mr. Syder—he is dead, miss."

She closed her eyes slowly, let them rest and savor the knowledge. Dead. He was dead. She let it wash through her, repeating the word. Dead. Dead. Dead.

"Miss. I—I am most sincerely sor—"

Without opening her eyes, she interrupted, "Is that everything, then? Have you anything else to tell me?"

His boots clomp-clomp-clomped further into the room. She opened her eyes to see what he was doing. He took an envelope from inside his coat and placed it carefully on the nearby desk. "He made arrangements. Set aside funds. The name of the solicitor is inside. It is all there for you when ... er, when you're ready."

Slowly, a smile emerged. "Thank you," she said softly, returning to her game. "That is excellent news. Excellent news, indeed."

Chapter Twenty-Five

"You see? I was right. You would do well not to question it in the future."

—THE DOWAGER MARCHIONESS OF WALLINGHAM to Lady Berne upon receiving confirmation of Lord Dunston's longstanding association with the Home Office.

"A BLOODY MESS IS WHAT IT WAS," DUNSTON COMPLAINED. "Literally. There was blood everywhere. Took some explaining, I don't mind telling you. Dashed nuisance."

The earl's relaxed posture as he lounged on a blue sofa in Clyde-Lacey House's drawing room was a bit casual for the level of tension in the room. Colin could not bring himself to care.

Harrison, on the other hand, appeared quite perturbed,

standing rigid with his hands firmly clasped behind his back. "You should be horsewhipped—"

"Now, now, Blackmore. I was only doing—"

"And then *dragged* by a horse—"

"—what I had to do—"

"—until every bit of skin is flayed from your—"

"—to ensure a villainous madman—"

"—miserable, lying carcass."

"—was stopped."

Harrison glared at his friend—a relationship about which Colin had serious doubts—and said in a soft, deadly tone, "You placed my brother in untenable danger."

"Well, yes, but only for the best of reasons."

"When you could have helped him pay his debt, perhaps avoiding Syder's notice, you did nothing."

Dunston tilted his head and scratched his chin, looking only slightly abashed. "Matters were ... delicate at that stage. To have aided the fair young Lacey might have exposed my position."

"So you allowed him to be chased from one end of England to the other."

"I gave him sound advice," Dunston retorted indignantly.

Harrison glowered. "What advice? When?"

"When we were all at Blackmore. July, wasn't it? I told him to ask you for the blunt. Which he did."

"He did not ask. I offered it to him."

Dunston threw up his hands in a wide, shrugging gesture. "There you have it. I knew very well you would not permit him to continue gallivanting across hill and dale without stepping in."

Atherbourne, seated in a large chair near the fire, cleared his throat as if preparing to speak. Standing with his elbow propped on the mantel, Colin gave him a sharp look and shook his head.

"Your *presumptions* nearly got him killed," gritted Harrison. "They caused Jane to be abducted. And now, Colin's wife has been injured."

Leaning forward and bracing his elbows on his knees, Dunston met Harrison's eyes directly. "Listen to me," he said, displaying the steel Colin had seen only a few times in their long acquaintance. "Nothing was done without necessity. Nothing. Syder consistently underestimated your brother, thought him useless and impulsive. That is what made Colin so effective. Syder assumed the young, feckless Lacey would charge off to rescue his truelove without a proper force behind him. Before that, he assumed Colin could not escape a slaughterhouse in Whitechapel."

Colin frowned. "Er—I did not escape, precisely."

"And before that, he assumed Colin would give him my name after a few measly hours of—what's that you say?" Dunston looked askance at Colin. "No escape. Did Syder *release* you?" His laugh underlined how absurd he considered the notion. "Surely not."

Scratching his head, Colin said, "His man Benning did. Said he was paid off by some mysterious 'nob.' I always assumed it was you." Clearly, it had not been Dunston. That left only one other possibility. Colin shook his head. He still could not believe it. Chatham was simply not the sort.

"However it occurred," said Atherbourne, "I think we can all agree the world is better off now that Syder is dead."

"Mmm," Dunston concurred, lounging back into his affable self. "Though, he did leave a ward behind. Haven't been able to locate her. Kept her well hidden, apparently. Aside from her, I doubt anyone will miss the offal." He sighed. Then adopted a grin with a sinister edge. "One last thing he did not expect? That Lacey here would be the one who put paid to that particular debt. A bit messy but well done, old chap. Arrogance was one of Syder's lesser faults. You used it to great advantage."

Turning back to stare down at the fire, Colin rubbed the two pieces of paper he held between his thumb and fingers. One was a note Syder had sent. It had arrived minutes after Colin and Harrison had bolted out the door of Clyde-Lacey House, intent on saving Sarah. It said only: *Located the loveliest Devonshire treasure this morning. Could not resist. Awaiting your reply.* Then, it gave Foote's Sloane Street address and was signed simply "S."

It was a reminder. Of how he had failed her. No matter what Dunston or anyone else said, he would live with that knowledge forever.

The second item was a letter from the headmaster of a school in Bath. It described a position that was ideally suited for Sarah. She had sent Thomas back into Miss Thurgood's house to retrieve it.

Just in case she decided to leave him. There could be no other reason.

Obviously, she did not trust him to provide for her, to care for her as she deserved. She had not believed in him before he had let her be attacked. He could not imagine she would believe in him now.

"Pardon me, gentlemen," said a gentle voice from the doorway. It was Eleanor, looking weary but pleased, her eyes crinkling in a smile. "Lord Colin, Sarah would like to speak with you. She has asked if you will come to her."

He swallowed, his mouth suddenly dry. Nodding, he crossed the expanse of the drawing room, pausing at the door when Eleanor touched his sleeve.

"Before you go," she said quietly, "I must tell you, she has missed you dreadfully these last few days. I know I am not your mother, but would you permit me to give you some small bit of advice?"

He nodded.

"When Mr. Battersby was first ... afflicted, I wondered if it was my fault. Had I unwittingly poisoned him with my cooking? Or perhaps I had not managed his sleep habits closely enough, or allowed him to work too much." She chuckled sadly. "It is natural to blame oneself, I suppose, when we bind ourselves together so tightly that we become part of each other. What I am saying is that sometimes the best thing you can do for the one you love is simply that—to love them. Completely. Without fear of what may come. Without recrimination for what has come before. Love her and let her love you in return." Sarah's mother sniffed, dabbed her eye with her knuckle, and patted his elbow. "That is my advice. Do with it what you will."

Again, he nodded, unable to reply. Then, he left the drawing room and traveled the corridor to their bedchamber. He paused as he reached the door, glancing again down at the papers in his hand.

Love her. He did. Of course he did. Who could not fall madly in love with his sweet, honeyed Sarah? Loving her was not the problem. Failing her was.

The knob, cool under his hand, turned. She was not there. He frowned, striding into the room, heading for the bed. Where the deuce had she gone?

"Colin," came a longed-for voice from his right.

His heart began beating again, pounding as his eyes devoured her. She sat on the divan beneath the window, a blanket across her lap, a letter in her hand. Her wild honey hair was down, pulled over her shoulder and tied with a white ribbon that matched her lace-trimmed dressing gown. He met her eyes, glowing gold as though she were happy to see him. The dark circles beneath had been greatly diminished, and she had regained a hint of bloom in her cheeks.

"Close the door, husband. I wish to speak with you." She certainly sounded like his Sarah, her voice smoothed of its prior roughness, her tone firm and authoritative. His little governess.

Hiding a grin, he complied then moved to sit on the side of the bed, facing her but keeping a careful distance. "Feeling better, I take it." *He* did not. Inside, he felt as shaky as a newborn colt.

"Why have you stayed away?" Her question was quiet, as though she'd been hurt by his absence.

"You needed rest. Time to heal."

"My healing occurs whether you are in the room or not, Colin."

Dropping his gaze to his hands, he nodded and released a sigh. "In truth, I have come to your door often, intending to enter. I suppose I did not wish to disturb you."

"Our door."

He met her eyes. "Pardon?"

"This bedchamber is *our* bedchamber." She pointed to the bed upon which he sat. "That is *our* bed. It is where you belong."

He froze, a bit stunned by her sudden, fiery spark. "You are angry."

"You are bloody well right."

Aside from the shock of hearing her utter a vulgarity, he reeled from the implication—that she had wanted him beside her. "I—Sarah, I did not mean to—"

"I needed you," she accused, her voice choking a bit. "I longed to have your arms around me, and you ..." Her little pointed chin trembled ominously. A sheen of moisture filled her eyes. "You weren't there."

Shoving himself from the bed, he tossed the papers aside and fell to his knees in front of her. His hands settled on her legs, reached for her hands, lowered his head to kiss the slender, callused fingers he adored. "Forgive me, sweet. Please don't cry. I only meant to give you the time and distance you deserve."

"Distance?" she said, sniffing. "If anything, I require proximity. Gargantuan amounts of proximity."

He gazed up at her, carefully brushed away a tear with his thumb. She captured his hand and held it against her cheek. He smiled, trembling before his wife. "I am sorry, Sarah. I shall remedy the problem immediately." Feeling the delicacy of her fine bones and soft skin beneath his palm, he asked, "Are you eating enough? I will tell Digby to—"

"Colin," she gritted, "do not start haranguing me again about food. I realize you only married me out of pity, but it is growing quite tiresome to have you treat me as some starving orphan whom you must fatten up forthwith."

"Pity?"

"I shall eat when I am hungry. Furthermore, you are my husband, whether you like it or not—"

The world had tipped sideways, a ship rolling on a sudden, steep wave. "I do not pity you."

"—and you will be my husband until the end, so you may resign yourself to a state of proximity for the foreseeable future."

"I did not marry you because I pity you, Sarah."

Her eyes welled again, her brow crumpling. "Naturally, you would say that. Your kindness is one of the reasons I love you. But you needn't lie to spare my feelings. We are married. That cannot be undone."

Was it brighter in the room, of a sudden? He thought it must be, for she glowed in his vision, her pixie face wreathed in light.

She loved him. She had said it, hadn't she? Perhaps he had misheard.

"Say it again," he rasped, fearing to blink and risk missing a sign that she had simply been rambling.

"What?"

"That ... that you love me. Say it again."

Her brow crinkled with confusion. "Of course I love you, you daft man. Why else would I have agreed to become your wife?"

Her last word was mumbled against his lips, for he could no longer resist kissing her. His *wife*. He took her face in his hands and kissed her until they were both breathless, until the light he had seen earlier pierced his heart and expanded outward, bursting throughout his body in a sparkling, radiant plume.

Moving to sit beside her on the divan, he gathered her delicate softness into his arms and pulled his mouth away from hers only so he could kiss every inch of her face.

"Colin," she panted, her hands clinging to his upper arms. "Wh-what is ... This is positively splendid, and I emphatically do not wish you to stop. But I don't understand."

"You love me." He laughed and kissed her wondrous, upturned nose. "You love me."

"Yes." She began smiling, the slow emergence of it resembling a sunrise. "I love you. This is a surprise?"

"I did not know. I thought you were only doing what you've often been forced to do—choosing the likeliest path to survival."

Her eyes softened, clung to his. "In a sense, that is true. For, I cannot live without you."

Shaking his head, he laid a tender kiss on her honeyed lips. "I will spend every day of my life earning your trust, my sweet. Of that you can be certain. You shall have no reason whatever to seek employment in Bath. I will build a life for us in which you will never want for another blessed thing—food, gowns, servants. We'll have one entire wing devoted to bolts of fabric."

Her eyes grew shadowed.

"And I shall protect you with my very life, Sarah." He traced her bandage with a feather-light touch. "Never again will you be placed in harm's way. I vow it."

She had paled considerably, her eyes dropping between them. She nodded in acknowledgment of his promise, but her reaction was the opposite of what he had intended.

"You are distressed. What did I say that disturbed you, sweet?"

"Nothing, I ... thank you, Colin. I realize you see me as a duty. I do trust you to provide for me." Those careful, subdued words cracked his chest wide open. Then, she lifted her eyes to his. She was wounded, bleeding. Not her neck, this time, but her heart. "And I do not mean to sound ungrateful. But what I need most is your love. That is the only thing necessary to my survival. The only thing I do not have."

By the time she was finished, a tear was falling. "You have it, Sarah," he whispered, unable to comprehend how she could possibly doubt it. "My love is yours. My body. My life. I belong to you, sweet. I have from the moment you pulled this battered, worthless scoundrel from the mud and declared him yours."

SARAH EXPECTED SHE WOULD FOREVER REMEMBER THIS moment—the moment when her life tipped on its axis. When she knew.

He loved her. He did.

"You love me," she babbled, grabbing his hair rather vigorously with both hands and forcing his face to come within an inch of hers. "You really do."

Eyes the color of summer at sea glowed and burned. For her.

"Er—easy, sweet." He reached up to loosen her fingers. "And yes, I love you. It's like a sickness, really. Haven't been able to shake it since Keddlescombe."

She clutched at him—climbed him—until she straddled his hips and held his face at the mercy of her lips. "Colin, my love." Kiss. "I love you so very much." Nibble. "And would like to thank you." Another kiss. "For loving me back." A little suckle at his perfect chin. "By making love to you now."

He chuckled, the sound rumbling from his chest through her rapidly hardening nipples, which pressed against him insistently. "Two points, sweet. First, you may make love to me whenever and however you like for whatever reasons you deem worthwhile. I am at your service. However, I would like to remind you of what I told you at your cottage, the night your father went wandering."

She pulled back long enough to frown. "Which part?"

He kissed her sweetly, letting his tongue linger and stroke until she was grinding herself against him insistently. "Do not thank a man for giving you what was yours at the start."

Beaming at him with all the love she had kept contained, she laughed with the joy of it. Then, she dove back into his mouth. Felt his lean, strong hands and muscled arms move along her back and in her hair and across her shoulders.

"Are you certain you are well enough?" he panted, his eyes once again blue fire, his hands gathering up the cloth of her dressing gown with impatient jerks.

"Yes. I need you." She did. She was clawing at him. Desperate for him. She ripped and tore at his cravat, at his shirt and waistcoat. It was not fast enough. Her need rose inside her, aching and begging. In her belly, in her breasts. But especially inside. Deep in her core, the emptiness wept for want of him.

Hard tension in his face relaxed just a bit. "Thank God." His hands gripped her hips then slid down onto the bared skin of her thighs. "Lock your legs around me." After several breaths, she managed it, crossing her ankles at the base of his back. Wrapping one hard arm around her, he stood in a single motion, dropping her blanket and carrying her to the bed. He laid her down upon the mattress as carefully as he might a porcelain vase, retreating only long enough to discard his tailcoat and cravat and unfasten the fall of his trousers.

She moaned as he covered her. Then gasped as he lifted her against him again, spinning until he sat on the bed with his back against the headboard and she sitting atop his lap, feeling his stone-hard staff slide against her folds with beseeching heat. "Oh!" she muttered, digging her fingers into his neck.

"If anything hurts, sweet, I want you to tell me." The words ground out of him. His eyes held a glint of concern that told her he meant what he said.

"I will."

Gently, he untied the bodice of her dressing gown, removing the layers of muslin until they pooled around her hips, and her breasts were there for his taking. His eyes darkened and burned as they fell upon the bruises.

"It does not matter, Colin," she whispered, stroking his cheek to soothe him.

"He must die."

"He is already dead."

"He must die again. Slower."

"Shh. Just touch me, my darling. Let me feel the pleasure only you can give me."

Slowly, the muscles in his abdomen relaxed and his hand came up to brush ever-so-lightly over her aching nipple. Then, he used his tongue to trace each fading bruise, to soothe and stroke and drive her mad with wanting.

His fingers plucked at the ribbon tying her hair, releasing it to spring outward and flow across her chest and back. He filled his hands with her curls, drawing her forward into his kiss.

His hands found her waist. Lifted her. Slid himself slowly, gently inside her heat, filling what was empty. Stretching her until she groaned his name.

He let her control their rhythm, resting his hands lightly on her hips. She leaned forward and ran her tongue along his neck, rubbed her nipples against his heaving chest. Ran her hands down over his abdomen, where three ridged scars served as a reminder of how much he had endured. She felt his thick, hard staff throb and pulse inside her like another heartbeat. His heartbeat.

"Please, Colin," she panted, running her fingers over his ears and his chin and down along his collarbone. She was trying, but she could not get the rhythm right. It was driving her mad to feel this need inside her. "You must ..."

"Must what, sweet?"

She growled her frustration, working her hips over him and missing something vital. "Please," she begged, not knowing what to ask for or how to make him understand. "I need you."

"Ah," he said teasingly. "The governess wishes to relinquish control, does she?"

"Yes. That is it precisely." She wriggled against him. "Now, do what you do. And be quick about it."

He laughed so hard, it shook the bed. She even felt it inside her, moving up from where they were joined and bubbling out of her throat. The sheer joy in his blue eyes became her joy. "As always, sweet Sarah, I serve at your pleasure."

With that, he gripped her waist and gave a startlingly deep thrust, slamming a gasp of delight from her throat. Then he did it again. And again. And five more times. And then she lost count because the wondrous, spiraling pleasure gathered and squeezed and imploded with sharp, pounding, breathtaking force. She screamed and wept her gratitude for his mastery, took his answering pleasure deep inside her body, took his answering shout into her mouth. And clung to the only man who had ever proved a temptation.

Afterward, they lay quietly beneath the blankets, he cradling her against his chest and playing with her hair. She suspected she had no bones remaining, having been reduced to flesh only. Warm, satisfied flesh.

"Do not ever leave me, Sarah. I beg of you." The hoarse plea brought her head up off his shoulder.

"Why would you—"

"I saw the letter. From the school in Bath."

His eyes held fear. Real fear and sadness. He believed she had meant to take the position, to abandon their marriage.

She traced a finger along his brow. "Retrieving the letter was a moment of doubt that I regret most profoundly. I feared that you did not love me and might tire of being my benefactor after the danger had passed. I was a fool."

"Never that, sweet."

She smiled and scooted so her eyes and lips could hover directly above his. "Besides, I cannot possibly leave you," she said softly, absorbing the miracle of their love. "Where would I go without my heart?"

Chapter Twenty-Six

"Happy Christmas? Bah! It shall be a far sight happier
when I have a grandchild, you ungrateful whelp.
And when will that be, hmm?"

—The Dowager Marchioness of Wallingham to herself upon
reading a recent letter from her son, Charles.

Watching her husband lovingly stroke the black hair of the babe he held in his arms, Sarah struggled for a sigh. Perhaps her sudden need for air could be blamed on sentiment. More likely, it was the immense quantity of roasted goose and plum pudding she had consumed at dinner. Her hand settled over her belly.

Gracious me, she thought, *I have never been stuffed so dreadfully full in my life*. At present, breathing would be a luxury. Of course, Colin had been incorrigible, insisting she eat more and more and still more until she had promised to do anything he wanted if he would only leave off. His wicked grin had carried promises of its own. But at least he had stopped.

"He will be a most devoted papa, I expect." The words came from Victoria, who sat in the red chair nearest Sarah. Startled by the unexpected comment from her sister-in-law, Sarah turned to gaze at her husband, sitting next to her on one of the blue sofas near the blazing fire of the drawing room, cradling Victoria's son.

"Mmm. Devoted," Sarah murmured. "If he is as devoted to them as he is to me, I fear they will all be as round as a Christmas pudding."

Colin looked at her and raised a brow. "I notice you are finally beginning to regain your color. You can thank me later."

She pursed her lips and waved toward the overlarge, uncomfortably warm fire that had reddened all their cheeks. "I shall place my thanks where it truly belongs, if you please."

A familiar, heated glint entered his eyes. "And if I don't please? May I still expect a proper thank-you?"

Her breathing quickened and her body burned for reasons other than the fireplace. "Well," she said, swallowing against a suddenly parched throat. "If you insist."

Victoria rose to retrieve her son from Colin's arms. The babe was wrapped in the quilt Sarah had made for him, a mix of blues and greens. Sarah was pleased with her work, and noted that some of the colors matched little Gregory's eyes.

"Time for Roseanna to put you to bed, my darling," Victoria said, carrying him to the waiting nursemaid.

"I have it!" announced Jane, entering the drawing room with Harrison, waving a letter in the air. "Lady Wallingham has come through. We shall not miss our entertainment for the evening."

They all settled in around the fire—Jane and Harrison, Lucien and Victoria, Sarah and Colin and Eleanor—to listen as

Jane shared the best tidbits from the Dowager Marchioness of Wallingham.

"She appears to be most concerned for the legacy of Lord Rutherford." News of the Marquess of Rutherford's death on the night of Lady Rutherford's rout had been the topic of much conversation over the last few weeks. Adjusting her spectacles, Jane continued, "Oh, dear. She does have a rather low opinion of the new Lord Rutherford. Listen to this: *Chatham—for I shall not be persuaded to refer to that reprobate by his father's previously estimable title—will undoubtedly prove irredeemable in every respect. Some have suggested he will undergo a miraculous transformation upon his inheritance, that a new jewel in his scepter shall turn a drunken, ravening wolf into something resembling a gentleman. His mother has a greater chance of joining a nunnery, and we all know of Lady Rutherford's predilections.*"

Jane paused for another, "Oh, dear," and a giggle before reading on. "She has knitted a cap for Humphrey. She says it is a bit lopsided, but she blames his 'sadly diminutive ears.'"

Laughing, Victoria said, "Perhaps I shall paint a portrait of Humphrey and add a bit of flattering length to his—"

"You will do no such thing," said Atherbourne.

"Whyever not?"

"Painting the dog means you will have to spend an inordinate amount of time in Lady Wallingham's company. Which means I must do the same."

Eleanor, watching the byplay, interjected, "I maintain Lady Wallingham cannot possibly be as bad you say. No one can."

"No, you are right. She is worse." Jane said.

"Yes," agreed Victoria. "Very dragon-like."

Even Harrison commented, "If visits are necessary, I recommend short durations. And, if need be, claim a sudden illness."

Everyone laughed—everyone except Harrison. "I am quite serious. The only one who may be more disagreeable to me is Lord Dunston."

Colin groaned. "Not this again."

"He deceived me for years. I never knew the man at all. How can you trust someone of that sort?"

Shaking his head, Colin replied, "If you intend to continue this hostility, perhaps you can wait another month or two before launching a full-scale estrangement."

"Why?"

Colin looked at Sarah for a long moment, then back at Harrison. "Dunston and I are in the midst of a ... transaction."

Not one to accept imprecision, Harrison snapped, "What transaction?"

Sighing, Colin again looked at Sarah, who frowned her confusion. "I was going to tell you, sweet." Then he turned to Harrison and the others. "Yardleigh Manor. I am purchasing it from him. The sale should be final in a few weeks."

Sarah's astonished "Oh, Colin" was lost amid questions from everyone. He answered them in turn—yes, Dunston was the owner. The earl had intended the Devonshire house as a refuge for himself and those who helped him in his projects. No, Colin did not think Dunston would lie about this, as he had about everything else. Yes, he intended Eleanor should live there, as well. Yes, if Sarah were agreeable, he believed they could use part of the house to reopen St. Catherine's Academy for Girls of Impeccable Deportment. And, yes, he concurred that the name of the school was both lengthy and majestic.

By the time he had finished answering their interrogation, Colin appeared dazed. At last, he smiled down at Sarah and asked the question that seemed to be most concerning to him. "Are you pleased, sweet?"

Instead of answering with words, she answered with a tearful kiss that lasted a bit longer than she had intended. When they finally separated, Sarah fanned herself with her hand. "Is anyone else a trifle warm?"

With cries of agreement, they all stood. Eleanor suggested music. Victoria insisted Colin take his seat at the pianoforte.

"Oh, do, Colin," she pleaded. "It has been much too long since I last heard you play."

Colin glanced down at Sarah, a small smile beginning to curl his lips, a question in his eyes.

She nodded. "Please, husband. It would make me so very happy."

He leaned down to whisper in her ear, "I am ever at your service."

Then, he sat before the keys, pausing for a breath, closing his eyes. He opened them and met hers. And began to play. It was similar to the song he had played the night of their wedding. But, if anything, it was richer, more complex.

With each passage, she could feel memories flowing through her veins, as warming as honey wine. Each note was a moment, a reason she loved him.

Rain upon a canvas. Waves upon a shore.

This man will seek to deserve you and when he falls short, he will seek your forgiveness.

Sunlight upon apples. Lips upon a mouth.

His mind will be strong so that he may attempt to equal yours.

Storm upon a roof. Pearls upon a neck.

His heart will be fierce and true for the same reason.

Snow upon a street. Blood upon a floor.

He will see your life as the only reason for his, and he will guard it accordingly.

Light upon a window. Hand upon a cheek.

You will see yourself in the mirror of his eyes, and you will be more beautiful, more precious than you were to me that early September morning.

Sarah looked into her husband's eyes and saw herself there. Beautiful. Precious.

You see, my darling girl? Impossible.

Wicked libertine Benedict Chatham is the new Marquess of Rutherford—and he's down to his last farthing. Who will come to his rescue? Perhaps a certain half-American heiress with a penchant for calamity and unfashionably red hair. But there's always a price to pay when you bargain with the devil. Read on for a **sneak peek!**

The Devil is a Marquess

ELISA BRADEN

Now available!

The Devil is a Marquess

AS THE FLAME-HAIRED AMAZON PIVOTED TO FACE HER FATHER, Chatham traced her womanly lines from long, pale neck to dark, silken hem. She possessed curves, certainly. He could see them when one hand braced on her hip, forcing the deep-purple cloth to caress natural fullness, to outline a not-displeasing backside and nicely proportioned waist.

"As our bargain was made in bad faith, Papa, I hereby withdraw my consent." Her voice, he noted, was pleasing as well, smooth and throaty with nary a hint of nasal whine. Unlike her father, she spoke proper English with no American inflection. Quite dulcet to the ear, actually.

"Balderdash. Our agreement has been struck, and you will—"

She was shaking her head, her simply knotted hair

shimmering like copper in the light of the fire. "You knew I would assume Lord Tannenbrook had reconsidered—"

"As Rutherford said, that was your mistake. Tannenbrook is only an earl," Lancaster scoffed. "And obstinate as that old horse your mother refused to sell."

"Hannibal was not obstinate. He was discerning about his friends. As is James."

James, is it? Chatham thought, downing the last of his whisky and carefully setting his glass on the floor beside his chair. *Interesting.*

"Hmmph," snorted Lancaster, giving his daughter a derisive once-over. "Discerning is one word for it. Tannenbrook refused to take you for any sum. Believe me, I pressed him."

Chatham watched as the amazon's bright-red head snapped back at the raw insult. It was the first time she had displayed weakness. He frowned, waiting for her to gather herself. He did not wait long.

Her shoulders, surprisingly slender now that he looked upon them, squared. "Lord Tannenbrook does not respond well to intimidation. Neither do I."

Lancaster's looming form edged toward his daughter. Reaching for his walking stick, Chatham felt his thigh muscles tense on the off chance he would have to step between them. Thankfully, no such action was required—the man stopped within a foot of her.

"I left the choice of husband to you, and you failed."

She sighed, her shoulders slumping out of square. "I have explained why a thousand times, Papa. The conversation has grown wearying."

The American's frown showed genuine consternation. "What is so difficult about wielding a woman's wiles? I see it every day. Girls younger than you, less intelligent. They flit here and there, wave their eyelashes about. It's simple. Men are simple."

A long silence filled the space, thickening amidst the dark and punctuated by the pop and sizzle from the fireplace. When she answered, her voice was quiet, as though the ground she tread had been worn so deep, the sound that emerged was muffled. "They do not want me. You may wrap my entire body in one-hundred-pound notes, and the reaction will be the same. Is that simple enough?"

In an instant, Chatham decided she was wrong. Charlotte Lancaster naked but for a few small bits of paper? They would want her. Perhaps not enough to marry her, but to bed her, most certainly. After the incident last winter, when she had taken a tumble beside the Serpentine and unveiled her lower half to a smattering of gape-jawed, gossipy lackwits, he'd endured endless rhapsodies from young bucks at Reaver's about how it would feel to climb between two limbs of such length. If she thought a man's cock gave a damn about whether her coloring was fashionable, she did not understand men in the slightest.

Now, Lancaster was shaking his head, rebuffing her answer. "You did not bother to try—"

"That is preposterous." She shook her skirts. "I wear the finest gowns."

"Beside the point."

"Attend balls and fetes and dinners and soirees and bloody musicales—"

"Mind your language, girl."

"—and have done for five years. I hate it. Every bloody bit of it. But I have done it, because it is what fine English ladies do when they seek a husband. And it has. Not. Worked."

"Obviously," Lancaster blustered. "You have been distracted by your mannish notions about entering trade. 'Preposterous' is imagining that a woman can manage an enterprise such as mine. You have only yourself to blame that we have come to this pass."

At this, her shoulders again stiffened. "It matters not who is at fault."

"It matters when you have engaged in sabotage to thwart my commands."

"Sabotage? I have done everything you asked! You simply

refuse to comprehend reality because it does not comport with your wishes. No matter. Here is where my compliance ends." Her long, slender arm shot out from her side and swung around to point in Chatham's direction. "I shall not marry him. He is a dishonorable—"

Lancaster protested, "Now, see here—"

"—scurrilous rake, and to spend one moment in his company—"

Chatham assumed she had forgotten he was still in the room. He cleared his throat pointedly.

"—much less an entire year is untenable."

"Miss Lancaster," he drawled.

She spun around, cracking her wrist against the back of her chair. Wincing, she cradled the injured arm and gave him a green-and-gold glare. "I have nothing to say to you."

"How refreshing."

Her chin elevated. "You are in your cups. I can smell it from here."

Unsurprised by her bluntness, he brushed imaginary lint from his knee. "Mmm. Makes the world more bearable. Perhaps you should try it."

"I will not marry a drunkard. Nor a lecherous scoundrel who collects followers to join him in debauchery."

Grinning, he replied, "Debauchery is best when shared, love."

She opened her mouth to parry, but Lancaster intruded first. "Whatever his past habits, Rutherford has agreed to cease all drunkenness and remain faithful to you for the year."

Charlotte's snort was accompanied by an eye-roll. Chatham found both oddly charming. "Benedict Chatham has no acquaintance with honor, Papa. If you are trusting him to keep his word, you shall be sorely—"

"Honor is weak tea, Miss Lancaster," Chatham interrupted. "As one who favors trade, you should understand a sizable dowry is a far superior incentive. If I succeed in surviving the year as your abstemious husband, my reward will be ... substantial."

She edged toward him, her silk rustling. "How substantial?"

Lancaster cleared his throat and began to protest, but Chatham did not give a damn what secrets the American wished to keep. "One hundred," he said smoothly.

A slim, freckled hand slid over her midsection as green-gold eyes rounded and red-orange brows arched. "Th-thousand?"

"Indeed. So, as you can see, my habits are to be sacrificed upon an altar of gold."

She drew several steps closer, her astonishment apparently tugging her like an invisible line. "Impossible," she whispered.

He chuckled and nodded toward the desk. "I thought the same, but the settlement has been drawn. Your father is bound to it, as am I."

She stopped before him, her skirts brushing his knees. "I don't wish to marry you." Her gaze was solemn, nearly apologetic, as though she denied him reluctantly.

But her denial could not be permitted. He despised being poor. It was one thing to be reviled by the ton for his scandalous behavior, entirely another to be pitied for lack of funds.

Slowly, he braced his hands on the arms of the chair and pushed himself to his feet. They now stood mere inches apart, her eyes flaring at their nearness. As she reeled awkwardly backward, he grasped her upper arms, forcing her to stillness. Then, he drew her closer and crooked his neck to meet her gaze. For a woman, she was abnormally tall, but her forehead still only came even with his nose. "Wishes have little bearing upon one's circumstances, Miss Lancaster. Your father holds the winning hand."

She shook her head, her breath quickening. "I cannot marry you. Not you."

His smile faded. "Yet, you were prepared to wed the giant."

"Lord Tannenbrook is a friend. You are ..."

Waiting, he loosened his hold, let his palms discover the softness of freckled skin and settle beneath her elbows. "Yes? I am?"

Her lips parted, her eyes searching his face. "A devil."

His grin returned, growing as he witnessed the tiny shiver she attempted to stifle. Carefully, he let his fingers linger on her skin a moment longer before dropping his hands to his sides.

She did not move, but swayed before him, her eyes riveted to his.

"Most observant, Miss Lancaster. A devil, indeed. But that does not change my title. Nor your father's leverage."

Lancaster chose that moment to reenter the conversation. "Charlotte, you will abide by the terms of our agreement. I have no desire to beggar your aunt and uncle. Do not force me to it."

Chatham watched her eyes close, saw coppery lashes settle briefly along freckled cheeks and felt a twinge of something foreign, like a vine sprouting through snow. It made him stroke her arm covertly with the back of his finger, made him tilt his head again to meet the despair painted in green and gold. Made him offer the one reassurance he could. "It is only a year."

Her mouth firmed, her delicately squared jaw clenching upon a visible swallow. Then, she nodded. Breathed. Licked pink lips and retreated a step. She faced her father and sealed their fates with two hoarse words: "Very well."

WANT MORE OF CHARLOTTE AND CHATHAM'S STORY?
THE DEVIL IS A MARQUESS IS AVAILABLE NOW!
FIND IT AT WWW.ELISABRADEN.COM

More from Elisa Braden

*Be first to hear about new releases, price specials,
and more—sign up for Elisa's free email newsletter at
www.elisabraden.com so you don't miss a thing!*

Midnight in Scotland Series
*In the enchanting new Midnight in Scotland series,
the unlikeliest matches generate the greatest heat.
All it takes is a spark of Highland magic.*

THE MAKING OF A HIGHLANDER (BOOK ONE)

Handsome adventurer John Huxley is locked in a land dispute in the Scottish Highlands with one way out: Win the Highland Games. When the local hoyden Mad Annie Tulloch offers to train him in exchange for "Lady Lessons," he agrees. But teaching the fiery, foul-mouthed, breeches-wearing lass how to land a lord seems impossible—especially when he starts dreaming of winning her for himself.

THE TAMING OF A HIGHLANDER (BOOK TWO)

Wrongfully imprisoned and tortured, Broderick MacPherson lives for one purpose—punishing the man responsible. When a wayward lass witnesses his revenge, he risks returning to the prison that nearly killed him. Kate Huxley has no wish to testify against a man who's already suffered too much. But the only remedy is to become his wife. And she can't possibly marry such a surly, damaged man...can she?

Rescued from Ruin Series

*Discover the scandalous predicaments, emotional redemptions,
and gripping love stories (with a dash of Lady Wallingham)
in the scorching series that started it all!*

EVER YOURS, ANNABELLE (PREQUEL)

As a girl, Annabelle Huxley chased Robert Conrad with reckless abandon, and he always rescued her when she pushed too far—until the accident that cost him everything. Seven years later, Robert discovers the girl with the habit of chasing trouble is now a siren he can't resist. But when a scandalous secret threatens her life, how far will he go to rescue her one last time?

THE MADNESS OF VISCOUNT ATHERBOURNE (BOOK ONE)

Victoria Lacey's life is perfect—perfectly boring. Agree to marry a lord who has yet to inspire a single, solitary tingle? It's all in a day's work for the oh-so-proper sister of the Duke of Blackmore. Surely no one suspects her secret longing for head-spinning passion. Except a dark stranger, on a terrace, at a ball where she should not be kissing a man she has just met. Especially one bent on revenge.

THE TRUTH ABOUT CADS AND DUKES (BOOK TWO)

Painfully shy Jane Huxley is in a most precarious position, thanks to dissolute charmer Colin Lacey's deceitful wager. Now, his brother, the icy Duke of Blackmore, must make it right, even if it means marrying her himself. Will their union end in frostbite? Perhaps. But after lingering glances and devastating kisses, Jane begins to suspect the truth: Her duke may not be as cold as he appears.

DESPERATELY SEEKING A SCOUNDREL (BOOK THREE)

Where Lord Colin Lacey goes, trouble follows. Tortured and hunted by a brutal criminal, he is rescued from death's door by the stubborn, fetching Sarah Battersby. In return, she asks one small favor: Pretend to be her fiancé. Temporarily, of course. With danger nipping his heels, he knows it is wrong to want her, wrong to agree to her terms. But when has Colin Lacey ever done the sensible thing?

THE DEVIL IS A MARQUESS (BOOK FOUR)

A walking scandal surviving on wits, whisky, and wicked skills in the bedchamber, Benedict Chatham must marry a fortune or risk ruin. Tall, redheaded disaster Charlotte Lancaster possesses such a fortune. The price? One year of fidelity and sobriety. Forced to end his libertine ways, Chatham proves he is more than the scandalous charmer she married, but will it be enough to keep his unwanted wife?

WHEN A GIRL LOVES AN EARL (BOOK FIVE)

Miss Viola Darling always gets what she wants, and what she wants most is to marry Lord Tannenbrook. James knows how determined the tiny beauty can be—she mangled his cravat at a perfectly respectable dinner before he escaped. But he has no desire to marry, less desire to be pursued, and will certainly not kiss her kissable lips until they are both breathless, no matter how tempted he may be.

TWELVE NIGHTS AS HIS MISTRESS (NOVELLA – BOOK SIX)

Charles Bainbridge, Lord Wallingham, spent two years wooing Julia Willoughby, yet she insists they are a dreadful match destined for misery. Now, rather than lose her, he makes a final offer: Spend twelve nights in his bed, and if she can deny they are perfect for each other, he will let her go. But not before tempting tidy, sensible Julia to trade predictability for the sweet chaos of true love.

CONFESSIONS OF A DANGEROUS LORD (BOOK SEVEN)

Known for flashy waistcoats and rapier wit, Henry Thorpe, the Earl of Dunston, is deadlier than he appears. For years, his sole focus has been hunting a ruthless killer through London's dark underworld. Then Maureen Huxley came along. To keep her safe, he must keep her at arm's length. But as she contemplates marrying another man, Henry's caught in the crossfire between his mission and his heart.

ANYTHING BUT A GENTLEMAN (BOOK EIGHT)

Augusta Widmore must force her sister's ne'er-do-well betrothed to the altar, or her sister will bear the consequences. She needs leverage only one man can provide—Sebastian Reaver. When she invades his office demanding a fortune in markers, he exacts a price a spinster will never pay—become the notorious club owner's mistress. And when she calls his bluff, a fiery battle for surrender begins.

A MARRIAGE MADE IN SCANDAL (BOOK NINE)

As the most feared lord in London, the Earl of Holstoke is having a devil of a time landing a wife. When a series of vicious murders brings suspicion to his door, only one woman is bold enough to defend him—Eugenia Huxley. Her offer to be his alibi risks scandal, and marriage is the remedy. But as a poisonous enemy coils closer, Holstoke finds his love for her might be the greatest danger of all.

A KISS FROM A ROGUE (BOOK TEN)

A cruel past left Hannah Gray with one simple longing—a normal life with a safe, normal husband. Finding one would be easy if she weren't distracted by wolf-in-rogue's-clothing Jonas Hawthorn. He's tried to forget the haughty Miss Gray. But once he tastes the heat and longing hidden beneath her icy mask, the only mystery this Bow Street man burns to solve is how a rogue might make Hannah his own.

About the Author

Reading romance novels came easily to Elisa Braden. Writing them? That took a little longer. After graduating with degrees in creative writing and history, Elisa spent entirely too many years in "real" jobs writing T-shirt copy ... and other people's resumes ... and articles about gift-ware displays. But that was before she woke up and started dreaming about the very *unreal* job of being a romance novelist. Better late than never.

Elisa lives in the gorgeous Pacific Northwest, where you're constitutionally required to like the colors green and gray. Good thing she does. Other items on the "like" list include cute dogs, strong coffee, and epic movies. Of course, her favorite thing of all is hearing from readers who love her characters as much as she does. If you're one of those, get in touch on Facebook and Twitter or visit **www.elisabraden.com**.

51603192R00182